I0622148

The Prince of Warwood

and

The War of Kings

J. Noel Clinton

Copyright© 2016 by **J. Noel Clinton**

All rights reserved by the author. No part of this publication may be reproduced, stored in a retrieval system or transmitted in any form or by any means electronic, mechanical, photocopying, recording or otherwise, without the prior written permission of the author.

ISBN

Paperback: 978-0-9773115-9-0

E-book/kindle: 978-0-9773115-5-2

LCCN: 2016902118

The Prince of Warwood

and

The War of Kings

J. Noel Clinton

Chapter 1

T he blade whizzed past his cheek, barely missing him. Xavier stumbled backwards, his heart hammering in his chest as he lifted his sword to defend himself. The large man attacked again with a full-arc swing. He deflected the blow, but the impact of sword against sword jarred him. Pain shot up his arms, and he fell to the hard stone surface. Weary and in pain, he sprawled across the cool surface, wishing he could lie there and forget about fighting, but he didn't have that luxury. Xavier Wells was special, very special. He was an empowered human who possessed supernatural abilities beyond imagination. What was more, he was the Chosen; it was his destiny to protect the future of all mankind. He had to fight! If he didn't stand up to the Dark King, if he didn't defeat him, humankind would be forced into slavery, darkness, and despair.

Xavier felt the next attack more than he saw it. He rolled quickly to his right a millisecond before hearing the sword ping and scrape against the stone floor. Lying flat on his back, he wasted no time and sent a fantastic, blue force at his attacker, freezing the man in mid-stride. Xavier smirked as he sprung to his feet in time to parry another attack by a second, smaller man. This man possessed more skill with the sword, and Xavier knew he couldn't count on his swordsmanship to overpower the man. His attacker feinted a strike to Xavier's left before arcing his sword at the last minute and nicking Xavier's right cheek. Xavier jerked backwards and rubbed his cheek, finding blood there. The man smiled down at him triumphantly. Instinctively, Xavier jutted his hand at the man and propelled an electro force toward him, but his opponent dodged the force and answered with a force of his own. It struck Xavier before he could counter a defense, and he was thrown backwards.

Slightly dazed and dizzy, he struggled to get to his feet, but his legs were too wobbly, and he collapsed to the floor. He raised his sword just as the man swung what would have been a kill strike. Fear clawed its way down his spine, and he felt a surge building inside him. He couldn't afford to lose control! He had worked too hard for too long to let his powers control him again. A pair of large doe-like eyes filled his memory and contentment settled over him, drowning out the unruly powers seeking to escape. However, in the precious time it took him to regain control, the man had formulated another attack. This time it was a compound maneuver that had Xavier jerking to block a high-body strike, but in a beautifully mastered movement, the sword swept low across his soft underbelly. Pain exploded in his midsection. Panic flooded his body once again, but he didn't have time to calm himself, for the man was swinging his sword again. Xavier managed to roll to his right a millisecond before the sword swept down, nicking his shoulder and then clanging off the floor. He had to get away from the man. He wouldn't survive the attack much longer in close proximity. Suddenly, Xavier found himself swaying unsteadily ten feet behind the man who stood poised, swinging at thin air where he had been just a second ago. He had teleported out of harm's way! The ability wasn't what surprised Xavier; he had acquired the ability about a year ago. What surprised him was that he had teleported so easily. The thought of putting distance between himself and the man had been only that—a thought. He hadn't actually mentally conjured it. But he didn't have time to ponder the possible ramifications; he had a fight to win. As the man turned to locate him, Xavier jutted his hand out, hitting him with a powerful electro force that slammed him into the wall and knocked him out cold.

"Good move, young sire!" the larger man, no longer frozen, stepped forward with a fleece blanket wrapped around his shoulders.

"Loren, would you see to mending Ephraim?" a voice of authority asked from the corner of the chamber that had served as Xavier's training room for a little more than six months. King Jeremiah Wells IV strolled across the room, his eyes fastened on Xavier's. Xavier's gaze flickered submissively away from the king's. With the training session at an end, Xavier's body slowly began to unwind and relax. Sighing and feeling suddenly exhausted, he dropped his sword heavily to the floor. The king lifted Xavier's chin with a forefinger and turned his face gently as he examined the nick on his cheek.

"You should have worn your mask, son," the king whispered.

"I hate masks! I can't see very well with one on," he protested softly.

Without a word, Jeremiah nodded and touched the wound gently. Knowing what was coming, Xavier closed his eyes just as a fantastically bright, warm light consumed the king's fingers and his cheek. Within seconds, the stinging pain evaporated from his face, and he knew the wound had been healed.

"Take off your vest and shirt so I can have a look at your stomach and shoulder," his father continued.

Xavier stripped the padded vest worn to protect his body

from being ripped to shreds by his opponent's blade and peeled away his sweat-soaked shirt. His belly revealed a large contusion that had already begun to turn black and blue. The wound on his shoulder oozed blood. The king took a quick look at his shoulder, placed his hand on the injury and healed it within seconds. Then the king frowned down at his abdomen. Xavier groaned as his father's fingers prodded and explored for more serious injuries. Then the healing light quickly flared again, but this time the healing force stung as it worked to heal a deeper wound. Hissing, Xavier waited for the healing process to complete. The injury was healed in moments, and he peered up at his father.

"Thanks, Dad. It feels better."

"Well, laddie, it wasn't a bad session," the smaller man announced, now conscious and rubbing his head gingerly, "but you've got to learn to stay on your bloody feet!"

"I would if you weren't so bloody good, Mr. Hardcastle," Xavier remarked with a smirk and watched as the man swelled with pride. "If you were a slow, bumbling oaf like Loren, I would have had you flat on your back in no time," he continued, nodding toward the large, blonde man standing next to him.

"Bumbling oaf?" Loren bellowed and lunged forward, playfully swinging an open hand at Xavier.

If Xavier hadn't quickly scrambled out of his reach, Loren's massive hand would have found its mark on the back of his head. Instead, Loren hit the king's shoulder, and Xavier burst out laughing as his father glared at his general.

"And why are you hitting me for the boy's cheek, General Jefferson?" he reprimanded. Though his father held his stern, professional demeanor, Xavier knew his father was amused. Within the last week, Xavier had acquired the ability to read other people's emotions. But he didn't need the ability to know that his father was teasing Loren. The twinkle in his eyes gave that away.

"He is *your* son, your highness," Loren commented dryly as he bowed mockingly at the king. Then he straightened and began to dance from foot to foot with his arms poised to fight. He jabbed a combination of punches at the empty air in front of the king.

With a bellowing laugh, Jeremiah shrugged out of his sweatshirt and nodded at Xavier. Hearing his father's telepathic message, Xavier raced grinning to the equipment chest, pulled out two pairs of boxing gloves and gave each man a pair. Then he and Ephraim backed away from the men as they pulled on the gloves and faced one another with boyish grins.

"You know, General Jefferson, I believe it's you who's too cheeky. I think you need to be taken down a peg or two," his father chided.

"If you think you're man enough to do it, sire," Loren retorted.

"Are you ladies going to box or gossip at each other?" Ephraim spat, chuckling.

Xavier burst out laughing and gave the general beside him a high five. "Good one, Mr. Hardcastle."

"Xavier, I've told you. You can call me 'Ephraim'."

During the last month of training at the mountain, both generals had asked him to call them by their first names. Loren was easy. He had begun using his first name over a year ago, but Ephraim Hardcastle was different. He was a serious, straight-laced man and a strict disciplinarian. His presence demanded respect from everyone. Whenever he tried to call him "Ephraim," the name seemed to stick in his mouth and would come out broken, stammered, and uncomfortable. It felt wrong and ill-suited to call him anything but "Mr. Hardcastle" or "General Hardcastle."

"Yes, sir. I know, but I just find it really hard to do. I guess I respect you too much," Xavier explained.

Ephraim grinned. "I see. Whereas Loren..."

Xavier matched his grin. "Exactly! Who would respect that bumbling oaf?"

"Hey! I heard that!" Loren bellowed and jabbed a hard right at the king's face.

"What's the matter, Loren? Does the truth hurt?" Ephraim chuckled.

It wasn't true though. Xavier respected Loren a great deal, but it was a different kind of respect.

Loren's head snapped back as the king landed a sharp punch to his face.

"Maybe you should worry more about what my dad's going to do to you than what we're talking about," Xavier blurted at Loren, laughing.

The king and Loren danced from foot to foot, surveying each other for weaknesses. The king was about an inch shorter and fifty pounds lighter, but he made up for it with speed and quick footwork. Jeremiah was obviously aware of his limitations and strengths, for he would dance within striking distance, jab, and then dance quickly out of range again. Soon both men's jovial faces turned hard with concentration as adrenaline rushed through their bodies in response to the competition. Loren surprised the king with a sudden attack and struck him with a hard blow to the ribs and another to his face. Jeremiah staggered away, shook his head, and regained his balance and composure. Then it was the king's turn. With a bob and a weave, he launched a combination move that had Xavier's jaw slack with astonishment. Loren never saw it coming. The first two blows brought Loren's hands down to protect his ribs and kidneys. This was a bad move on the general's part, for the last punch landed squarely between Loren's eyes, and he simply collapsed. Jeremiah dropped his hands and looked down at his fallen friend before looking at Ephraim.

"He's going to be in a piss-poor mood when we bring him to. Maybe the boy should do it," he joked.

"Nooo, way!" Xavier blurted, hiding behind Ephraim. "You're the one who knocked him out! You wake him up."

His father laughed. Then with a sigh and a shake of his head, he knelt next to Loren, placed his hands on his head, and the healing white light shrouded both men. When the light dissipated, Loren sat up and rubbed his head.

"You seem to be having a bad day, mate," Ephraim called out jovially.

Loren glared up at his friend. "I think I need to stop being so easy on the Wells boys. They sure don't return the favor!"

Later that evening, Xavier climbed into bed as his father entered the small chamber that had served as his bedroom for the last six months.

"Ready for bed?" his father asked.

"Yep. The sooner I go to sleep, the sooner morning comes, and the sooner I can finally go home," he stated with a grin.

"Well, I need to talk to you about that, son."

"Please, don't tell me that I have to stay here another week or two..."

The king waved away Xavier's rebuttal. "No. We are going home tomorrow morning. But I want you to be prepared for what it will be like for you."

"Oh, Dad! You've told me this already."

"Humor me! You know that most of the damage your influx of powers created has been repaired, but there are still signs of the destruction. There are a few large cracks in the land that have yet to be filled in, and they're the most obvious."

"Dad, really, I get it. I know my surge of powers really wrecked the place. I know that I'm not to blame."

"You're not," his father said firmly.

"I know that," Xavier responded a bit testily.

"Xavier," the king sighed warily. "Please, hear me out. I know better than anyone what challenges you'll face when we return to Warwood. Will you listen?"

His father's tone sent a chill through him, and he drew his legs up to his chest, wrapping his arms around them. His father was about to give him some bad news. The king's tired, slumped shoulders made it evident, and his wary eyes screamed it. Something was wrong! He could feel it. Something had changed in Warwood. Unable to speak past the lump that had lodged in his throat, Xavier simply nodded and waited for his father to continue.

The king sighed again and stared at his hands clasped in his lap as he continued, "The citizens are uneasy. Now, the High Council has been told of your destiny, and there are others in high positions who have surmised who and what you are."

"So they know that I'm the Chosen?"

Jeremiah nodded. "Yes, some have concluded that, but there are others who have come to believe the contrary."

"The contrary?" Xavier frowned, unsure at first what his father meant. Then his meaning crashed over him, and he felt sick. He looked at his father, appalled. "They think... I'm... that I'm the Dark King?"

Jeremiah nodded.

"But why would..." Xavier paused. Why wouldn't they think it? Hadn't he thought the very same thing when his powers became so uncontrollable that he attacked innocent people and nearly destroyed the entire kingdom? Xavier met his father's wary eyes. "What do I do?"

"I didn't want your identity compromised this soon. Your

identity, your destiny, is too important to handle lightly. The way we choose to handle it could make a difference to your survival. Initially, I had hoped to keep it a secret. It would have been safer. However, I don't think that's an option now. I'm certain the events six months ago have reached our enemies. Danson may be a moron, but Dr. Angelo is not. She will have figured it out by now and started preparing Fox."

Xavier nodded, trying to swallow the lump in his throat. "They've known for longer than that, Dad. They called me the Chosen when... when they tortured and killed Milton. So... what are we going to do, Dad?"

The king nodded and sighed a third time. "Regardless of how we decide to handle it, I'm afraid your life in Warwood has changed permanently."

"Yeah, well, I should be used to that," Xavier muttered before addressing his father again. "What are my options?"

"Well, we could do nothing and allow the rumors and speculation to continue to spread. However, that means you'll have to cope with the attention from those who believe you're the Dark King as well as from those who believe you to be the Chosen. Or, we can perform a public ceremony, recognizing you as the Chosen—the King of the Light. The downside of making it publicly known that you are in fact the Chosen is you'll know no peace. You will become even more of a celebrity. You will become famous, a legend. There will be little privacy."

Xavier frowned. Man, this sucked! He had been looking forward to returning to Warwood so much! Now, he just felt anxious, afraid.

"Would it be better for the citizens to know who I am in preparing for war?" he asked his father.

Jeremiah smiled sadly down at him and stroked his worried brow. "No. I fear if it is publicly known that the Chosen exists, people will become relaxed and overly confident. Their training could become substandard as a result. So, in my opinion, I think we should let the rumors alone for now. There have always been rumors floating around about the Chosen. When the war grows closer and our people need encouragement, then we will present you to the kingdom as the Chosen."

Xavier nodded. "Okay. That sounds good."

His father stroked his hair. "I love you, son. Just remember, you're not alone in any of this. You can always come to me."

"I know, Dad. Thanks."

The king kissed his forehead, stroked his cheek, and then stood to leave. "You best get some sleep. Good night, son."

"Dad? Can I at least tell my friends that I'm the Chosen? I don't like lying to them. It feels disloyal," Xavier asked.

"Do you trust them with your life to tell them this secret?" the king asked soberly.

"Yeah. Yeah I do," he answered, unwaveringly.

"Then tell them, but impress upon them how important it is to keep the truth to themselves, no matter what happens or what they hear."

Chapter 2

There was so much blood! Xavier clamped both his hands over the wound and pressed down, but the blood simply pumped out between his fingers.

"Oh, God! Dad!" he cried out.

"Xavier, don't cry, son. I wouldn't... h... have changed a thing," Jeremiah spat out weakly. "B... be brave. Everything... will be... fine."

"No! It will never be fine!" Xavier wailed. "Dad, I need you! I can't lose you! I *won't* lose you!"

Xavier wiped at the tears streaming down his cheeks and repositioned his hands on top of the profusely bleeding wound in the king's abdomen.

"It won't work," a hoarse voice commented warily behind him.

Xavier bolted upright in bed, shivering and panting. Sighing miserably, he fell back into the bed and rubbed his eyes vigorously. It had been a dream, only a dream. He tried to reassure himself, but he knew that whatever it had been, it hadn't been just a dream. It had felt too real. With a shuddering moan, Xavier wiped the tears from his cheeks. He had witnessed a premonition. He had experienced enough of them in the past to know the difference. He had seen his father's death! His father would die; he would die soon.

The next morning came too soon in Xavier's opinion, and his father was shaking him awake.

"Up you get, sleepyhead," he chuckled.

Xavier moaned disgruntledly and rolled away from his father.

"Now, come on, son. We're heading home. I thought you were looking forward to seeing a certain brunette with large brown eyes," Jeremiah teased.

Xavier lifted his head and squinted up at his father.

"I am," he began hoarsely. "I just didn't sleep too well."

"Ah, too wound up to sleep, eh?" his father concluded.

"Yeah, I guess you could say that," he muttered, sitting up and yawning.

"Well, you better get a move on. We leave in twenty minutes," the king chirped, patting the boy's head before leaving the room.

Nearly twenty minutes later, the king, General Hardcastle, Henrick, and Xavier exited King's Mountain and stood on the summit. Miles and miles of wilderness could be seen in every direction. Xavier shivered and snuggled deeper into his coat.

"All right. We will teleport to the airfield where the jet is waiting to fly us back to Warwood," his father announced. "Xavier, you'll need to pair up with me since I'm familiar with the landing area."

"Why don't we just teleport back to Warwood, Dad? Why even bother with a plane?" Xavier questioned.

"Teleporting can be very dangerous, young sire," Ephraim answered.

"Dangerous? How can it be dangerous? I mean, the worst that can happen is I'd accidently teleport to the wrong place. Big whoop!" Xavier scoffed.

"Xavier!" his father warned. "Do not dismiss General Hardcastle's warning!"

Xavier's cockiness deflated, and he muttered, "Sorry, Mr. Hardcastle."

"It's understandable to think that teleportation is benign and not dangerous, but you'd think wrong," Ephraim responded.

"I don't understand, though. How is it dangerous?"

"Son, what's the greatest distance you've ever teleported?" his father asked.

Xavier blinked. "Ah, I don't know. I guess a couple of miles. I teleported from the academy to Center Square once."

Jeremiah's brows rose. "You did? When did you do that?"

Xavier shuffled his feet. "Ah, just before I accidently started a food fight at Warwood Café," he answered bashfully.

Henrick snickered. "Yeah, I remember that, and so does my forehead," he interjected, pointing at the faint, thin scar on his brow.

"Yeah, ah... sorry about that, Henrick," Xavier muttered, cringing.

"Son, if you teleport into an area you're not familiar with or an area that is constantly changing, like Center Square, you could teleport into something or someone."

Xavier snickered at the thought. "What would happen if I teleported into Loren? Would I end up with his nose or something? Man, that would suck," he joked.

"No, son, you and Loren could be severely injured or killed. However, it's more likely that you'd receive more devastating injuries since your body mass is quite a bit less than Loren's. Son, teleporting into other people, or worse yet, into solid objects is what makes teleporting so dangerous. People have killed themselves doing it. Think back to your first experience with teleporting. Do you remember it?"

Xavier thought back to over a year ago when he had accidently teleported into his father's Latin class. He had run into his father and ended up with an enormous bruise down his left side as a result.

"That was a painful experience, wasn't it? You hadn't teleported into me, but within inches of me, and it still caused you pain. Teleporting into someone or something else can rip the teleporter apart."

"Oh," Xavier gasped. "I didn't know that."

"But to answer your question, we can't teleport to the kingdom because quite simply, we're close to three thousand miles away from Warwood, and teleporting is extremely inaccurate and volatile at those distances. Most teleporters can't teleport more than a few miles. We've had teleporters who tried to push their limits with disastrous results. One man ended up in the middle of the Atlantic when he tried to teleport himself to France for a holiday. The stress he put on his body was so great that he had a stroke and passed out. He drowned."

"Oh, wow! I... I didn't realize," Xavier responded.

"Well, now you do, and that is why we don't simply teleport back to Warwood. Once we're within range, we could teleport to the palace. There are designated teleport areas throughout the kingdom were teleporters can safely use their power without fear of accidents. But I think we'll simply drive through the kingdom to announce your return."

"Oh, okay."

Jeremiah inhaled deeply. "Now, are you ready to go home?" The king held out his arms invitingly with a wink.

"I don't know. Now, I'm scared to teleport," Xavier

commented with a dry snicker as he stepped into his father's arms.

The moment the king's arms wrapped around him, he felt the tugging and pulling sensation of teleportation, and he closed his eyes to the sensations. Seconds later, he stood in a large open field with a small leer jet warming up a hundred meters from them. As Jeremiah led him to the jet, a soft pop behind them announced Henrick and Ephraim's arrival.

Once on board, Xavier sank into a leather-covered chair and buckled his seat belt while his father went into the cockpit, settled into the pilot's seat, pulled on a head set, and began flipping switches.

"Dad knows how to fly a plane?" Xavier questioned as Ephraim settled into a seat across the aisle from him.

Ephraim smiled. "Oh, yes. He's been a pilot for years."

"Wow, I didn't know that. That's so cool! Do you think he'd teach me to fly?"

"From what I hear, your highness, he doesn't need to," Henrick interrupted with a wink.

Once the plane was in the air, Xavier reclined his chair and watched his father with fascination as he operated the plane with competence and ease. Between the hum of the engines and the light vibrations of a smooth flight, Xavier's eyes soon grew heavy, and he dropped off to sleep. In what seemed like seconds, his father was shaking him awake.

"We're home, son."

Xavier peered out the window and saw a limo waiting with Loren and Robbie standing next to it. Xavier grinned and tried to jump to his feet, but he was still buckled in. He hastily unfastened the belt's clasp, raced to the door of the plane, jumped down the steps to the ground, and raced to Robbie. His first thought as he hugged her was that she smelled really good.

Robbie giggled against his shoulder. "Did you miss me? You realize it's only been a week since I visited?"

Xavier pulled away and looked down at her smiling. "Yeah, I know, but before that I hadn't seen you, hugged you, or kissed you for months," he responded, and he couldn't help but laugh with her.

"Well, don't hold back on my account, sire. Kiss away," Loren teased from beside them.

Xavier blinked up at the large man. "Loren? When did you get here?" he teased.

"Ah, thank you so much, young sire. After all I've done for you, this is the thanks I get? I'm completely forgotten when a pretty girl is within a mile of you. I'm nothing more than chopped liver to you!" Loren complained, doing his best to contrive a forlorn expression.

"No, of course you're not chopped liver, Loren," he told the general with a wicked grin. "I can tolerate chopped liver!"

"You little..." Loren spat and lunged at Xavier, but the boy was quick on his feet and jumped out of his reach, raising his hands defensively.

"Whoa, Loren. You don't want me to turn you into a human popsicle again, do ya?"

"Son, stop harassing my general," Jeremiah ordered before adding with a wink, "He's very delicate after all."

"Delicate! Jeremy, should I describe the time I kicked your butt in front of most of the kingdom? Then we can decide which one of us is the delicate one!" Loren retorted.

"That was nearly twenty years ago! I wasn't much older than Xavier, and if I remember correctly, you were nearly six feet tall and outweighed me by at least fifty pounds!"

"Excuses, excuses," Loren taunted as he opened the back door for the king, Xavier, Robbie and Ephraim.

Shaking his head, Jeremiah slid into the limo, and Xavier

clambered in after him. Robbie scooted into the seat next to Xavier, while Ephraim settled beside the king. The men began leafing through a large folder of papers. Henrick sat in the front passenger seat next to Loren.

Xavier couldn't help himself. He sat grinning like a fool, staring at Robbie and holding her hand. His father and Ephraim exchanged amused looks before returning to the papers on the king's lap.

"God, it's so good to see you," Xavier whispered feverishly. Then looking at the men to make sure they were occupied, he leaned toward her and added softly, "I really want to get you alone."

Robbie blushed and giggled. Then she settled for playful innocence. "Whatever for, your highness?"

Xavier leaned in closer so that his lips were centimeters from her ear. "I'd like to kiss you."

Jeremiah suddenly cleared his throat loudly, and the sound made Xavier spring away from Robbie, blushing.

"Control your telepathy, son. You're broadcasting those thoughts again," his father informed him through his thoughts.

Xavier's blush deepened while Robbie exchanged a curious look between father and son. Fifteen minutes later, the limo pulled slowly up to the grand entrance to Warwood. A large steel door squealed in protest as it swung down. The car slowly pulled through the gatehouse and onto the main roadway adjacent to the open market at Center Square. As the limo crept past the bustling market, the crowd suddenly stilled and watched. Two small children running happily around a vendor table were hastily ushered away from the vehicle by a plump woman. Several people scurried away from the limo as if it were a bomb. Xavier didn't need his abilities to know that his people were afraid. They were afraid of him! He sighed heavily. This wasn't going to be easy.

Robbie's hand slipped into his and squeezed. His eyes swept to hers, and she gave him a reassuring smile. He smiled back. It was hard to be forlorn about anything when she smiled. She was so beautiful. Minutes later, they pulled through the palace gates and continued the short distance to the palace. Xavier looked out the window at the building he called home. He reminisced to his first ride to the palace. He had been so nervous, excited, and in utter awe over the grand building with its stained-glass windows and gargoyle storm drains. He smiled at the memory. As fantastic as the palace was, now it seemed a bit smaller. But then, he wasn't that same starry-eyed kid he had been nearly two years before. The limo rolled to a stop in front of the palace doors, Loren opened the door and the group piled out.

"Welcome home, young sire," Loren smiled as he ruffled the boy's hair.

Xavier laughed. "Thanks! It's good to be home."

"Come on, son. Emma is dying to see you," Jeremiah called, beckoning him.

Xavier took Robbie's hand and hurried forward. As he approached the door, he noticed two royal guards standing next to the entrance. His smile slipped as he drew closer, and one of the guards shuffled slightly away from him. Xavier stopped and studied the man. He recognized the guard. He had been one of the guards who had hoisted an unconscious king onto his shoulders and carried him to safety during the height of Xavier's attack on the kingdom. The guard was young, no more than twenty-five. His entire body was tense, and he seemed to be holding his breath.

"Hi," Xavier whispered, releasing Robbie's hand to move toward the young guard.

The man stood about four inches taller than Xavier and had a wiry, slight frame. The guard was well trained and kept his eyes forward.

"At ease," Xavier glanced at the man's badge, "Guard Pickens."

Pickens looked down at him briefly, but no other part of him seemed at ease at all. "Yes, sire?" he inquired, his voice a bit unsteady.

Xavier held his hand out, and the young man stiffened more, if that was even possible, and looked down at the prince's hand, puzzled.

"Sire?" his eyes finally met Xavier's and stayed.

Xavier smiled at the man. "I wanted to shake the hand of the man who got my father to safety when I..." Xavier broke eye contact this time and ran his hand through his hair before looking back at the guard. "Look, I know what I did was horrible, and even though it was beyond my control to have stopped it, I promise you I will work my butt off to earn your trust and respect. I give you my solemn oath that I will never attack my people again." Xavier sighed and nervously ran his hand through his hair again. "Anyway, thanks for saving my father's life. I... I don't know what I would have done if I'd been responsible for killing him."

The guard gave him a curt nod before returning to attention at his post.

Recognizing his conversation with the guard was over, Xavier turned, took Robbie's hand, and entered the palace.

Robbie squeezed his hand. "Don't worry, Xavier. They'll come around. You're a great king, or at least, you will be. I know it!"

Xavier stopped her halfway down the corridor that led to the royal residence and the residences for both General Hardcastle and General Jefferson. "Thanks, Robbie. I needed to hear that," he whispered before kissing her. He felt a spike of sensations, and he hugged her closer.

"Son? If we keep Emma waiting any longer, she will smack both of us. Now, release Robbie and get a move on,"

his father's voice announced, invading his thoughts.

Xavier released Robbie abruptly and groaned.

"What is it?" Robbie whispered breathlessly.

Xavier smiled dryly down at her. "Dad," he answered simply. "Come on before he has a stroke." He took her hand and pulled her down the corridor and into the large open foyer. A grand ornate staircase stood in front of them. To the right was the entrance to the Jefferson residence, and the Hardcastle residence was on the left. Xavier led Robbie past the doors and up the wide staircase. Another guard stood at the summit of the stairs next to a large oak door that led into the royal residence—his home. His father stood on the platform peering down at the teens with smiling, knowing eyes.

"We really need to work on controlling your telepathy when you're in the company of Robbie, son. It's quite disturbing to have your thoughts blaring into my head," he said softly, and Xavier's face ignited.

Robbie looked between the king and Xavier opened-mouth. "He's... transmitting his thoughts about me? How come I can't hear it? What's he saying about me?"

Xavier's blush grew; he could feel it creeping down his neck.

Jeremiah smirked. "I think the last question is best answered by Xavier. As for why you can't hear him, my guess would be either he's just transmitting those thoughts only strong enough for telepaths to hear, or you're not really listening to him. Could you be a bit preoccupied?" After seeing Robbie's face become just as red as his son's, the king turned to Ephraim. "Are you able to get anything from him?"

"Only brief impressions, but yes, he's broadcasting his thoughts well enough that I'm receiving some thoughts," Ephraim answered.

"Oh, great," Xavier muttered, released Robbie's hand, and moped up the remaining steps.

Robbie followed, perplexed and curious. She would have to ask Xavier what he had been thinking about later. Right now, she wanted to see his face when he entered the residence. She hurried up the steps and took his hand again, grinning. Xavier couldn't help but grin back.

Xavier opened the door to the residence as his father stepped aside to have a word with the guard on duty. As he stepped inside, a loud chorus of voices called out, "Welcome home!" Xavier froze in his tracks and stared, dumbfounded at the two dozen or so faces all grinning back at him. The guys were there, Beck's flaming red hair standing out. Daniel was standing in front of Mike, hopping in place with excitement. Then all at once, the group converged on him, patting his back, hugging him, and welcoming him home.

"Good to have you back. We can finally have a decent rugby match," Mac blurted, thumping Xavier's shoulder.

"Xavier! Xavier!" Daniel chirped, twisting his way through the crowd of bodies, and then throwing himself at Xavier.

"Hey, Daniel," he responded, staggering backwards from the smaller boy's weight.

"Man, it's so good to have you home, cousin." Daniel exclaimed. "Dad wouldn't let me visit you at the mountain. He was being such... a... a..."

"Careful, Daniel," Mike whispered. "You may want to think about how to finish that since I'm standing right behind you and in prime position to bust your little butt if I don't like what I hear." Mike's relaxed posture and wicked gleam in his eye belied the reprimand.

"Hey, Uncle Mike," Xavier greeted, smiling.

"Hey kiddo. Glad you survived months of isolation with my brother. I can't begin to describe the pity I felt for you," he responded conspiratorially, giving Xavier a brief hug.

Xavier's eyes widened. Michael Spencer made a joke. He was actually teasing the king!

"Welcome home, sweetie," Lana whispered, hugging him close and kissing his cheek. "I've missed you so much."

"Thanks, Lana. I missed you too." Xavier responded quietly as he hugged her back. There was such warmth, such comfort in that hug. It filled him with calm and peace that only a mother's love could do.

Suddenly, there was another flood of bodies rushing at him, and Xavier was knocked flat on his back while he was playfully assaulted with wet-willies, noogies, and thumps.

Laughing, Xavier yelled, "Ouch! Hey, I'd like to keep my ribs intact, guys. Come on, get off!"

Slowly the group of boys climbed off Xavier, and Court helped him to his feet, grinning. "All right there, mate?"

"Boys!" Erica gasped, rolling her eyes before hugging Xavier awkwardly. "Good to have one of my favorite scapegoats back."

Xavier laughed. Erica was Loren Jefferson's youngest daughter, and like Loren, she had a wicked sense of humor and a knack for mischief. "Thanks a lot, but do you really think I need to be your scapegoat? I get into enough trouble without your help."

"Amen!" the king bellowed with a smirk.

"He gets it honestly, Jeremiah Wells!" a soft reprimand directed at the king parted the crowd. Mrs. Sommers' eyes widened the moment she spotted Xavier, and she squealed, cupping her hands to her mouth as her eyes filled with tears. "Oh, my!" she gasped, bustling forward and capturing Xavier in a tight hug. Xavier felt his own eyes water. Although Mrs. Sommers was his governess, she had been the mothering influence he had so desperately needed after his mother died. He loved her dearly. Her body shuddered against him as a soft sob escaped her, but within seconds, she contained her emotions and pushed him at arm's length to look him over. "Let me have a look at you," she demanded past her tears. "Prince Wells, you've gotten so big! Your school uniforms will never do now! You'll need a new set and shoes as well," she finished, looking down at his feet.

Xavier laughed, hugging and kissing the older woman on the cheek. "I missed you too, Mrs. Sommers."

Finally, she swatted him away. "Oh you! Stop that or you'll have a blubbering old woman on your hands!" She briskly turned toward the crowd and announced, "There are refreshments and snacks in the dining hall. Help yourselves!"

The crowd began to disperse in different directions, some heading to the dining hall, some moving toward the king and his generals standing nearby, and a few began dancing when someone turned on some music.

"Sire?" an overly sweet voice called behind him.

Xavier turned and saw Loren's oldest daughter, Sara, standing behind him. Sara was only about a year and a half older than Xavier, but she often acted superior, as if she were much older. Basically, she was a little stuck up. Xavier wasn't sure why she was that way. Both Loren and his wife, Lucy, were down-to-earth, nice people.

"Hello, Miss Jefferson," Xavier responded, nodding formally to her.

Sara looked him up and down, and then surprising him, she hugged him.

"I'm glad you're back," she whispered, her lips so close to his ear he felt each word breathed against his cheek. Chills shivered down his spine before rushing out to the tips of his fingers and toes.

Robbie cleared her throat loudly from beside them. Sara lingered briefly to kiss his cheek before giving him a coy,

23

sweet smile as she stepped away. Xavier went flushed and his mind blank.

"Ah... ah... yeah. Thanks, Sara. I'm glad to be back," he stammered.

"Excuse me," Robbie interrupted rudely, glaring at Sara. "I'd like to dance with *my boyfriend*." Then she dragged Xavier into the small crowd of dancers. The couch and arm chairs had been shoved to the perimeter to provide ample dancing space.

Xavier pulled Robbie close and began to sway in time to the lulling love ballad, but Robbie continued to glower at Sara.

"What's wrong?" Xavier whispered.

"Nothing," Robbie responded a bit too quickly, but when her eyes met his, she smiled shyly. "I'm glad you're home. I missed you so much!"

"I missed you too," Xavier choked out as Robbie nestled against him, laying her head against his shoulder. Her soft warm breath caressed his neck, and he had to close his eyes against the heat building inside him. Abruptly, he pulled away, grabbed her hand, and pulled her into the library, closing the door behind them. He then turned to her and yanked her against him, kissing her. He had dreamed of this! And now that the dream was finally a reality, it was even better than he had imagined. Her lips were softer. Her body wasn't just warm; it was hot and alive against him.

"Robbie," he moaned against her lips. "I love you."

He felt Robbie's body tremble before she answered, "Oh God, Xavier. I've loved you all my life!"

When they kissed again, Xavier thought he would combust from the heat pumping through his veins. When his lips finally left hers, he had to hold onto her to steady himself, and he opened his eyes. It was at this exact moment that Robbie gasped and stepped out of his arms, her face lifting with shock.

Xavier frowned. "What?"

"Your... your eyes!" she stuttered. "Your eyes are glowing, Xavier!"

"What!" His heart thumped hard in his chest, and he ran to the nearest shiny object, a brass lamppost. Sure enough, his eyes glowed bright pink. He blinked and stared again. Yep, it was still there but fainter.

"Oh no!" he gasped miserably. "Crap! I glow like dad! How sick is that?"

Robbie started giggling.

Xavier turned and glared at her. "Why are you laughing? This is embarrassing!"

Robbie tried to stop laughing, but she couldn't, and in the end, Xavier had to chuckle with her. She was so beautiful when she laughed. He went to her, pulled her back into his arms and kissed her. She stopped laughing.

When he released her, she stared up at him absentmindedly. Then she mumbled, "They're not glowing now. Why did they glow before and not now?"

Blushing, Xavier opened his mouth to answer, but suddenly the door swung open, knocking him into Robbie, and they tumbled to the floor. He would have landed on top of her if he hadn't stopped himself. Without thinking, he activated his levitation ability and hovered a few inches above her before rolling to the side and falling to the floor next to her. His father and Mike stood in the doorway, staring down at Xavier with nothing short of awe.

Finally, his father broke the stunned silence that filled the room. "Son, you have other guests here besides Robbie. I think you should return to the party."

Xavier scrambled to his feet. "Y... yes, sir. Sorry." Then he turned and helped Robbie to her feet, and the pair scrambled from the room and away from the men's all-knowing smirks.

"There you are!" Daniel blurted loudly the instant Xavier and Robbie emerged from the library.

Every eye in the room swept toward the couple, and Xavier felt his face combust into tingling heat once again. Oblivious to the attention, Daniel danced up to Xavier.

"Hey, Xavier! Guess what?" But Daniel didn't wait for Xavier to guess before he was rambling on. "Dad built me a new fort. It's even better than the first one! You should see it! It's got this rope swing, a rope ladder, two different floors, and all kinds of stuff! It's really cool!"

"Sounds like it," Xavier agreed with an indulging smile. "Maybe the guys and I can come over sometime and camp out in your fort."

Daniel's eyes lit up, and he looked like he would explode with excitement. "Oh, wow! Seriously? That would be awesome!"

"Well, I'll talk it over with the guys and let you know."

"Sweet!" the smaller boy exclaimed and hurried toward his dad.

Xavier could hear him animatedly explaining to Mike that he was going to have a sleep over with Xavier and all his friends.

The party began to wind down close to eleven. The few who remained were Xavier's closest friends. Xavier sat in an armchair with Robbie next to him while Court, Erica, Garrett, Beck, Harry, and Frankie sat around him.

"Look, guys, I have something I need to tell you," Xavier began, suddenly very nervous about what he had to say. He looked at Beck. "I lied to you, Beck. You asked me at the mountain if I was the Chosen. I couldn't tell you then; no one was supposed to know. It would have been safer for all of us that way, but after what I did to the kingdom, I don't think I can hide it. You were right. I *am* the Chosen."

The group just looked up at him blankly.

"Didn't you guys hear me?"

Garrett was the first to answer, "Geez, X. We kind of already figured that out for ourselves."

"Yeah," Beck added. "You're a horrible liar, mate. Besides, how can you not be the Chosen with all those abilities! How many do you have now?"

Xavier shrugged, frowning at the thought that no one was surprised by his announcement. His father was right. There was no way he could hide who and what he was any longer. "Ah... to be honest, I've never counted," he answered Beck's question distractedly. "I don't think I really want to know."

"Dang! That many?" Garrett gasped.

"Well, we all figured out that you had to be the Chosen a long time ago. All of us except Frankie that is. That git thought that you could be the Dark King!"

"No, I didn't!" Frankie protested. "I said that my cousin thought he might be the Dark King. I don't think... I've never thought that!"

Beck smirked at Xavier and gave him a he's-so-easy-to-torment look. Xavier had to grin. God, it was great to be back to a normal life. Well, maybe not exactly normal, but normal for him.

Chapter 3

The sword glinted orange in the dusk light as it sliced through the air, striking the king across the abdomen. Jeremiah cringed and doubled over in pain as the sword arced around and swept across his back. The king recoiled from the blow, arching backwards. His sword clattered to the brick tiled floor. Danson sneered triumphantly as he plunged the sword into the king's chest. Jeremiah fell in a heap onto the ground.

"NOOO!" Xavier screamed, sitting up in bed drenched in sweat. For a couple of panicked moments, he glanced around the dark room, confused and disoriented. Then he remembered. He was home. He was safe. His father was safe and sleeping in the next room. He wasn't slain and dying on the palace's garden patio. The war wasn't yet upon them. With a loud sigh, Xavier flopped back into his pillows and ran his hands over his face.

"Hello, young sire," a deep voice spoke softly from the corner of his room.

Xavier's body was suddenly alive as fear and adrenaline crawled across his skin like a swarm of insects. Instinctively and without thought, he catapulted from his bed, summoning a blaring electro force at the ready in his palm.

"Who's there?" he demanded, sounding braver than he felt.

"Easy boy," the voice responded softly. Then with a soft pop, every light in the room switched on.

Xavier blinked rapidly against the sudden brightness. The prophet, Abraham Vincent, stood leaning casually against Xavier's computer desk.

"Could you put that away, sire? I'm not terribly fond of being electrocuted," the prophet remarked with a smirk.

Xavier extinguished the force and dropped his hand to his side. "What are you doing here?"

The man chuckled. "I haven't been able to visit you for six months, and that is all you can think of saying?"

The prophet grinned. Xavier wasn't sure he had ever seen the old man grin before. He was struck by how young he appeared when smiling. He was handsome for an old guy.

"How have you been? Lord, you've gotten taller," he remarked as he sauntered toward him.

Xavier blinked. Did he just ask him how he had been? When did the prophet inquire into his well-being?

"Ah..., I'm fine," he answered nervously.

"Good to be home, eh?"

"Yeah, it is."

The prophet chuckled softly and ran a hand through his short-cropped gray hair, giving it a spiked, rolled-out-of-bed look. "I can see my idle chatter is making you nervous, so I'll get to the point." He looked down at Xavier with a solemn expression. "I know what your nightmare was about. I'd like to tell you that it was only a dream, but I'd be lying, and I'm sure you already know that it wasn't just a dream."

The prophet paused and looked down at him as if expecting a response. He didn't want to talk about this! "Y... yeah," he managed to croak out.

Abe nodded and continued, "I'd like to tell you it won't happen, but I'm afraid it will."

He felt pain tighten in his chest, and he bit back a sob building there. Abruptly, he turned away from the prophet and busied himself by straightening his sparse nightstand, but the picture of his mother was his undoing, and he buried his face in his hands, vainly fighting against the tears.

"Xavier? Ah, come on, boy. Don't do that!" the prophet whispered, his voice thick with remorse. He grabbed Xavier's shoulders and spun him around.

A blinding flash erupted from the prophet's hands the instant his hands came into contact with Xavier, and he yanked his hands away as if burned. Xavier gasped, his grief momentarily forgotten.

"Wh... what was that?" he exclaimed, looking up into the prophet's shocked face.

"I... I'm not exactly sure. But if I were to venture a guess, I'd say that it appears that you and I create a paradox now that your influx is complete and you've acquired all your abilities. I fear that if I were to touch you again, it would end my ability to time travel, and I would cease to exist in this realm," Abe stated, still staring down at his hands. He looked at Xavier and suddenly grinned. "Let's not do that again, eh?"

Xavier understood very little of the older man's words but couldn't help but smile. "Prophet Vincent... sir... can it be stopped? Can I prevent my father from being killed?

The prophet sighed. "I don't know, Xavier, but if anyone has a chance at stopping it, it would be you. I'll do what I can to help you so long as it doesn't lead to your demise."

Xavier nodded. Maybe he could get his father out of the kingdom before the battle began.

The prophet cleared his throat and added, "Let me amend my last statement, sire. I will do what I can to help you so long as it doesn't lead to your death, the downfall of the kingdom, or the success of the Dark King in his conquest for world domination."

Xavier frowned. He didn't give a damn about the kingdom or the world if his father wasn't in it. How did the prophet know what he was thinking?

"Prince Wells," the old man sighed, closing his eyes to reign in the irritation that painted his face and laced his words. "I am telepathic. This kingdom is your responsibility whether you want it or not. You should care about the safety and the future of its citizens! Can you honestly tell me you'd choose the death of numerous innocent men, women, and children in exchange for your father's life?"

Xavier squirmed under the prophet's heated glare before answering, "No, sir."

The prophet exhaled the tension that had built up inside him. "All right, look. You need to understand how things are for a time bender," he announced as he grabbed Xavier's desk chair and dragged it next to the bed.

Xavier sank onto the edge of the bed as once again something about the prophet sparked a memory. The man reminded him of someone... Then it struck him. Abe reminded him of his father! As the old man settled in the chair in front of him, Xavier studied the prophet's features closely. His eyes looked remarkably like his dad's. His voice, the way he spoke, was similar to the king's voice, and the way he kept running his hand through his hair was a gesture he had seen Jeremiah do numerous times.

"What is it, boy?" Abe questioned, his brow frowning with concern, much like his father's would.

"Ah..." Xavier stammered, hopeful. "Um, are you... are you my father?"

Abe's eyes widened with surprise before humor danced into his features. "What?" he blurted with a chuckle. "You think that I'm Jeremiah Wells IV?"

His reaction was answer enough. The prophet was not

his father, and Xavier felt his hope sink. Feeling dangerously close to tears, Xavier muttered, "No, I guess not."

"Why did you think I was your father, young sire?" the prophet asked softly, seeing the boy's forlorn expression.

Xavier shrugged in response.

"Xavier? Look at me," Abe ordered gently.

Xavier's eyes reluctantly met the prophet's.

"Why did you think I was your father?"

Xavier fought back the tears that pooled in his eyes. "I... I guess... you remind me of him—the way you talk, your eyes... I don't know. I guess I was just hoping that you were because if you're my dad then... then there's still a chance he can be saved... that he won't die."

"Xavier," the prophet chided gently. "I'm not your father. I've told you, your father is dead in my world and has been for a long time. He was killed during the great war, the War of Kings."

Xavier lost his battle against his tears, and they flowed freely down his cheeks. "What do I do? There's got to be some way of saving him!" he moaned, wiping the tears from his cheeks.

"There is a chance. I'm not sure it will work, but I have an idea. Your father is a very stubborn man," Abe told him before adding bitterly, "The man nearly got himself killed at the climax of your influx. I told him long ago that he needed to obtain additional powers from the Key, but he refused to listen until it was almost too late." The prophet shook his head irritably. "So, reasoning with him will be futile. We'll need to be stealthier, devious if you will. But before you can do what I have in mind, before I can tell you my plan, you must strengthen your telepathic abilities, especially those blocking abilities! If I were to tell you the plan now, Jeremiah would most assuredly pry it from you, and it would fail. Do you think you can do that, young sire? Do you think you can work on your telepathy?"

Xavier nodded enthusiastically as hope for the future swelled inside him. "Yes, sir! I can. I will. I'll do anything if it means Dad won't die."

Abe nodded. "I know you will, Xavier. I know. I want you to have a better life than what you have in my world. A happy king is a great king."

"What's my life like... in the future?"

The prophet hesitated before answering with great care. "Sire, knowing too much about the future can have unexpected and often dire effects on events. I can't describe your life in great detail. I can only give you the necessary facts that will help you save your father. I don't yet know what the effects of saving your father will have on your future or the future of this kingdom. I believe his life could only be beneficial, but I cannot make that assumption. I must get a vision or see it first-hand."

"So... are you saying... what are you saying?"

"I'm saying I will know if my plan works when I return to my time. Time travel is messy and complicated, young sire." Abe paused to study the boy. Xavier needed to know the rules that govern time bending and time changing. He must tell the boy and pray he was old enough to understand.

With a deep breath, Abe began carefully. "Remember what I told you at Mirror Lake? About the three types of destinies? I don't think the survival of the king would create adverse effects, but I must be certain it won't before I can follow through with my plan. At the same time, I must commit to the plan in order to see if it will work."

"Uh, so... what you're saying is you've got to decide to tell me to do something to change the future before you can tell if it'll work?" Xavier surmised.

Abe raised a brow, impressed. The boy was bright, very bright. He chuckled at the irony in such a thought. "Yes, that's exactly it."

"But... you've decided, right? So why don't you know if it will work out?"

"I won't know until I return to my time, my world."

Xavier frowned. "But... you knew at King's Mountain... that time you disappeared," Xavier shuddered at the memory of the prophet's death, his slaughter.

The prophet nodded gravely. "Yes, well, that was a very different circumstance, young sire. What happened that day was a result of a very poor decision on your part. It nearly got you killed! If your father and his generals hadn't seen my demise, they wouldn't have taken such heed. If they hadn't witnessed my death, they would have spent hours debating and determining where you'd gone. You and I both know that if they had been even one minute later, you would have been killed," the prophet remarked in a rough voice.

Xavier looked up at the old man and was taken aback by the anger he saw in the man's face. He quickly looked away from Abe's intense gaze.

"That decision nearly got us both killed! You need to realize that a man's actions don't just affect him! His actions affect the people closest to him. This is exponentially true for you, sire. You are the Chosen! Your decisions affect all of mankind!"

Xavier's shoulders dropped as guilt weighed heavier and heavier on him. Finally, he managed a soft, "Sorry."

The prophet expelled a large sigh and stretched back in the chair, the spindles creaking in protest at the movement. "I know you are, Xavier," he said softly. Leaning forward in the chair once more, the prophet returned the conversation back to time bending laws. "But as for time bending and changing, when I return to my time, having made the decision to intervene, I will be able to see the results of that intervention." Abe saw the hope gush into the boy's face, and he rushed to interrupt his excessive enthusiasm. "No, Xavier. He will not be alive. He won't be alive until after the plan is implemented and completed. However, I have the ability to see alternate realities once I've committed to intervening. So I'll be able to determine if the actions are successful and what it will do to the future of the kingdom."

"Sir? You told me at Mirror Lake that you'd only interfere with destinies that must be changed. Why are you helping me now with Dad? Is he one of those destinies that have to be changed?" Xavier questioned.

The prophet seemed to shrink. He looked guiltily back at Xavier before responding. "No. His destiny does not adversely affect the future of the kingdom. There were a few issues early on, but it all worked out."

"Then why are you doing all this? Why are you helping me?" Xavier asked.

At first, Xavier didn't think he would answer. But finally, after a deep breath, Abe responded, "I guess I'm just as anxious as you to see that the stubborn, hard-headed git lives to torment us all for years to come."

Xavier laughed. "Yeah, imagine being that git's son. The tormenting is much worse!"

Abe's smirk widened. "No imagining necessary, young sire."

Xavier laughed and watched as the prophet stood and returned the chair to its rightful place.

"Well, you better get back to bed. You've got a lot of work to do," he announced, winking at him.

Xavier grinned. "Yes, sir. Good night."

"Good night, Xavier," the prophet responded and then vanished with a soft pop. Xavier stared at the empty air where the prophet had stood just a heartbeat ago.

Chapter 4

The next morning, Xavier strolled into the dining hall with a large smile. "Morning, Dad!" he said cheerfully, kissing the king noisily on the cheek.

Jeremiah choked on his tea. "Morning, son. What's put you in such a good mood?" he asked, eyeing the boy with amused suspicion.

"What can I say? Home life agrees with me!" Xavier beamed.

Jeremiah laughed. "Yeah, I can see that," he commented, glancing at his watch. "But since when did you get up before the crack of eight without a cattle prod?" he joked.

"Well... never, but I wanted to ask you something before you left for work."

The king laid down his fork and wiped his mouth with his napkin before giving Xavier his full attention. "All right. What is it, son?"

"Can the guys and I have a campout by the lake tonight?"

With a grin, the king answered, "I don't see why not." Seeing the boy's eager expression, he probed, "Is there something more you wish to discuss?"

"Well, yeah. I was wondering if... sometime today... if you had time in your schedule, could we do a bit of training? I'd like to start working on my telepathy and blocking capabilities."

Jeremiah looked at his son, dumbfounded. The boy had always fought him on working on his telepathic abilities. "You're asking me to work with you on your blocking power?"

"Yes, sir. I..." Xavier's mind raced for a reason. "I don't want Fox to be able to get into my head and use Robbie and how I feel about her against me."

Jeremiah nodded. "No, neither do I. It's a hard thing to live with when it happens," he told him roughly.

Xavier realized his father wasn't speaking hypothetically. He had experienced it first-hand with Xavier's mother. A hard lump constricted his throat. Xavier had always felt responsible for how his mother had been taken, tortured, and killed by William LeMasters. He never told anyone that he had witnessed what had been done to her before and during her slaughter. He knew she had been beaten, tortured, abused, and raped. He had seen it all unfold in his dreams—his visions. But he had never considered the guilt his father carried over her death. Suddenly his father made a lot of sense to him. He couldn't help but feel his sadness and loneliness. Xavier sank into the chair next to his father.

"That's why you pushed Lana away at the mountain, isn't it?" Xavier whispered.

The king stared at him for a moment before answering. "Yes. All the memories and feelings I felt when I found your mother came rushing back when I saw what William was doing to those he captured who had remained loyal to me. I couldn't allow Lana to suffer for loving me the way your mother had."

Xavier stared unseeingly at his feet for a moment. He shuddered at the thought of those things happening to Robbie. He looked up at his father.

"I saw what happened to her, to mom, in that nightmare

I had at my grandparents when you went after her. I... I saw everything they did to her. How they tied her down and sent electro forces into her body; how that... that witch Dr. Angelo sent pain into her over and over again until Mom just... passed out. But they wouldn't let her stay unconscious. They'd bring her back and do it all over again. And," Xavier took a shaky breath, trying to calm the emotions rippling through him. "Both Danson and William... they... they raped her."

Pain and devastation flashed across the king's features. "Yes, they did," he remarked, his voice breaking. After a deep breath, the king continued, "Dub told me he believed that you had a post-monition that night. And, from what little I got from you, I knew you'd seen the worst."

Xavier rushed to continue. "I had always thought it would have never happened if I hadn't run away, if she hadn't been out looking for me. I blamed myself for her death for the longest time."

"Xavier, it was never..."

"Dad, let me finish, please!" Xavier urged, and the king nodded. "I had always thought I was at fault for her death, and that they killed her because of me. Then Maggie and Dublin were both killed too. That's why I ran off to face LeMasters on my own. I didn't want anyone else dying for me, sacrificing themselves to protect me. But I now realize that none of that was my fault. William would have taken Mom no matter what I did. So I guess what I'm trying to say is that it wasn't me... and it wasn't you either, Dad. It was that evil, sick man who was responsible. I'm not completely sure that he wasn't truly the Dark King. I mean, everything he touched turned evil or was destroyed. But it was never our fault," Xavier finished, his voice wavering.

Tears had filled the king's eyes, and he stared at his son with awe and admiration. "When did you get so smart?" he ribbed with a watery smile. "Come here and give your dad a hug."

Grinning sheepishly, Xavier stood and stepped toward Jeremiah. Jeremiah yanked him into his lap and kissed him on the forehead before nearly squeezing the life out of him.

"Ah, Dad," Xavier squeaked. "I can't breathe!"

The king released him with a good-natured smack to the butt before standing, clearing his throat, and returning to the subject. "I have meetings all morning, but I should be free for a couple of hours after lunch. I can be home by one, and we can work on your telepathy for an hour and follow with an hour of combat training. I'd like Sir Blair to come so we can expand your combat techniques. I think you've grown too familiar with Loren and Ephraim's fighting styles."

Xavier grimaced in response. He never got along with Sir Blair. He was quite certain the professor didn't like him much.

"Plus, at nine this morning, you'll accompany Ephraim and his family to Nottingham's to be fitted for new school uniforms."

"But there's only a couple months left of school. What's the point?" Xavier whined.

"Son, your old uniforms will no longer fit you, and you need to go to school," Jeremiah said with barely contained patience. "Besides, while you were at the mountain, the legislature voted to extend schooling to a year-round schedule with a two-week break at the end of each term. We felt it best in order to prepare students for war. When the war comes, the enemy won't just attack and kill adults. Everyone needs to be able to defend themselves and their kingdom."

Xavier nodded.

"While I'm on the topic of school, I'm working with

Michael to make some necessary changes to your schedule."

Xavier felt the blood leave his face. "Changes? Like what?"

"You will go to school in the morning for your core classes, but your empowerment classes are no longer challenging enough. So after lunch you will report to the Governing Hall. We will work for an hour on telepathy. Then for a couple of hours, you will shadow me so that you can learn the duties of a king."

Xavier snickered. "Will there be quizzes?"

"Son, your crown, your rule will be your quiz," his father remarked, raising a brow. "And the last hour and a half, you will work on your combat training. Your empowerments will be worked into that training."

"Wait! So... I'm only going to school half the day, but I still end up working for over an hour longer than I would have if I'd just stayed in school all day?" Xavier frowned. "Dad, with at least an hour of homework each night from my core classes, I won't have any time to hang out with my friends or Robbie!"

Jeremiah sighed. He could feel a teenage temper tantrum building in the boy. "Xavier, there's a war coming! You must be prepared to fight and succeed. You must learn how to take over my rule if something were to happen to me."

Xavier froze. An intense sinking feeling left him reeling and depressed. Then he remembered the prophet's plans, and he shook away the negative feelings. "Yeah. Okay. You're right."

Jeremiah's brow rose with surprise, and he shook his head. "All right then. Be back at the palace at one, and we'll practice telepathy before working on your combat training. Then you're a free man to spend the rest of your day as you wish."

Xavier grinned and saluted his father mockingly. "Yes, sire!"

Jeremiah rolled his eyes as he kissed Xavier's head. "Cheeky prince. I'll see you later."

At a quarter till nine, Xavier followed the Hardcastles out of the palace and into a waiting limo. Henrick drove the group the short distance to Nottingham's.

"Okay, boys. Xavier, Court, and Dennis need to be fitted for uniforms. I'll take you three. Caleb, your mom will take you to get your new tennis shoes. Drew, you can handle your errands on your own. Don't lollygag! Get what you need and meet us back here. Be on your best behavior, boys, or I'll bust your backsides! Clear?"

"Yes, sir," the boys mumbled together.

The group split into their separate ways as Xavier followed Ephraim, Dennis and Court into the shop. The shop was void of customers, but almost immediately, Mr. Nottingham hurried toward them with an enormous smile.

"Ephraim! It's good to see you! I'm sure you're happy to be back with your family full-time," he bellowed, shaking the general's hand.

"Thanks, Jon. I sure am," Ephraim answered before nodding to the boys. "Two of mine need re-fitting. They've outgrown their uniforms."

Mr. Nottingham's eyes smiled down at the boys. As his eyes fell on Xavier, his grin broadened. "Hello, young sire! It's so good to have you home!" he commented, shaking Xavier's hand enthusiastically.

"Thank you, Mr. Nottingham. It's great to be home!"

Jon Nottingham's eyes raked down the prince's body before commenting, "No need to tell me why you're here, Prince Wells. It looks as if you've grown half a foot since I saw you last. You're going to need a complete set of new uniforms."

Xavier smiled. "Yes, sir."

"Right this way then, sire," he ordered, bowing and gesturing toward the back of the room.

Xavier led the group into the measurement room. Both Court and Dennis flopped into chairs against the wall while Mr. Nottingham led Xavier to a stool. Xavier stepped onto the stool while Mr. Nottingham collected a tablet and a measuring tape. He whistled softly as he set to work measuring every inch of Xavier's body.

For no other reason than to take his mind off of the intrusive task, Xavier asked his friend, "Hey, Court. Dad says I have tonight free. What do you think about having a campout at the lake with the guys?"

Court's face lit up. "That would be sweet." Court looked up expectantly at his father. "Can I go, Dad?"

Ephraim smiled. "As long as you and Caleb finish cleaning up that pigsty you call a room, and you do what your mother asked you to do this morning without giving her cheek."

"Yes, sir," Court answered dutifully, but the moment his father's back was turned he made a face and mimicked him.

Dennis stared at his younger brother before rolling his eyes and returning back to the book he was reading.

"You want to come, Dennis?" Xavier asked suddenly.

Court's jaw dropped. Dennis looked just as surprised as his brother, his gaze jumping between Court and Xavier. Finally, he answered, "Um... no, thank you, Prince Wells. I don't think that's such a good idea."

Xavier saw Court exhale visibly, but he ignored it. "I think it is. Look, if you want to come, you should come. It'll be fun."

Again, Dennis's eyes darted between Xavier and his brother. "I don't know..."

"Hey, Dennis," Xavier probed gently, "do you want to go with us to the lake?"

Dennis's eyes fixed on Xavier as he considered the question. "Well, kinda, yeah. Can I invite Terry?"

"Sure. Why not?"

Dennis grinned. "Great! Okay. What time?"

Court groaned and rolled his eyes.

Again, Xavier ignored him. "I'll come get you and Court at say... 6:30. Okay?"

"All right. I'm all done, sire. You can step down, now," Mr. Nottingham announced, patting Xavier's shoulder. Xavier stepped down and turned and shook the man's hand. "Thank you, Mr. Nottingham."

The man grinned broadly. "Any time, sire."

"Courtney? Dennis? Who's next?" Ephraim questioned.

"Dennis can go," Court grumbled, eyeing Xavier grumpily.

Dennis stood and went to where Jon Nottingham stood waiting. Xavier slouched into the chair next to Court.

"Why in the hell did you do that?" he hissed quietly.

"What?" Xavier whispered.

"Invite the king of geeks, you git!"

"Because he wanted to come," Xavier answered.

"No, he didn't, not until you asked him anyways," Court spat.

Xavier glared at his friend. "I'm soooo sorry," he sang condescendingly. "When did you become telepathic?"

"I don't have to be to know that he and Terry will be dead weight! He'll probably tell Dad and Mum everything we do! He's the world's biggest wanker!"

"He won't tell on you. He feels left out, Court. Come on, mate. Don't be like this."

"Easy for you to say. You're an only child. You have no idea what it's like to have someone always ratting on you.

God! Why don't you just invite Caleb while you're at it?" Court complained, sulking.

"Okay, Courtney. You're up," Ephraim's voice called him over to the stool as Dennis moved to sit next to Xavier.

Dennis eyed his younger brother while he stomped to where his father and Mr. Nottingham stood waiting.

"Look, Prince Wells, I know Court doesn't want me to go with you guys tonight. We don't have a lot in common. I think he sees me as swot, a nerd because I enjoy reading and learning about things. I don't like confrontation, and he knows that. Well, all my brothers know that. They either ignore me or order me around because I'm acquiescent and would rather do what they say than fight. I want my brothers to like me. Dad says I have to learn to stick up for myself. I guess I would if it were something I really cared about or that was really important. You know? But I'd like to be more than just a bookworm. I guess after all that's happened in the last couple of years, I want to do more than just read about other people's bravery and adventures. I want to live it. Crickey, I'm fifteen years old! I should be living my life to the fullest, not just reading about other peoples' lives. Does any of this make any sense?"

Xavier nodded. "Yeah, it does. I wouldn't have invited you if I didn't want you to come," he replied, reading the boy's insecure thoughts. "And forget about Court. He has a hot head sometimes, but when he cools off, he always comes around."

Dennis smiled. "Yeah, I know. He's the most like Dad. Mother believes that's why they fight so much."

"Dennis?" Ephraim's voice made both boys jump.

Dennis looked guiltily up at his father. "Yes, sir?"

"Why don't you go outside to the car and see if the others are back yet?" Mr. Hardcastle suggested.

"Yes, sir," Dennis answered before looking back at

Xavier. "Thank you for inviting me tonight, Prince Wells."

"Hey, you might as well call me 'Xavier' or 'X.' The rest of the guys do."

Dennis grinned. "Okay. Thanks, Xavier." Then he left the store.

Ephraim settled into Dennis's chair next to Xavier, stretching his legs out in front of him. He smirked as Court grimaced as Mr. Nottingham measured his inseam.

"That was very kind of you to invite Dennis and his friend to your campout, Xavier. Aside from Terry, he rarely gets invited to things. He's a smart lad, but he's also incredibly shy. His brothers would walk all over him if his mother and I didn't put a stop to it."

"I know. I could see it in his thoughts. He doesn't mind his brothers doing that most the time, but he wishes he could be more like them—more outgoing. I thought if Court could get past his irritation, we could help him do that."

Ephraim looked down at Xavier with nothing short of respect. "Prince Wells, you are going to make one fine king someday," he concluded and ruffled Xavier's hair.

Chapter 5

A fter lunch and playing video games with Drew, Court, and Caleb for a bit, Xavier finally exited the Hardcastle residence, sauntered up the stairwell, and entered the royal residence five minutes after one.

"Hello, son," Jeremiah greeted stiffly.

Xavier turned and found his father lounging on the sofa with his feet propped up on the wooden coffee table and a newspaper in hand. By all accounts, the king looked relaxed and calm, but Xavier sensed his father's body language was nothing more than a ruse.

Xavier hesitated and studied his father closely before asking, "Are you angry at me?"

Jeremiah swiftly stood, tossing his newspaper onto the coffee table before giving him a dry smile. "You tell me," he answered flatly, holding his arms out to his sides in an invitation.

Xavier allowed his telepathic abilities to stretch across the room and connect to his father, who mentally pushed back, not allowing him access. Xavier frowned. "Dad, if you want me to use my abilities, why are you blocking me?"

"Who said I wanted you to use telepathy?"

"You did!"

"Did I? I believe I asked for your opinion. Now, if you want to use telepathy to find out the answer to your question, then I suggest you push harder, boy," Jeremiah snapped.

"Ah... no, that's okay. I don't need telepathy to know you're pissed at me," Xavier mumbled.

"Do it, boy!" his father barked.

Xavier jumped and glared at the king. "Geez, Dad! Did Lana tell you off this morning or something? Why are you so freaking mad at me?"

The king stomped toward Xavier until he stood large and imposing in front of him. "Do it!" he snarled.

Xavier bit back a retort and glared at his father. *"All right then. If he wants telepathy, if he wants me to push, I will,"* Xavier thought as he squared his shoulders and pushed hard into his father's thoughts. He felt his father's surprise, but Xavier was too angry to stop at the king's surface thoughts. *"By God, you wanted me to push! I am,"* Xavier thought, forgetting that his father would hear every word. Suddenly, Xavier pushed into a fog that seemed to serve as a barrier to the king's memories and deeper thoughts. The first image he saw was that of Lana and his father standing on the patio, dancing and kissing to the faint music drifting out from the king's room.

"God, I really don't want to see where this goes," Xavier thought and pushed on quickly.

"Xavier, stop!" His father's voice sounded muffled and far away.

Xavier ignored him and kept pushing. Soon he found himself in the hospital. His father was sat next to a bed, his head on an unconscious Xavier's chest, and he was sobbing.

"Xavier, stop now!" his father's voice came again, clearer this time.

But Xavier pressed on. He continued past the memory of his father, mother, and him on the beach when he was an infant until he came to a large wall. Puzzled, Xavier peered up at the wall and wondered why his father had a wall in his memories. Cautiously he approached it and pushed it. It was solid. Idly Xavier wondered if his abilities would work in his father's brain.

"No! Xavier, I forbid you!" his father ordered.

Ignoring his father, Xavier pressed against the wall with all his might, and it tumbled, revealing a classroom filled with students. Puzzled he entered the memory filled with quiet, working students. Father O'Brien stood at the front of the room, watching the students. Then Xavier spotted a teenage version of his father sitting in the back next to a tall lanky blonde boy. Loren! Xavier had to laugh at the youthful, skinny image of one of his father's closest friends. Eager to find more familiar faces, Xavier quickly scanned the rest of the class, hoping to find Mr. Hardcastle or possibly Henrick among the students. But as his sight swept over a dark-haired, dark-eyed boy, he froze. Sitting a row over and a seat up from his father was none other than William LeMasters. Fear prickled up and down Xavier's neck before he could remind himself that he was in no danger and that he was witnessing a memory.

"Prince Wells!" O'Brien snapped loudly, causing most of the class and Xavier to jump. "Sit up straight!"

Xavier watched as his father grimaced but straightened in his seat without rebuttal.

Looking thoroughly satisfied, Father O'Brien sat behind the desk and began grading papers. As soon as the priest was occupied, William LeMasters glanced back at Jeremiah, who was busily working on his assignment.

Suddenly, Jeremiah shouted, "Bloody Hell! Who did that?"

"Sire Wells! I don't appreciate the outburst, and that language is unbecoming for the Prince of Warwood," O'Brien spat.

Jeremiah glared at the priest before answering, "Yes, Father O'Brien. Sorry, sir."

With a nod of satisfaction, the priest returned to grading the papers. Jeremiah's glare swept toward William, who smirked back at him before returning to his work. With a flick of his finger, William's book rose up and smacked him in the forehead. Jeremiah stifled a snicker and returned to his work, but William wasn't going to let it end and suddenly the papers and books on Jeremiah's desk flew forward, smacking the boy in front of him in the back of the head before slamming loudly to the floor.

"Ow! What did you do that for?" the boy whined.

"I... I didn't..."

"Prince Wells!" Father O'Brien barked from his desk. "Come here. Now!"

Reluctantly, Jeremiah stood and approached the front of the room. O'Brien picked up his ruler and walked around the desk to stand in front him.

"Hold out your hand!" he commanded roughly.

A muscle rolled in Jeremiah's cheek as he slowly presented his hand to the priest.

Father O'Brien grabbed his wrist and held his hand in place as he struck the palm of his hand with the ruler half a dozen times. Though he didn't make a sound, Jeremiah winced with each blow and tears pooled in his eyes.

"I hope this punishment has reminded you, sire, that this is my classroom. You hold no authority here, boy. I want you in my office at the end of the day for detention. Understood?"

Jeremiah blinked back the tears and scowled back at the priest. "Yes, Father O'Brien," he whispered bitterly.

"Good. Now return to your seat and do not interrupt my class again."

Jeremiah turned and walked toward his seat.

"How's the hand?" William whispered. "I'm sure your *girlfriend* Loren will be upset that you can't use it on your date tonight."

Suddenly, Jeremiah pivoted on his heel and lunged at the other boy, knocking him out of his chair and slamming him to the floor. The class erupted to their feet and surrounded the fighting boys.

"Prince Wells!" the priest shouted, scrambling to his feet and shoving his way through the crowd.

Jeremiah pummeled William's face into a bloody mess before O'Brien finally reached them, grabbed Jeremiah, and yanked him off LeMasters.

"Get off me, you fat ass!" he shouted, whipping around and sending an uncontrolled force into the priest's chest.

Father O'Brien stumbled backwards, his face screwed up in pain as Jeremiah turned back to William and continued to punch him unmercifully.

"Jeremy! Jeremy, please stop!" a beautiful young girl pleaded, grabbing his arm in mid-punch.

"I said, get off!" Jeremiah screamed, turning and backhanding the girl and simultaneously striking her with an electro force. The girl collapsed immediately, and Jeremiah froze, staring down at the unconscious girl in horror.

"Lucy?" he whispered, leaping off a moaning and barely conscious William. He knelt next to the fallen girl and timidly stroked her hair from her face. "Oh, God! Lucy? I'm so, so sorry! Please, wake up!"

"Move away, boy!" Father O'Brien ordered harshly as he shoved Jeremiah hard to the side and began examining the unconscious girl. Then he looked at a boy standing behind Jeremiah. "Mitch, go get the nurse."

The boy nodded importantly and raced from the room.

O'Brien looked at the rest of the class. "I want everyone

in their seats, now!" he barked.

The class quickly moved to comply except Jeremiah, who was still on the floor where the priest had shoved him, staring fixedly at Lucy. Loren stood behind Father O'Brien, his eyes also fixed on Lucy.

"Sir? Father? Is she going to be okay?" Loren asked, his voice thin and broken.

Father O'Brien didn't answer as he continued to study the girl.

Then the nurse raced into the room and knelt next to O'Brien. "What happened, Father?" she asked as she busily scanned Lucy with her hand, using some kind of x-ray ability.

"She was attacked with an electro force," he answered, his eyes settling menacingly on Jeremiah.

Jeremiah still hadn't moved. He sat stiffly, watching the nurse examining and applying aid to the deathly still girl.

Finally the nurse relaxed and sighed. "Her vitals are good, but she has a concussion. I'll wake her and call her parents to come and get her. She needs to be examined by a trained healer."

"All right. If they have any questions about the incident, refer them to me. Take Mr. LeMasters with you to the infirmary. He was assaulted by Prince Wells as well, and I'm sure the king will want that on record," Father O'Brien stated before standing and regarding the rest of the students. "Class, I want you to take your belongings to the library. You're to work on the assignment I've given you until dismissal for lunch. Understood?"

"Yes, Father," the children chorused and began to exit the room as the nurse brought Lucy back to consciousness.

Jeremiah slowly got to his feet.

"Not you!" O'Brien spat as he grabbed him painfully by the arm. "You are coming with me to the office while I call the king!"

William moaned as he struggled to sit up. He wiped the blood off of his face with the back of his sleeve and sniffed.

"Mitch, help Mr. LeMasters to the infirmary," the priest ordered before yanking Jeremiah out of the room. Xavier followed the priest and his father down the corridor of Wells Academy, listening to O'Brien's loud reprimands.

"How dare you use your powers against your own people! How dare you attack me! Your father will beat you until you're within an inch of your life, boy. Just you wait! You'll regret the day you ever thought that because you're a prince, you can get away with being a hoodlum."

They entered the headmaster's office, and Father O'Brien slammed the door behind them. "Sit down!" he barked, shoving young Jeremiah into a chair, waddling around the walnut finished desk, opening a file drawer, and slamming two folders onto the desk before sitting. He opened the top file, picked up the phone on his desk, and called Lucy's parents.

Jeremiah squirmed guiltily in his seat as Father O'Brien explained what happened and who was responsible for their daughter's injuries. After informing them to pick up their daughter from the kingdom's infirmary, he bid them farewell and hung up. Jeremiah looked close to tears as the priest shuffled the folders and opened a considerably thicker file. Again, he picked up the phone and dialed.

"Hello, Deborah. I need to speak to King Wells, please. It's rather important. We've had an incident involving the prince here at the school." O'Brien paused. "Yes, thank you, I'll hold." After nearly two minutes, Father O'Brien's face lit up and he straightened in his seat as though he were at attention. "Good day, King Wells. This is Father O'Brien, headmaster of the academy." The priest paused before continuing in a rush, "Yes, sire. I know you're a busy man.

I'm so sorry to interrupt you, but I have a serious problem with Prince Wells that I was certain you'd want to know about." He paused as the king responded briefly. "Well, sire, in my class today, the prince displayed disrespectful and disruptive behaviors. I corrected him, but it had no effect, for no more than a minute later, he started beating another boy in the class. Then, when I attempted to stop him, he assaulted me with his powers and went on to do the same to a young girl. The girl had to be sent to the kingdom's infirmary."

"HE DID WHAT!" a voice bellowed so loudly that even Xavier could hear it. Jeremiah slumped deeper into his seat, doing his best not to cry. "You tell Prince Wells I will be there shortly and there will be hell to pay!" the voice continued from the phone.

"Yes, sire. See you soon," Father O'Brien responded, hung up the phone and peered down at the boy in front of him with triumph.

In less than three minutes, a middle-aged man wearing a royal purple cloak and crown stomped into the office.

Xavier studied his grandfather with interest. He was tall and his shoulders were broad, but he carried a few extra pounds around his middle. His hair was cropped short, and he had a neatly trimmed beard. His eyes were identical to that of his son and grandson—a stormy, dark gray. He would have been a handsome man if it weren't for the look of disgust and anger that twisted his features.

"Get to your feet, boy! Now!" he boomed loudly.

Immediately, Jeremiah jumped to his feet. "Father…"

"Silence!" he shouted. "I don't want to hear your pathetic excuses and lies! Follow me!" the king interrupted viciously, turned on his heel, and walked out of the office. "You as well, O'Brien," he added loudly from the hall.

Xavier followed the two men and a solemn Jeremiah,

who shadowed his father and the priest with his head hanging low with shame. The king led them down the hall and into the busy cafeteria. Every student in the school sat chattering and laughing over their lunches, but the moment the king entered, a hush rippled through the room.

"Good afternoon, young citizens," King Jeremiah Wells III greeted them. "I have been called away from my job as your king to keep your kingdom running safely and smoothly because Prince Wells has decided he's above the rules and laws of this academy and this kingdom." The king looked down at Jeremiah before adding, "You're not above the laws of *my* kingdom, son. You are not king yet." The king addressed the silent students again. "So I am here to pass judgment and execute punishment for the prince's crimes. It is your duty to bear witness."

King Wells took off his cloak and crown and handed them to Father O'Brien. Then he turned to Jeremiah. "Drop your pants and face the wall."

Jeremiah's eyes bulged as he looked up at his father in horror. "Sir?"

"You heard me, boy!" he spat, unbuckling his belt and pulling it from his protruding waist. "Drop them and face the wall!"

Jeremiah glanced around anxiously. "Father, please!" he pleaded, his eyes filling with tears of humiliation.

"Now!" the king bellowed, his imposing, authoritative voice sending a wave of flinches through the room.

Tears streamed down his face as Jeremiah slowly turned, awkwardly unfastened and dropped his trousers down to his boxers, and despondently leaned his flushing face against the wall.

The king beat him with the belt in his hand. He beat the boy so hard that welts turned into opened wounds, but the king didn't pause, didn't hesitate as he continued to violently punish his son. Jeremiah fell to the floor after the fifteenth blow and cowered into the fetal position as the king continued to strike him.

"No," Xavier moaned. "Stop! Please stop!"

The whipping continued, and Jeremiah was sobbing loudly with each lash.

Forgetting that it was only a memory, Xavier thrust his hand at his grandfather and screamed, "Stop! Stop hitting him!"

Suddenly the king straightened and looked around the silent, terrified group watching the whipping. "Who said that?" he demanded roughly. "Who dares to intervene?"

Xavier took a step back, bewildered. Had his grandfather heard him? How was that even possible? Surely not!

"Well? I demand to know who yelled out!" the king continued, scanning the crowd of children.

"S... sire?" Father O'Brien spoke up timidly. "No one yelled. I... I didn't hear anyone yell, sire."

His grandfather had heard him! Xavier staggered backwards in shock and collided against a solid form. He turned and looked up at his father.

"Time to go," he ordered softly and instantaneously the scene dissolved as they withdrew from the king's memories.

Panting and confused, Xavier staggered into the receiving room and sank heavily onto the sofa. His grandfather had heard him! How?

"Xavier?" his father whispered. He gazed down at him, perspiration beading on his forehead.

Xavier shook his head bewilderedly. "I forgot it was a memory. I was afraid grandfather would kill you. I just wanted him to stop! How could he hear me?"

Jeremiah shook his head with awe. "Son, you are the most powerful empowered in the world. God only knows what powers you possess."

Xavier frowned. It bothered him when his own father looked at him like he was an anomaly. Clearing his throat, Xavier changed the subject. "Why did grandfather do that? Why was he so... so cruel?"

Jeremiah's gaze flickered. "He was old-fashioned and had a very short temper—two qualities that made it hard to be his son. But he wasn't always like that. There were times when he was kind and gentle."

Xavier looked up at his father doubtfully. "Like when?"

"Well, when I was twelve, he took me to an amusement park. He rode every ride with me and loved it. I was petrified of heights then, but seeing my father acting like a big kid, I got over my fear quickly. I think that was his plan all along." Jeremiah smiled at the memory. "Plus, after the punishment you just witnessed, my father came into the bathroom where Mrs. Sommers had me soaking in an oatmeal bath. Father gave me ointment for the wounds. When I told him I couldn't reach the ones on my back, he did it for me. His touch was so gentle, it nearly made me cry. He didn't apologize for punishing me like he did. That wasn't his way, but his touch, his actions were his apology. It proved to me that he did love me."

Xavier nodded. "Mrs. Sommers was right. You're not like him. You'd never do that to me! Even when I intentionally attacked Drew, you weren't as hard on me as your dad was to you. You made everyone leave the dormitory, and you didn't beat me like that." Xavier glanced up at his father. "Would he have killed you if... if he hadn't stopped?"

Jeremiah frowned. "No, son. He wouldn't have killed me. Although, at the time, I thought he might if it hadn't been for the boy who yelled out for him to stop." Jeremiah shook his head and chuckled. "It's strange to realize now that the boy who stopped the beating was my own son."

"Yeah... it's kind of freaky," Xavier remarked smiling weakly. "Dad, is that why you and Lucy broke up?"

"Yes. She never fully trusted me again. I didn't blame her. She suffered bruised ribs and a fractured skull from my attack. Loren wouldn't speak to me for months afterwards. I came to find out that he had been in love with Lucy since we were in primary school. When I discovered he had started dating Lucy, I made matters worse with my jealousy and feelings of betrayal." The king gave a dry smile. "I wasn't much different than you when I was your age. Anyways, I'm not too proud of that year of my life. I made a lot of bad decisions."

"What did you do when you found out Loren was dating Lucy?"

"I picked a fight with him, and he kicked my butt," Jeremiah answered bluntly.

"Dad?"

"Hmm?"

"I'm sorry I was late. You were angry because I was late and disrespected the time you had set aside from your duties to work with me. Right?"

Jeremiah nodded.

"Well, I'm sorry. It won't happen again. I promise."

Another grueling thirty minutes of telepathic technique ensued, and by the end of the lesson, Xavier was relieved to be done and looked forward to the physical exercise he would get in combat training. A little after two o'clock, he stood in the middle of the palace's ballroom clad in protective gear. The room had been cleared of all its furniture. Sir Blaire stood opposite of him dressed similarly with five cages behind him. The irony that one of the animals was a fruit bat didn't escape Xavier.

"All right, boy," Sir Blaire announced. "You've had

training on this skill in class against a dummy and against Andrew Hardcastle during one unfortunate lapse of judgment on your part."

Xavier swore he saw Sir Blaire smirk, but the protective mask obscured most of his face.

"Today, we will use animals as a weapon in combat. I've chosen some less dangerous animals to start with. Come and chose an animal as your companion, your highness."

Xavier approached the cages and examined the animals. Aside from the bat, Sir Blaire had brought a crow, a large rat, a snake, and a squirrel. After studying each animal closely, he selected the crow, thinking the bird's beak would make a good weapon, and he could have it fly into Sir Blaire's line of sight.

"Loren, Henrick, Ephraim," Jeremiah announced as Sir Blaire and Xavier took a moment to develop a bond with their animals. "Our task is not to interfere in this exercise, but to be on hand if things get too out of control."

The men nodded and spaced themselves around the room. The king shut the door and stood in front of it.

Xavier bonded easily with the crow, and it nipped affectionately at his fingers as he spoke to it. "Now, listen. I need you to keep flying in his face so that he's blinded to my attacks. Whenever he casts an empowerment at me, bite, poke, screech, and do whatever you have to do to distract him. Okay?"

"Right. Play. I like play," the crow chirped at him excitedly.

Xavier smiled. "Yeah, that's right. Play. Be as playful as you can. Good bird."

Still grinning, he squared his shoulders, adjusted the crow onto his left arm and faced Sir Blaire, who waited patiently with the squirrel.

"Ready, your highness?" he asked.

Hell yeah, he was ready! He was ready to get a little payback for all the times Sir Blaire barked at him, made him clean animal cages, or told him off in front of everyone. With a nod, Xavier answered, "Ready."

In a movement almost too fast for Xavier to see, Sir Blaire cast an electro force at him with a simple flick of his finger. Xavier was knocked completely off his feet and slammed onto his back, knocking the breath out of him. The crow flew off cawing in distress.

Gasping desperately for air, Xavier struggled to put up a blocking force just as another electro force barreled from Blaire. He felt his force shudder upon impact, and he grimaced to hold a block in place as he tried to get his bearings. Then the crow came to his rescue, diving from the ceiling, fluttering madly in front of Sir Blaire's face and cawing loudly. Xavier scrambled to his feet and called to the bird to fly to safety as he launched a ball of fire at Sir Blaire.

The empowerment hit the professor and launched him into the air, sending him a good ten feet back. Xavier stalked toward the fallen man ready to finish him off when out of nowhere Blaire's squirrel leaped at him and scurried up to his face. Staggering, Xavier worked to peel the hissing, biting creature from his face, thankful he was wearing a mask.

Finally, he tossed the squirrel aside to find Sir Blaire standing, his protective gear smoking slightly. Before he could react, Sir Blaire pointed at Xavier and pain shot instantly through his body. Xavier screamed and fell to his knees. Then the squirrel attacked again. Overwhelmed, Xavier curled into a ball. Finally, the pain subsided, and the squirrel scurried off him. He pushed his languid body into a seated position but froze at the sword inches from his throat.

"You, my dear prince, are dead," Sir Blaire whispered.

Groaning in defeat, Xavier collapsed onto the floor. He heard Blaire sheath his sword and looked back up at the man, who was holding his hand out to help him to his feet. Xavier took it, and Blaire hauled him to his feet with ease. The king strolled toward them with an easy grin.

"Why, thank you, Jack. We were beginning to think the boy was invincible. He spanked Loren like a little girl during their last bout," Jeremiah joked, and Xavier had to grin.

"Hey! That's not exactly true! I wanted to give the kid some confidence. That's all," Loren protested.

"Yeah? Was lying flat on your back whimpering part of that plan?" Ephraim ribbed.

"Yeah!" Loren insisted as the group laughed heartily.

The laughter faded when the door opened and Mrs. Sommers stood in the doorway peering around the room with dismay. The men uneasily followed her gaze and took in the damage done to the room. There were scorch marks on the walls and floor. A portrait of the king was all but destroyed and still smoking at the corners. There was glass on the floor that must have been a vase or bowl of some variety at one time. The chandelier hung haphazardly from the ceiling, and several of its crystals were missing or broken. The king quickly righted the dangling chandelier before looking sheepishly at the perturbed governess.

She eyed the group in silence as they shuffled guiltily under her scrutiny. Finally, her eyes narrowed on the king. "Jeremiah Wells," she chastised quietly. "Why on earth would you ever consider having combat training in the ballroom?"

Jeremiah opened his mouth to speak but didn't.

Xavier snickered and was rewarded with a soft jab to his side by his father.

"Well? What do you have to say for yourselves?" she asked impatiently.

"Sorry, Mrs. Sommers," the men muttered, and Xavier's shoulders began to shake with barely contained laughter.

Jeremiah finally found his voice enough to respond, "In hindsight, it wasn't the best place to do this. We'll move the training to the coliseum from now on."

"See that you do!" Mrs. Sommers snapped. Then she impatiently waved the men out of the room. "Come on, boys. Out of the room so it can be cleaned and repaired."

After pausing briefly to help Sir Blaire cage his animals, the group shuffled out of the ballroom and past Mrs. Sommers with their heads down. Once out of the room, Xavier unleashed the jubilance that had swelled inside him and was met by five daggering glares, which only made him laugh that much harder.

Chapter 6

After dinner, Xavier clambered out of the residence and down the royal staircase carrying a sleeping bag and a duffle. As usual, the Hardcastle residence was in an uproar with loud, arguing voices spilling into the foyer.

"Caleb Hardcastle!" Mrs. Hardcastle yelled, followed by a muffled thud and a loud, "Ow, Mom!"

"If you think that hurt, just you wait until your father gets home, young man!" his mother scolded. The Hardcastle residence always seemed a bit chaotic. With four ornery boys, Ephraim and Rebecca were always on their toes.

Snickering at the thought, Xavier knocked on the door.

"I'll get it!" Court hollered from inside.

Xavier listened to his heavy footsteps approach the door before it flew open.

"Hey, X! Come on in. I think Dennis has been ready since noon. I still have to find my sleeping bag," Court chattered, leading him into the residence. Xavier closed the door and followed.

"Hey, Prince... I mean, Xavier," Dennis greeted before turning to a gangly blond boy standing next to him. "This is Terry Malone. He's in my year at the Academy."

Xavier recognized the boy from his advanced math class. He never spoke or answered questions in class, but he always seemed to get excellent marks on all his tests. "Yeah, we have math class together," he commented, shaking the other boy's hand.

"Y... yes, s... s... sire," he stammered badly. He blushed. "I... I'm s... sorry..., s... sire. It g... g... gets w... worse when I'm n... n... nervous."

Xavier shrugged. "Don't worry about it. I sometimes stutter when I'm nervous." Xavier grinned. "Imagine facing my father after turning Jonas McKnight into a jackass."

The boys burst into hysterics.

"That was great to watch though," Dennis remarked. "He deserved it. He's a jerk."

"Yeah, he is, but my father didn't see it that way." Xavier snickered uneasily. "Seriously, the man is scary when he's angry."

"Yeah, wh... when we w... were all at the m... m... mountain and you z... zapped Drew with your p... powers, I about p... p... pissed my p... pants when he y... y... yelled for everyone to get out of the d... dorm... D... Dennis said y... you got caned."

"Terry!" Dennis hissed, elbowing his friend. He looked at Xavier's reddening face and shrugged apologetically.

Xavier found it hard to meet the older boys' eyes. "Does... uh... does everyone know what happened... afterwards?" he asked.

Dennis glanced darkly at Terry before answering, "Well, not specifically. There're guesses, but I swore Terry to secrecy, and I never told anyone else what happened. I swear it!"

"Don't worry about it, Dennis," Xavier sighed, adjusting the strap of his duffle higher onto his shoulder.

"Ready!" Court announced, entering the room with his backpack and sleeping bag, but he noticed the tension in the room. "What? What's going on?"

"It's nothing. Come on, let's go," Xavier announced,

leading them out of the residence, down the hall, and out of the palace.

"Xavier! Geez, slow down, mate! What's up? Did Dennis and T... T... Terry say something to tick you off?"

Xavier stopped and faced his friend. "Don't do that! Don't make fun of Terry like that."

Court blanched. "Sorry, mate," he muttered. "I was just joking. What's wrong?"

Xavier nodded for Court to step beside him as they made their way around the palace.

"It's nothing, really," he told Court. "I guess I just have to get used to people talking about me is all."

Court nodded. "Yeah. It can't be easy to have your business and everything you do a topic of conversation for everyone."

"Yeah. I keep thinking I'll get used to it, but... I never do." Xavier sighed and forced a smile. "Let's just forget about all that and have some fun."

Court grinned broadly. "You bet! It's going to be brilliant!"

The boys slipped through the secret passage in the palace's wall and raced across the field to the woods. It didn't escape Xavier's attention that the cracks he had created during the height of his influx were still noticeable. Someone had attempted to refill them with soil, but the soil had settled a bit lower than the rest of the ground. Then, when the group entered the woods, Xavier stopped abruptly and peered around with unease.

"What?" Court questioned, stopping next to him.

"The wood is... different. It's less... dense."

"Well," Court began awkwardly, "the fire burned away all the underbrush and dead fallen trees and stuff. Dad says it's actually good for a forest to be cleaned out from time to time. It allows the trees to flourish and gain more nutrients from the ground."

Nodding, Xavier followed the boys to the lake and found Beck and Garrett already there, building a campfire.

"Hey, X!" Garrett greeted. "Frankie got grounded by his mom. He won't be here. Harry and Mac should be here any minute though."

Beck dropped a pile of wood onto the ground next to where Garrett was carefully arranging branches into a campfire. He grinned devilishly at the boys. "Yeah, and the girls are coming later tonight once Erica's parents go to bed."

Court and Xavier exchanged elated expressions before grinning back at Beck.

"Excellent!" Court exclaimed.

Garrett shook his head with a laugh. "God! You blokes are hopeless," he surmised. Then he mocked at them in a high-pitched voice, "Oh, I love you so much!" He smacked kisses at the trio before mimicking making out with his hand.

The three boys looked at one another, and after a nod from Beck, they charged the smaller boy, scooped him onto their shoulders, carried him to the water, and tossed him in.

"Hey!" Garrett protested, but then thought better. "Ha, ha. I was getting hot anyways."

The boys rolled their eyes at him and returned to building the campfire.

"X, can you light that?" Beck asked after he arranged the last of the wood into the stack Garrett had built.

"Sure, no problem," Xavier answered and with a simple flick from his finger, flame erupted from the wood.

"Great, we need to get more wood to feed the fire as the night goes on. It'll be cold as hell when we climb out of the lake," Beck stated.

"Terry and I will do that," Dennis announced, elbowing

his friend and taking off into the woods.

Beck gave Court a questioning look.

"Don't look at me. I didn't invite them. Xavier did!" Court muttered defensively.

Beck's gaze swept to the prince. "*You* invited them? Why would you do that?"

"Why wouldn't I?" he retorted. "God, you guys act like I invited William LeMasters here or something. He wanted to come, so I invited him. What's the big deal?"

Beck and Court exchanged looks. "Well, I wasn't lying when I said Dennis snitches on me all the time when I do something remotely wrong. But even if he manages to keep his mouth shut, there's Terry. He's... he's strange."

"Why? Because he stutters?" Xavier snapped.

"No, mate," Beck interrupted. "Terry is a sneak and a stoolpigeon. When Madam Stokes was headmaster, he used to give her names of students who violated school rules. We don't trust him. All I'm saying is that you need to watch your back if you plan to hang out with them."

After Mac and Harry showed up, the boys braved the cold water for a swim. Within seconds, their teeth were chattering as they splashed and dunked one another.

"Which one of you sissies wants to race me to the rocks and back?" Beck challenged.

The other boys groaned and rolled their eyes.

"No way," Mac grumbled.

"Do I look mental?" Court spat.

"Why not? Are you *girls* chicken?" he chastised.

"No, we're not chicken," Garrett answered. "I think I speak for all of us when I say we'd prefer not to sit and listen to you brag about what a great, strong swimmer you are for the rest of the night."

The rest of the group grumbled their affirmation to Garrett's words.

"Can I help it if it's true?" Beck countered.

The boys moaned loudly and trudged exasperatedly out of the water.

"I'll race you," Xavier announced with a grin.

Beck beamed. "You're on! Garrett, will you start us off?" he asked as he and Xavier sloshed out of the lake and stood at the water's edge to begin the race.

"Yeah, sure thing," he answered as he and the other boys settled around the warmth of the fire.

Both boys leaned forward, ready to spring at the word go. With a smirk, Beck gave Xavier a good-natured shove with his forearm, and Xavier staggered slightly.

"Balance, your highness," Beck ordered, doing an excellent imitation of Henrick Davies.

Grinning, Xavier shoved his friend back and muttered, "You're going down, Wilson."

"In your dreams, Wells," he retorted.

The group behind them snickered appreciatively and egged the boys on with banters and insults.

Garrett called out over the ruckus, "Okay, on your marks. Get set. Go!"

Xavier paused a few seconds to give Beck a head start and watched as his friend high-stepped through the shallow portion of the lake before diving into deeper water.

"Xavier, what are you doing, mate? Go!" Court yelled.

Xavier gave his best friend a grin and a wink before turning back to the lake, leaping past the shallow water, and driving into deeper water. The group's thoughts of awe slammed into his thoughts as he swam through the water, and he grinned. Feeling cocky and confident, he decided to give his friends a good show. He dove deeper and deeper into the water before changing direction and dolphin kicking faster and faster to the surface. His body broke through and propelled almost ten feet above the water. After effortlessly completing a double axel and a flip, he drove back into the water.

A collective, "Whoa!" followed him into the depths of the lake, and Xavier laughed. That should keep them talking for days. Now, he just had to win the race. In three dolphin kicks, Xavier propelled fifteen feet forward, passing Beck, who had reached the rock and was now on his way back to shore. Xavier tagged the rocks, and in two more kicks, he pulled up next to Beck, who laboriously pounded the water. Xavier reverted to a freestyle swim and splashed along with his friend for a few strokes. Beck was a strong swimmer, but Xavier was much, much stronger. Deciding to have a little fun at Beck's expense, Xavier kicked deeper underwater before arcing upward, and in two kicks propelling his body out of the water, leaping over Beck, and diving back into the water on the opposite side of him. He repeated this maneuver two more times, basking in the cheers and laughter from the boys on shore. Finally, he dove underwater again and positioned himself about a foot beneath Beck, turned onto his back, and lazily kicked his feet to keep in time with him. It took Beck a couple of strokes before he noticed Xavier. Xavier smiled and waved at the other boy. Beck completely freaked out. Bubbles and a scream erupted from his mouth before he erupted to the surface coughing and sputtering.

"Xavier!" he bellowed, irritably. "You're a cheat!"

Xavier popped to the surface and regarded his friend. "Cheat? How did I cheat? I touched the rocks! Ask Garrett!"

"You're a cheat because you were messing with me during the race!" Beck spat.

"I didn't mess with you! I never touched you or got in your way when you swam! I swam around you... over you... and under you, but I never touched you." Xavier couldn't keep the wide grin from his face, and with the others in hysterics behind him, his battle against the erupting laughter was lost.

"Fine! I quit!" Beck growled, and after swimming around Xavier, he climbed from the lake. "Shut it, you guys!" he hissed, snapping his towel at Garrett.

"What's so funny?" Erica called as she, Robbie, Melissa Dorne, Rene Jones, and another girl Xavier recognized but didn't know by name emerged from the tree line. Xavier slowly waded out of the water and inched toward the warmth of the fire.

"Oh, man! You missed it. Xavier totally schooled Beck in a swimming race. He literally swam circles around Beck. It was hysterical!" Court blurted.

"Shut it, Hardcastle, or I'll shut it for you!"

Erica interrupted Court's rebuttal before he could needle Beck further. "You guys actually went swimming? It's freezing!"

"Yeah, and Garrett has nuts the size of peas to prove it," Beck jeered. "Oh, wait. They're normally the size of peas."

"That's not what your girlfriend said last night," Garrett spat, and the boys laughed appreciatively.

"Hey! Don't pull me into this!" Melissa protested.

"Ignore them," a pretty little blonde beside Melissa whispered. "Boys are crude and obnoxious."

Beck's ears went red, but he backed off.

"Do you want to go swimming?" Court asked the girls. "You'll have to take off your clothes so you have dry clothes to put on afterwards. You don't want to get hypothermia after all. Safety first!" Court directed his ornery grin at Erica.

"You're off your head, Courtney, if you think we're going to strip down to our underwear and swim in freezing water," Erica announced.

"I could heat up the water!" Xavier blurted suddenly.

All the children gaped at him.

"You can do that?" Robbie asked, voicing the surprise from the group.

"Yeah... I mean, I've never done it, but I'm pretty sure I can."

"Is that a good idea?" Dennis asked quietly.

"Shut it, Dennis! Of course it is! Do you want us all to die of hypothermia? Warming up the water wouldn't hurt anything," Court reasoned.

"But..."

"I said shut it! God! I knew you'd be like this! Why do you always have to over-think things?" Court spat again.

Dennis's face blanched, and he swallowed his protests.

The group erupted at once, all in favor of Xavier's idea.

"Do it, Xavier!"

"That would be so awesome!"

"Why didn't you think of it earlier, mate?"

"Cool! We'll have our very own hot tub!"

Encouraged by the attention and the whoops of support, Xavier waded knee-deep into the lake, submerged his hands, closed his eyes and concentrated on warming the water. Instantly, he felt energy build in his chest, sweep down his arms and into the water. Slowly, the water eddying around his legs grew warmer and warmer until it felt more like bathwater than lake water. He opened his eyes and found steam rising from the surface of the lake. He turned and faced the group, who had watched in silence, jaws now slacking.

Garrett was the first to respond. "Last one in the lake has to collect more wood for the fire!"

All at once, the boys galloped into the lake. The girls stripped down to their underclothes before racing in after them. Only Dennis and Terry remained, whispering feverishly with each other.

"Hi," Robbie murmured softly as she sidled up next to

Xavier in the water.

"Hi." Xavier grinned broadly.

"You should have brought a spare T-shirt to swim in," Robbie remarked, tracing a finger down his chest, giving Xavier goosebumps.

"Wh... why?"

Robbie rolled her eyes at him and snickered. "You didn't even notice, did you? Melissa, Rene, and Natalie were all ogling over your bare chest."

"No, they weren't. Really?" he blurted disbelievingly.

"Yes, they were, Xavier. You're hot! Not that you weren't always hot, but now other girls are starting to see it too. I don't think I like it," she snickered.

Xavier laughed and hugged her close. "I'm so glad you came! How did you sneak away so early? We thought you were waiting for Loren and Lucy to fall asleep."

"We changed our tactics. I told my mom I was spending the night with Erica, Erica said she was spending the night at my house, Melissa told her mom she was staying with Natalie..."

"Okay, okay. I get the idea." Xavier laughed and hugged her close to him. "Is the water warm enough for you?"

"Oh yeah! It's nice! I'm not cold at all!"

"Good," he whispered and kissed her.

"Hey, Xavier," Dennis called softly from the shoreline.

The first thing Xavier noticed was that Dennis had his pack on his back, and his sleeping bag was rolled up and tucked under his arm. Frowning, Xavier released Robbie and waded to shore.

"You're not going, are you?"

"Yeah. Terry can't stay the night. He's got a doctor's appointment tomorrow, and I'd feel like a third wheel if I stayed. Ya know?"

Xavier nodded, understanding. Terry was his friend. The

other guys seemed to be barely tolerating their presence, and so Dennis felt out of place. Gritting his teeth at his friends' insensitivity, he decided he would have a word with the guys about it later.

"I understand how you feel, but you're not a third wheel in my eyes, mate. I wish you'd stay, but if you don't feel comfortable without your best mate, I can understand that." He looked at Terry, who had gathered the last of his belongings and moved next to Dennis.

"Th... thanks, X," Terry said with a warm smile.

"Any time, Terry. Maybe you can come again sometime when you both can stay the night."

"Y... yeah. Th... that would be g... g... great."

"See you later," Dennis said softly. "Tell Court I can keep secrets, and Dad will never find out from me that the girls snuck out here."

Grinning, Xavier responded, "Thanks. That would be great. See you guys later."

Chapter 7

The next morning just before sunrise, a reporting boom and low resounding rumble jolted the kids awake.

"What in the hell was that?" Beck blurted.

Xavier stood and listened intently. Another boom echoed from the direction of the gatehouse and Center Square.

The group got to their feet and looked around, confused and scared.

Then Xavier felt it. He felt the fear and panic from the guards on duty at the gatehouse. There was a full frontal assault on the gatehouse by three dozen dark soldiers. The attackers had only one plan, to determine any weaknesses in security.

"We're under attack again. I have to go!" Xavier blurted fiercely as he raced into the dark, dense woods.

"No, Xavier! Wait!" Robbie called, her voice catching.

Xavier got five feet into the forest before he remembered he could just teleport there. Knowing that the safest spot to teleport would be next to the greenhouses a few yards from the kingdom's entrance, he closed his eyes to conjure up his teleportation just as Robbie grabbed him by the shoulder. He felt the pull of the force yank him out of the woods and set him down into nothing short of chaos.

A thump and weak groan behind him had Xavier

spinning with his hands raised, an electro force spinning at the ready in his palm. Robbie was sprawled on the ground.

"Xavier, it's me!" Robbie shouted over the battle taking place around them.

He dropped his hand, the force dying instantly.

"Jesus, Robbie? How... what... what are you doing here?" he hissed, helping her to her feet.

"I was trying to stop you! Please, don't do anything stupid. Please, please let the guards handle it."

"I can't do that! Robbie, this is what I've been training to do—to protect the kingdom. It's my job! It's my destiny! I can't turn my back on this!" Xavier insisted.

"But... you're... you're only fourteen!"

"Age doesn't matter. I'm the Chosen. I have to do this!" His eyes softened at her worried, frightened face. "I'll be fine. Really! Just... just stay here and stay hidden. I'll come back for you when it's over. Okay? Don't move!" And, not waiting for Robbie to talk him out of it, Xavier sprinted into the chaos.

Forces and empowerments lit up the darkened sky all around the gatehouse, and one whizzed uncomfortably close to Xavier's cheek. With his heart thumping violently in his chest, he waved his hand quickly to create a blocking force around him. His blocking force wasn't strong, but it would do the job in protecting him from a stray force. As he approached the gate, he found it aflame but luckily still intact. Several guards with swords drawn fought against men outfitted in black pants, shirts, and masks. The men in black were beating the guards backwards and gaining further access into the kingdom.

Xavier picked up a sword of a fallen guard and raced forward.

"Young sire! You mustn't be here!" A guard yelled at him, but Xavier ignored him and continued forward.

Quick succeeding pops announced the arrival of the king, Loren, Ephraim, and Henrick. The four men rushed forward with swords drawn. Xavier watched in awe as the men joined in the battle to maintain the security of the gatehouse. His father wielded his sword with expertise and finesse. He struck down three dark soldiers with less than half a dozen parries and one astounding complex maneuver before propelling several dark soldiers backwards and slamming them into the stone wall with telekinesis.

"Hold the line, men! They mustn't get through!" Jeremiah blared as Xavier plunged into the heart of the battle, blocking what would have been a killing blow from a very skillful dark soldier. The young royal guard looked at his prince in nothing short of astonishment. Xavier lunged his sword at the man, who superbly parried the attack before sweeping into an attack of his own. Xavier blocked his sword, feeling the impact jarring up into his shoulder. Quickly he extended his hand and blasted the dark soldier with an electro force as the young guard recovered from the shock and buried his sword into the soldier's chest. The dark man dropped to the ground, lifeless.

"Watch out, sire!" the young guard shouted.

Xavier spun, instinctively knowing the direction of the assault, but he was too late as the soldier's blade sliced across his chest. The wound was only a graze, but if he hadn't moved at the last second, he would be lying on the ground bleeding out. Out of anger, or maybe fear, a resounding blast erupted from Xavier's hand, propelling the dark soldier twenty feet into the air. The dark man landed with a resolving crack. Cautiously, the prince approached the fallen man and verified what he already knew—the man was dead. He had killed his first man in battle.

He stared down at the man, emotions warring inside him. Did he have a family? What had led him to join forces with the LeMasters? Did he truly believe in their warped views of world domination and superiority, or was he a victim himself?

Unable to look at the dead man any longer, Xavier turned and found the remaining dark soldiers retreating into the pre-dawn night. Cheers erupted from the men.

"Long live King Wells!" the men began to chant, taunting the retreating forms.

"Xavier?" Robbie called as she ran across the street to where he stood. "Are you all right? Oh my God, you're bleeding!"

His eyes followed hers to the wound on his chest. "It's nothing," he murmured as he placed his hand over the wound, emitting a bright white light and healing the wound.

The king congratulated his men one at a time, shaking hands and thumping their backs. When his eyes settled on Xavier, his face went white before quickly flushing in anger, and he stomped toward him.

"What in the hell are you doing here?" he shouted, grabbing Xavier painfully by the arm.

"Helping," Xavier managed to say, pulling his arm free. "I am the Chosen after all. It's my destiny to fight the Dark Army."

"No!" his father barked. "Your job is to fight and kill the Dark King. The Dark Army is my responsibility. I'm still king of this kingdom. What if you'd been severely injured or killed? What do you suppose would happen to your destiny then?" Then Jeremiah noticed the ripped shirt and blood on the boy's chest.

"Oh, dear God! You're injured!"

"It's nothing!" Xavier spat, jerking out of his father's grasp. "It was just a scratch! How am I supposed to get real practice in combat if I'm never allowed to be in combat?"

"That is also my concern!" his father yelled.

"Oh, thank you, your highness," he snapped as he condescendingly bowed before his father. "I'll sleep better at night knowing that!"

"Watch it, boy!"

"What am I supposed to do then? Huh?" Xavier shouted back. "Just sit around like a good little prince and expect Daddy to handle everything?"

"Yes!"

"Well, it's not going to happen, *King Wells*!"

The king swelled to his full height and glared down at his insolent son. "First, if you don't take care in how you speak to me, Chosen or not, you'll find yourself across my knee," he spat, glaring pointedly down at Xavier. "Secondly, you're only a boy, my boy, and you will do what I tell you to because, quite simply, I know what's best for you. Understood?"

Impulsively, Xavier rolled his eyes, but Loren intervened before Jeremiah could respond to the blatant gesture of disrespect from the boy.

"Sire, maybe this discussion is best suited for another time. We've got work to do," Loren whispered discreetly.

After studying Xavier's stony expression, the king nodded. "You're right. Let's get started," he told Loren before speaking to Xavier. "I want you to get your things from the lake and return to the palace. We'll finish this later," he warned before turning to give his guard assignments in investigating the attack.

Loren studied Xavier a moment before his eyes settled on Robbie standing timidly behind the boy. His brows rose. "Robbie? Why are you here? Where's my daughter?" he asked suspiciously.

Robbie faltered. "Uh, she..."

Loren smiled dryly. "Let me guess. She told her mother and me that she was staying with you, and you probably told your mother you were staying with her so that the pair of you could sneak off into the woods to camp out with the boys."

Robbie stared uneasily up at Loren but said nothing.

"That's what I thought," he groaned rubbing his face wearily. "Robbie, please tell my daughter to get herself home immediately. She and I will need to have a long talk about lying and being where she says she'll be."

"Yes, sir," Robbie whispered.

"Son?" the king blared, looking back at him from a group of royal guards he was preparing for searches. "Home. Now!"

Xavier muttered curses under his breath as he started to turn toward Robbie.

"Xavier!" his father shouted angrily. Xavier's eyes met the king's. "I can hear what you're saying!" he finished in a loaded undertone.

Father and son stared at one another in silence for several long seconds. Finally, the king, looking smug that his point was made, returned to his discussion with his guards. Seething, Xavier took Robbie by the arm.

"Come on, Robbie. I'll teleport us back to the woods," he muttered, his eyes still on his father. Then a brilliant plot to get even came to mind, and he grinned wickedly. He pulled Robbie into his arms, flicked a finger at his father, laughed, and teleported to the lake.

"Oh, my God! Did you do that?" Robbie blurted with a mix of horror and awe.

Xavier smiled innocently. "Do what?"

"What happened?" Court asked eagerly, but both Robbie and Xavier ignored him.

"You turned the king's hair bright pink!" She couldn't help it, and she began to giggle. "Oh, my God, Xavier. He's going to kill you!"

"You did what?" Garrett hissed with a whistle.

"No way! You didn't do that!" Beck challenged.

Xavier nodded. "Yeah, I did. He pissed me off yelling and ordering me around."

"Robbie's right, mate. You're dead. It's been nice knowing you," Mac muttered with exaggerated despair, shaking his head.

"Naw. I'm the Chosen. He can't kill me," he answered with a wink. "But I've been ordered home, guys. You too, Erica. Loren knows how you worked him so that you could come here."

Erica went pale.

Fifteen minutes later, as Xavier clambered up the royal staircase, he heard his father's voice drifting heatedly from the residence.

"It's not funny, Lana! The boy was out of line! He had no business being there, and this prank is the last straw!"

Xavier stumbled slightly and stopped at the top of the steps.

"Good morning, Prince Wells," Henrick greeted stiffly, a smirk playing at the corners of his mouth.

"Hi, Henrick," Xavier moaned, glancing from Henrick back to the door. "Do you reckon I should wait until Lana cools him down before I go in?"

Henrick's battle against his smile was lost, and he chuckled. "I don't know, kid. That's your call."

With a huge sigh, Xavier opened the door and shuffled into the residence.

"Jeremiah, just calm down," Lana said to a very agitated, pacing king.

The moment the residence door closed, his father turned and glared down at Xavier. It took every ounce of will power not to burst out laughing. The alteration to the king's hair had been fantastically done. It wasn't just pink! It was bright, fluorescent pink.

"Undo this now!" the king spat, stomping toward him.

Xavier straightened and refused to flinch. "No. Not until you apologize for going off on me in front of the entire royal guard!"

Jeremiah gaped at him. "Excuse me?"

"You screamed at me like I was just a kid, only a kid. I'm not! Haven't you been drilling that into my head over the last seven months? I am the Chosen, Dad. Maybe you're the one who needs to come to terms with that!"

Dumbfounded, his father stared silently down at him.

"Xavier," Lana interrupted as she approached her two men with amusement. Could father and son be any more alike? They had no idea how much they resembled one another with the same stubborn attitudes, the unwavering moral compass, and compassionate, loving hearts. Even now as father and son stared at one another, each with his hands on his hips and determined eyes, they looked so much alike. "Turning your father's hair pink wasn't the act of the Chosen; it was an act of a boy—a child. If you want your father to treat you with the respect of a man, you'll need to act more like it."

What? Lana was taking his father's side? He had thought for sure she would help him out on this one. "But, Lana," Xavier protested, "he was yelling at me in front of everyone and ordering me home like a baby! I was embarrassed. I... I... just thought..."

"You just thought you'd get even with him?" she asked knowingly.

Xavier's mouth clamped shut, and he blushed.

"Sweetheart, you are the Chosen, and you have a lot on your shoulders as a result, but you're still a boy too. You haven't had enough training to go toe to toe in battle against a man."

"I did today," Xavier whispered, remembering the dead soldier's blank eyes with a shudder.

Jeremiah stiffened. "You killed a man today?"

Xavier nodded, unwanted tears swelling in his eyes. Why was he crying? The man had been a dark soldier, a follower of the Dark King. He would have killed Xavier if the young royal guard hadn't warned him.

With a sigh, Jeremiah pulled him into his arms and held him close as the tears dropped heavily on his father's shoulder. For several long seconds, his father soothed him without words. He continued to hold him and stroke his head and back.

Finally, he murmured into Xavier's ear, "It's a hard thing, taking a man's life, son. I'd be worried about you if you weren't affected by it. You care about people, good or bad, and that is what makes you different from Fox. That is why you will succeed. That," he pulled Xavier arms-length and wiped the tears from his cheeks with his thumbs before finishing, "is why I am so proud to be your father."

"Thanks, Dad." Xavier smiled weakly up at his father.

Jeremiah kissed his forehead before looking back down at him with a crooked smirk. "Now, I have a favor to ask of you. Get rid of my pink hair before I bust your butt."

Xavier's smile burst into laughter. "Yeah. Okay. Sorry about that."

"No, you're not, but I'm going to let it slide this one time. If you do something like this again, your backside will be as pink as my hair. Got it?"

"Yes, sir." Xavier saluted his father mockingly before returning his hair to its normal state.

Chapter 8

The next morning, Xavier clambered down the stairs dressed for Mass. He straightened his royalty sash as he entered the dining hall and found his father already seated at the table with Lana to his left.

"Morning," Xavier announced as he took his place at the table. He shyly met Lana's eyes and smiled. "Morning, Lana."

"Good morning, Xavier. Did you sleep well?" she asked, smiling sweetly back.

Xavier nodded as he eagerly watched the kitchen servant enter the room with a cart of covered dishes. He lifted his napkin and placed it on his lap as the servant laid a plate in front of him and lifted its lid. Xavier's stomach groaned at the sight of eggs benedict, sausages, and an oatmeal cup topped with brown sugar, nuts, and fruit.

"Son?" Jeremiah began clearing his throat. "I... we need to talk to you."

His father's nervous, stuttering voice nearly had Xavier forgetting the food in front of him. Something was up.

"What? Is there something wrong, Dad?" he asked, laying his fork and knife back onto the table.

"No, nothing's wrong. I..." he looked nervously at Lana before drawing a breath and continuing, "I want your blessing to marry Lana, son. I asked her last night. She said yes."

Xavier's eyes darted from his father to Lana and back again. "Really? You're really getting married?"

The king nodded. "Yes, we are. How do you feel about that?"

The grin that split across the boy's face was enormous. "I think it's brilliant, Dad! I've always hoped you'd marry. So, yeah, I feel awesome about it! Congratulations!" he responded, jumping to his feet and nearly tackling his father, chair and all, to the floor in a bear hug. He went to Lana with more poise and tenderness, hugged her tightly, and kissed her cheek.

"Are you *really* happy about this, honey? It wouldn't hurt my feelings. I'm not trying to take your mom's place. I just hope we can continue to be friends."

Xavier was surprised by the hurt he felt at her words that she wasn't trying to take his mom's place. He had hoped she would take her place—sort of. He wanted a mom. He wanted someone who'd hug him in front of his friends, clean dirt off his face with her napkin and spit, he wanted the unconditional love that only a mother could give. He swallowed and tried to mask his disappointment and guilt. "Sure. Of course we can continue to be friends, Lana." He looked back to his father. "So? When are you going to marry?"

Jeremiah grinned at Lana and winked. "Well, I will announce the engagement after services today. I hope to have the ceremony in a couple of months."

"Great!" Xavier exclaimed, grinning and hugging his father again.

"Come now, son. Let's eat breakfast before it gets cold," the king laughed, patting his son's back.

Xavier followed his father and Lana into the church with

a smirk. They were hand in hand, and it didn't escape the group converging into the church that Lana wore an elaborate engagement ring on her left hand. Whispers chased after them even after they entered the nave and found their seats in the front pew.

"Hey, Xavier," Robbie greeted rushing over to sit next to him. "Can I sit with you during the sermon?"

"Yeah, sure!" Xavier grinned and scooted over to make room for her.

"So? Did you get into trouble for changing your dad's hair?" she asked, trying not to giggle but failing.

"Hey, I hear that giggle!" the king reprimanded, playfully elbowing Robbie and making her giggle more.

"Jeremiah! Leave the poor girl alone. She can't help it if you look ridiculous with bright pink hair," Lana laughed, swatting the king playfully.

As Robbie's eyes fell on Lana's engagement ring, her eyes widened. "Oh my gosh! You... you're wearing a... a ring!" she blurted.

Jeremiah grinned down at Robbie and covered Lana's hand with his. "That's right. We're making the announcement after services today."

"Oh, wow! Oh, that's great! Congratulations, sire!" Robbie gushed before looking at Xavier. "Are you okay with it, Xavier?"

Xavier grinned. "I'm more than okay. I'm ecstatic!"

"Oh, good. I think Lana will be good for your dad. Don't you?"

"Oh, yeah. She's just what he needs," Xavier replied, giving his father an enormous grin. "So? What happened when your mom found out that you and Erica lied so that you could meet us at the lake?"

Robbie smiled sheepishly. "I'm grounded for a month."

"A month? Just for sneaking out to go swimming at the

lake? God, that sucks," Xavier groaned indignantly.

Robbie shrugged. "Well, I think she was more upset because she didn't know where I was when the invasion occurred. So was Loren. He yelled at both Erica and me. He's kind of scary when he's mad."

"Yeah. I know. It stills sucks that you're grounded. I was hoping we could go out after school tomorrow."

"Sorry, Xavier."

"It's okay. Don't worry about it. I'll find something to do," he told her when he saw her face fall with guilt. He gave her his most charming smile and winked. "It won't be nearly as enjoyable as being with you, but I'll cope."

Robbie laughed and kissed him on the cheek.

Father Reinhart approached the pulpit, and the congregation grew silent. Xavier didn't hear a word the priest uttered. Robbie kept stroking the palm of his hand, and it sent heated sensations through his body. It took all his willpower to keep the raging inferno in his body under control. Though it had been months since he unintentionally expelled a power, he wasn't willing to take the risk, especially in a church with a large percentage of the kingdom present.

Ten minutes into the sermon, the king had had enough of his son's thoughts projecting themselves into his mind. Clearing his throat, he whispered softly to Robbie, "Robbie, why don't you sit next to Lana and get a good look at that ring? I need to sit next to Xavier."

Nodding, Robbie released Xavier's hand, and as inconspicuously as possible slid between the king and Lana.

Xavier regarded his father with questioning eyes. With a smirk, he cleared his throat and nodded to the pulpit where the priest was still addressing the congregation with a lesson on the pitfalls of vanity and pride. He followed his father's eyes to the priest as his father's voice pushed into his thoughts.

"You really need to work on controlling the feelings Robbie creates, son."

Xavier blushed crimson as he ducked his head and studied the toe of his highly polished dress shoe. *"Yeah. Sorry, Dad."*

When Father Reinhart finished his sermon, he gave the king a nod before announcing, "Before I dismiss you all to enjoy the rest of your Sunday, King Wells has an announcement he'd like to make. Sire?"

It was the first time Xavier ever remembered seeing his father nervous. The king stood slowly, wiping his sweating palms on his pant legs. He held out a hand to Lana, who took it with a reassuring smile. The couple approached the pulpit and turned to face the silently waiting crowd. As nervous as the king was, little of it showed as he stood tall and regally, preparing to address the people.

"Good morning, my faithful supporters. Today, I have wonderful news I wish to share with all of you." He glanced down at Lana and smiled. "I had the honor to offer my hand in marriage to Lana Applegate."

The entire church erupted in applause and cheers. The king's grin grew, and Lana blushed. When the crowd quieted, Loren's voice called out cheerfully, "So what did she say?"

The king laughed and held up Lana's left hand. "She said, yes!"

The church exploded in cheers and applause again. Once the congregation settled again, Father Reinhart announced, "King Wells and Ms. Applegate will receive your well wishes and congratulations in the vestibule. Have a pleasant week."

It took nearly a half an hour to get through the line of people offering their best wishes to the happy couple. The people left the church in high spirits and chattered happily about the upcoming wedding and what a wonderful queen Lana would make. She had attained a great amount of respect from the common citizens, and that was obvious.

"So you're really okay with your dad marrying Lana?" Robbie asked him as she slipped her hand in his.

Xavier dragged his eyes from his father and Lana to Robbie and grinned. "Yeah, I really am. I like Lana. No, I love Lana. She's really nice and sweet, and she's good for Dad." Xavier laughed. "He can't get away with anything with her around. It's funny to see someone boss my dad around—someone who's not *afraid* to boss him around."

Robbie snickered. "Yeah. I bet that's an entertaining sight."

"Oh, it is!" he blurted happily.

"Xavier?" his father called from the entrance to the church. Most the crowd had gone home and all who remained included Father Reinhart, Robbie's mom and sister, Loren, Ephraim, and their families. "Come here, please."

"Come on," Xavier said as he gently pulled Robbie across the lawn to where the others stood.

"What do you think about having a picnic at the coliseum and playing some rugby?" his father asked.

"That would be great! Can I invite Garrett, Beck, and the rest of the guys?"

"I don't see why not," his father responded before turning back to Father Reinhart. "Lana and I will be in to see you about arranging the wedding details early this week," Jeremiah told the priest.

"I look forward to it, your highness," Reinhart responded.

"Is Erica allowed to come?" Court asked Loren.

The general eyed Court, causing the boy to visibly gulp. Before speaking, Loren folded his arms across his massive chest. "She's grounded, Courtney."

"Yes, sir," Court agreed meekly before continuing quickly. "But she has to eat, doesn't she? And... and you'll be there so you can make sure..." Court faltered.

"I'll tell you what, Courtney. I'll make you a deal. She can come to the picnic if you and I come to an understanding. The next time she does something stupid or impulsive, *you* talk her out of it!"

"Uh... I... I'll try, sir, but you know Erica. There's not much that can stop her when she has her mind made up."

Loren stepped up to Court and glared down at him. "Well, in a case such as that, you call me!"

Court hesitated. Loren was asking him to betray his girlfriend. How could he do that? If Erica found out about this deal, she would kill him. He tried another tactic.

"Sir, you can trust me to look out for Erica. I'd never let anything happen to her."

The general nodded. "You better had, boy, but that's not the deal I'm making. I want you to call me if she refuses to listen to reason."

"Ah... w... with all due respect, sir, Erica would be sorely pissed if I did that. I want to help you out, but I can't betray her like that. I... I'm sorry, sir," Court responded timidly.

Loren stared down at Court in silence for a long moment before Lucy shoved her husband irritably. "Loren Douglas Jefferson! Leave the boy alone. It is not his fault your daughter is mischievous and stubborn. The girl takes after her father!" she spat before turning and looking kindly down at Court. "Courtney, Erica will be at the picnic. She will join us all in celebrating the king's engagement." Then after a dirty look at her husband, Lucy pulled him away from the children.

Xavier snickered. "Mate, you looked close to wetting your pants just then."

"Shut it, Xavier. He scares me when he looks at me like that, and he looks at me like that almost all the time now... now that Erica and I are dating officially."

Ephraim's hand clamped down on his son's shoulder, and Court jerked with a start.

"Holy hell, Dad! You scared the life out of me," Court gasped.

Ephraim chuckled. "What's the matter, son? Did you think Loren was having a go at you?"

"Well, yeah. He looks at me like I'm a roach—a roach he'd like to squash!"

"Then I suggest that you behave like a gentleman and mind your manners with his daughter. Come on. Let's get home and help your mother pack up some food for the picnic," his father responded, patting Courtney's shoulder before bowing slightly toward Xavier. "Sire."

"General Hardcastle," Xavier returned with a nod.

That afternoon, Xavier, his father, and Lana exited the palace with the Jeffersons and the Hardcastles. As they walked down the drive toward the palace gates, Xavier watched with fascination and delight as his father took the picnic basket from Lana and kissed her briefly before taking her hand in his.

"They look really good together," Erica remarked. "Are you sure you want them to go through with it? You'll have two parents, and that only means double the punishments when you get caught."

Xavier frowned at Erica. "Of course I want Dad and Lana to marry. I'll take my chances on the punishment thing."

Erica shook her head melodramatically. "All right, but it's your funeral."

Mrs. Minnows, Robbie, and Brittany were waiting for the group next to the gates, and as they approached, Mrs.

Hardcastle draped an arm around her sister. Brittany stayed close to the women while Robbie drifted next to Xavier.

"Hi," she whispered, taking his hand.

"Hi. Glad your mom is letting you come."

"Well, she said if it weren't a celebration for the king's engagement, I'd be sitting in my room instead of coming. Remind me to thank your dad for getting engaged," she joked.

When they arrived at the coliseum, the rest of Xavier's friends were already there messing about on the field.

"Oi, Wilson!" Courtney called out as the group entered the rugby pitch.

The group of boys froze at the sight of the group approaching and stared reverently at the king. Then to Xavier's dismay, they sank to a knee.

"King Wells," Beck whispered. "Thank you for inviting us to join your picnic and celebration."

"You're very welcome, Beckley. Please, stand, all of you," Jeremiah responded.

The boys stood and shuffled uneasily before the king.

Xavier rolled his eyes. "Geesh, guys," he blurted, snatching the rugby ball out of Garrett's hands. "Come on. Let's have a game before we eat." He turned to his father. "Are you going to play, Dad?"

The king grinned broadly. "Of course."

"Count me in," Loren announced, draping an arm over the king's shoulders.

Moments later, the men and children had divided themselves into equal teams as those not playing set up for the picnic and drank iced lemonade as they talked, laughed, and watched the game in progress.

"Son, pass it here!" Jeremiah shouted as he swung out wide behind Xavier, who had three opposing players closing in on him.

Xavier turned and tossed the ball to his father and looped around behind him. The king lunged forward about ten feet before Loren charged at him and forced him to the ground. Xavier was ready and snatched up the ball as his father released it and ran across the goal line, scoring a try.

"Well done," Jeremiah commented, grinning and clapping his son on the back.

"You fouled me!" Beck blared loudly, shoving Mac.

"I did not! You ran into the back of me! I didn't do anything illegal!"

"Bloody hell if you didn't!" Beck spat, shoving Mac.

"You shove me again, Beckley, your hands will come back as bloody stumps," Mac threatened, bumping his chest into the other boy.

Beck shoved Mac and a fight broke out.

"Hey! Boys! Enough!" Jeremiah shouted, racing to the scuffling boys and pulling each to his feet by their collars. As the boys struggled to get at each other, the king shook them. "I said that's enough, boys! It's only a game."

Instantly the boys stilled and looked up at Jeremiah with a mingling of shame and respect.

"Sorry, sire," they muttered in near unison.

"I think we should take a break and have a bite to eat. Maybe we can continue the game with cooler heads afterwards," Jeremiah announced, releasing the two boys.

The group sat together on the lawn of the rugby pitch eating sandwiches, chips, pasta salad, and pies of every imaginable flavor.

"Xavier Wells!" Lana gasped as she watched the prince cut the apple pie in half and scoop half onto his plate.

"What?" Xavier questioned innocently.

"Don't you think you should start with a smaller piece?"

"But I love apple pie. It's my favorite."

"I can see that," Lana commented dryly. "But there are

other people who might want some of that pie."

Xavier looked at her slightly bewildered. "There's still half of the pie left."

Jeremiah snickered and shook his head, amused.

Lana gave him a quick glare that had the king struggling not to laugh harder.

As Xavier settled in next to Robbie, she snickered and said, "I'd have to agree with Lana, Xavier. That's an awfully big piece of pie."

"I can't help it. I'm starving!" he commented past a large bite he had just shoveled into his mouth.

Still laughing, she kissed his cheek. "I'm going after more lemonade. You want some?"

"Sure," he answered, giving her his charming grin that had the butterflies in her stomach doing somersaults.

As Robbie meandered toward the drinks, she wondered if Xavier knew he had that effect over her. He probably did since he had telepathy and could read her thoughts. Then she smiled to herself. Xavier Wells might know how easily he could make her knees go weak, but he glowed around her! That had to mean something! After all, if the rumor about the king glowing when he was in the company of a woman he loved was true, it would have to mean that Xavier was in love with her. Right? Besides, hadn't the king complained that Xavier's thoughts were so strong around her that he was unwittingly broadcasting them? Boy, what she wouldn't give to know what those thoughts were. She would have to corner him sometime and ask.

Robbie poured two large cups of lemonade. Irritation and jealousy crawled up her neck when she turned and found Sara Jefferson sitting in her place next to Xavier with her hand on his arm. Xavier was blushing and smiling at something she was saying to him. Trying not to crush the paper cups in her grip, Robbie briskly walked over to the couple.

"...and I told Jonas that I'd never go out with him because he was a complete jackass, and that it was a shame your transfiguration wasn't permanent because he made a much better jackass than a boy."

Xavier erupted with laughter. "That's great! I bet he was pissed."

Sara nodded melodramatically. "Oh, he was! His face went red, and he stomped away like a little boy." She rolled her eyes, and the hand on Xavier's arm slid up to rub his bicep. "He's such a man-child! You'd think at eighteen, he'd be more mature!"

Robbie cleared her throat loudly. "Excuse me, but you're in my seat!"

Sara blinked up at Robbie. "There aren't any assigned seats, Roberta. We are not in school."

"Here, Robbie. Sit here," Xavier suggested, patting the ground on the other side of him.

Robbie's temper flared, and she glared at Xavier. Sara batted her eyes at Robbie and smiled. Robbie then mirrored Sara's phony smile and dumped lemonade over both their heads. Sara squealed indignantly and ran to her parents as Robbie smiled smugly.

"Ah! Why did you do that?" Xavier blared, jumping to his feet as the cold liquid ran down his back and shoulders.

She looked at her boyfriend triumphantly. "You looked as if you needed to cool off." And, with that, Robbie stomped away, leaving Xavier to stare after her dumbfounded. He looked down at Court and Erica, both unsuccessfully stifling snickers.

"What in the heck was that about? What did I do?"

Erica rolled her eyes. "Boys! You really are clueless, aren't you?"

Chapter 9

The next morning, Xavier woke to his father drawing back the drapes in his bedroom and sending sunlight blasting into his room and across his bed. He stretched noisily.

"Morning, Dad," he muttered.

"Morning, son. Are you ready to start back to school?"

"Yes, sir. It'll be nice to do something somewhat normal!"

Jeremiah smiled. "Well, remember, you are in classes at the Academy until after lunch. Once you've eaten and had your break, you're to report to my office in the Governing Hall. We'll work on telepathy and begin your apprenticeship. For the first week or two, you will shadow me and watch, but I will be asking you questions about what you learn and see during each day. So pay attention."

"Yes, sir," Xavier responded.

"Then, at three, we'll go to the coliseum for combat training. I can arrange to have royal guards with specific abilities. So if there's anything in particular you'd like to work on, you better let me know now," his father told him.

"Ah, no. I'll let you choose," he answered. "Dad? Why haven't I sparred with you since the first few weeks at the mountain?"

The king sighed, crossed the room, and sat on the edge

of the bed. "Well, Ephraim believed with the stress you were under that you needed someone you could trust, someone who hadn't hurt you during training, someone you'd *know* wouldn't hurt you. It just made sense it would be me. If a boy can't depend on and trust his father, then what good is the father?"

Xavier nodded. "Would you train me if I asked?"

The king regarded him for a moment before answering, "Yes. I would. If you wished to work on telepathy during combat, then I'd be the only viable option. Mike's leg would prevent him from being a good sparring partner. Why are you asking me this, son? Do you wish to spar with me?"

"Yeah, I do, but not yet. I want to work my way up to you."

The king smiled. "All right. You better get a move on, boy. You don't want to be late your first day back," he announced, patting the boy's leg and standing.

An hour later, Xavier maneuvered through the secret passage with Court, Court's brothers, Erica and Sara. Robbie wasn't speaking to him and refused to come to the phone when he had tried calling her that morning. What in the world was her problem? He hadn't done anything wrong! She was the one who had dumped lemonade on his head and embarrassed him in front of everybody. If anyone should be mad, it was him!

"You're awfully quiet, your highness," Sara remarked, snapping him out of the internal pity party he was holding for himself.

Xavier looked at the girl next to him. She looked remarkably like her mother. She was breathtaking. "I was lost in thought, I guess."

Sara nodded. "Thinking about Robbie?"

"Is it that obvious?"

Sara shrugged. "I don't understand why she behaved like

she did at the picnic. You didn't deserve to be embarrassed like that. It's not right. You deserve better treatment. You're our prince after all."

Yeah! Xavier thought indignantly. He hadn't deserved any of it! What in the world had gotten into her? Well, one thing was for sure, he wasn't going to be the one to apologize! She was the one who acted like a jerk, not him. Feeling smug with himself, Xavier smiled down at Sara.

"Thanks, Sara. I needed to hear that," he told her.

Sara gave him her most devastating smile and batted her eyes. "I'm only speaking the truth, sire."

"Please, just call me 'Xavier.' I'm not my dad," he told her as they approached the entrance to the academy.

Sara giggled. "Yeah, but you're looking more and more like him though."

Xavier made a face and laughed. "Please tell me you're trying to pay me a compliment."

"Oh, yes, I am! Most of the girls in my year think the king is hot. One of my friends is depressed that he and Lana are engaged. But if you ask me, she's delusional. She doesn't stand a chance with King Wells. Do you know who Marilynn Murray is?"

Still trying to get past the fact that some of the girls in his school thought of his father in that way, he stammered, "Ah... ah, yeah. She's in Drew's year. Right?"

"Yep, that's the one," she continued, lowering her voice as they entered the academy and made their way down the hall. "She snuck into the castle once. Her cousin was a servant for the king at the time. She says she helped her cousin change the king's sheets and stole a pair of his boxer shorts."

Xavier choked out, "What? That's disgusting! Why would she do that?"

Sara shrugged. "She had a major crush on him."

"Did my dad ever find out?"

"No," Sara told him and grabbed his arm. "You won't tell him, will you? I mean this was at least three years ago. You weren't even here when she did it. It's like ancient history. Please, don't tell the king. She'd be devastated if he knew."

"Heck, no! I'm not going to tell him that some girl stole his underwear three years ago. Even if I wanted to tell him, how in the heck would I start a conversation like that?" he blurted, revolted by the thought. He found this entire conversation disconcerting and longed to end it. "Well, I better get to the headmaster's office and get a copy of my schedule. See you later, Sara."

Sara flashed him a grin, and before he knew it, she leaned against him and kissed him. His stomach fluttered madly. Then she pulled away, still smiling at him. "See you later, Xavier." And, before he could untie his tongue and regain his wits, Sara turned and sauntered down the hall in such a way that had nearly every male student watching her walk.

"Holy hell, X! What was that?" Drew hissed appreciatively, draping an arm over Xavier's shoulders.

"Beats me," he answered, shrugging his shoulders.

As the morning wore on, rumors began to spread around the school that Sara and Xavier were dating.

"I'm not dating Sara! Robbie is my girlfriend!" Xavier insisted for the fifth time that morning.

"Then why does Beth say she saw you kissing her in the middle of the hall next to the headmaster's office?" asked Melissa Dorne.

"I... I didn't kiss her. She kissed me!"

"I don't think Robbie sees it like that, Xavier. You better talk to her. She's really upset!" Rene Jones whispered.

"I've tried!" he blared loudly. "She's acting crazy! She

dumped lemonade on me for no reason Sunday! Why is it my job to chase after her like a starved puppy? She's the one who started it! She should be apologizing to me! Now, if you two don't mind, I've got to get to History class!"

Xavier hurried down the hall, away from the staring eyes and prying girls. He didn't owe Robbie anything. If she wanted to believe the rumors and blow the situation between Sara and him out of proportion, then he would let her. With that thought, he moodily entered the classroom and slumped into an empty seat in the back next to the windows. Court came in a few seconds behind him with Erica and Robbie on his heels. Court strode directly to the seat next to Xavier whereas the girls, giving him a dark look, sat at the front of the room.

"Mate," Court began sympathetically after seeing Xavier's expression to Robbie's obvious rejection, "I don't know how it happened, but you sure pissed that girl off."

"No! Really? How could you tell? Was it the lemonade she dumped on my head yesterday? Or maybe the fact she won't answer my phone calls and seems hell-bent on ignoring me?" Xavier spat, taking out his frustrations on his best friend. Then, sighing deeply, he looked apologetically at Court. "Sorry. It's just so frustrating! I don't have the foggiest idea what I supposedly did to get her mad."

"I don't know either. She won't talk to me, and Erica has been sworn to secrecy. But I think they're planning something, mate. Why don't you use your telepathy and find out why she's mad and what she and Erica are planning?"

It was tempting, very tempting, but he had promised Robbie that he would never invade her thoughts in that way. "I... I can't. I promised her," he moaned dejectedly.

Court shrugged. "Okay, but I'm telling you they're plotting revenge. So if I were you, mate, I'd sleep with my eyes open tonight."

By lunchtime, the tension between Xavier and Robbie was so thick that most of the school knew the prince and Robbie were at odds with each other. The majority of female students eyed Xavier like he was something just scraped off the bottom of their shoes. Sighing heavily, Xavier sought refuge with his closest friends and sank onto the bench next to Garrett.

"Hey, X! We were just talking about you," Beck piped up gleefully.

"You have to tell us everything. Don't leave out a single detail," Frankie said eagerly.

"Tell you what?"

"About kissing Sara," Frankie prompted.

"I didn't kiss her. She kissed me," Xavier mumbled.

"What was it like?" Frankie all but begged.

"Shut it, Frankie," Court stated, settling onto the bench next to Xavier. "Everyone knows you've always had the hots for Sara."

"Yeah, only Frankie and about every other boy in the school!" Beck piped up. When Court glared at him, Beck protested, "What? The girl's freaking hot! Have you ever watched her walk? And she knows what it does to all us guys too. Go on, Xavier, tell us!"

Xavier shrugged. "It was nothing really," he stated.

"There's no way it could be nothing! Did she use tongue?" Beck inquired gleefully.

"No, seriously. It wasn't that kind of kiss. She doesn't like me in that way anyways. I think she's got a thing for my dad."

The other boys gaped at him. Beck was the first to break the silence. "That's sick! He's like... an old man!"

Xavier nodded. "Yeah, I know. But on the walk to school, it was all she could talk about. She kept telling me how all the girls in her year think," Xavier made a repulsive face, "that he's hot." He exaggerated the shudder running through him at the thought.

All the boys nodded sympathetically.

"Well, he is really buff, and girls seem to like that kind of thing," Frankie commented.

Beck stared at Frankie in disgust. "*Francine*, you scare me sometimes. Do you know that?"

After lunch, Xavier followed Robbie around the courtyard. He planned to be close to her so when she finally came to her senses, she'd be able to find him. But from the looks of things, Robbie wouldn't be doing that anytime soon.

"Xavier?"

He turned and nearly knocked Sara down. He grabbed her quickly to steady her. "I'm sorry. Are you okay?"

She smiled up sweetly, her hands squeezing his biceps. "Wow, you've got some serious muscles under your uniform. I bet you could lift me without much effort, huh?"

Xavier stumbled on the compliment. "Ah, well, there... there wasn't a lot to do at the mountain by myself except work out and read." He shrugged in an attempt to be modest.

"Well, you look and feel really good," Sara said, moving her hands so that they rested on his chest. "Do you have a six-pack set of abs too?"

Xavier straightened and his chest expanded with pride. "Well, yeah, I guess I have a bit of one started."

Suddenly, Sara grabbed at his shirt, yanked it loose from his pants, and lifted it.

"Hey!" Xavier blurted, jumping back and pulling his shirt free of her hands. "What are you doing?"

"Just checking to see if you're lying," she giggled.

"Hello, Sara," Robbie stated stiffly from behind them.

"Oh, hello, Roberta," Sara greeted with a giggle and pushed at Xavier playfully. "Xavier, you're so funny."

Okay, Xavier was officially lost. Funny? What did he say that was funny?

"Yeah, he's a riot!" Robbie blurted dryly. "Did you get a good look at my boyfriend's chest or would you like another look?"

Xavier felt a tingling sensation race down his neck. He knew that look.

"Uh, no. She doesn't need another look. She didn't have permission to look the first time," Xavier rushed to say, but he was too late. Suddenly he stood in the middle of the courtyard bare-chested.

The group around them snickered lightly.

"Robbie..." Xavier warned in fear she would go further with her act of revenge. "Robbie, don't."

"Oh, you are so right, your highness. It's not fair that you should show off your beautiful chest when Sara isn't," Robbie spat.

Suddenly there was a collective groan of male appreciation around him. Xavier spun to a stunned Sara, who now wore only her bra from the waist up. Blushing from head to toe, Sara tried to cover herself as she ran to the entrance of the school.

"He's *my* boyfriend, Sara. You understand? He's mine! So you better keep your slimly little hands off of him! Got it?" Robbie yelled after her.

"Robbie! Stop!" Xavier demanded, grasping her firmly by the shoulders. "What is wrong with you?"

Robbie shoved his hands away. "What's wrong with me? Are you serious? Are you really that stupid, Prince Wells?"

Xavier felt his temper rising but worked to keep it buried. "I must be because I have no idea what I did to make you mad and want to embarrass me like this."

"You... are... flirting... with... Sara! You let her kiss you! Everyone is talking about it. And, just now, I stood there and watched while you let her put her hands on you!"

"I didn't let her do anything, Robbie! I might have a lot of powers, but I don't have the power to control what other people do!" Actually he did, but somehow it didn't seem very helpful to mention that.

"Roberta Minnows!" Headmaster Spencer barked from the doorway. "Get yourself to my office immediately!" When Robbie didn't move and continued to glare at Xavier. Michael Spencer barked, "NOW!"

With a huff, Robbie stomped to the door and brushed angrily past the headmaster.

"Sire Wells? Go to the nurse's station, and she'll give you another shirt. Then I suggest you get yourself to the Governing Hall. Your father will be expecting you."

"Yes, sir," he responded. He avoided eye contact with the group who had witnessed the exchange, entered the school, and made his way to the nurse's station.

Chapter 10

Xavier teleported onto a stone platform reserved for just that purpose in the center of the garden located in the palace's enormous horseshoe-shaped drive. Nearly a year ago, William LeMasters had slaughtered countless victims in this very spot. A few feet away from the platform stood a beautiful white marble memorial with the names of all the lives lost during the invasion. Dublin's name, Robbie's father, was among them, as was Milton's, his father's personal assistant, who had been like a father to him. He tore his eyes away from the memorial and started across the drive to a large cylindrical shaped building with dark tinted windows. As he approached the entrance, he became more and more aware of people stopping to stare at him. He hated when people did that. He wasn't an endangered species in a zoo for God's sake! Instead of cowering and shyly hurrying away from the prying eyes as he had done in the past, Xavier tried a different tactic. After straightening his tie and combing his fingers through his hair, he looked at a group of women boldly and greeted them jovially.

"Good afternoon! How are you beautiful ladies today?" he asked, giving them a devil-may-care grin.

The women grinned back at him. "We're doing lovely, your highness. Thank you," one woman responded before the group turned and, with a giggle, continued with their business.

Pleased with the reaction, Xavier continued toward the Governing Hall in this fashion, greeting those who openly gawked at him. When he entered the building, he was grinning broadly and strolled confidently down the first floor commons to a pair of large wooden doors. He opened the door and bounded up the large marble staircase, taking two steps at a time until he reached the second floor, where his father's office was located. He opened another pair of doors that led into the commons for that floor. The Governing Hall was beautifully designed and decorated. Each floor had its own purpose and function, and the artwork in the commons reflected that purpose. The first floor was the judicial level and handled disputes and trials, so the mosaic artworks along its walls were of men and women in robes presiding over a court of law. The second floor served as the legislative department of the Governing Hall, so the artwork here depicted men and women writing laws, debating, and voting, and in the center of each mosaic design was the image of the king. Although people didn't stop and gawk here, they did nod to him respectfully as he made his way down the hall toward his father's office.

"Sire? You can't go in there right now. King Wells is in a confidential meeting," the secretary informed him when Xavier started toward the office door.

"Oh. Okay," he muttered and grinned at the secretary. "Hi, Alexandria. How are you doing?"

Alexandria smiled at the boy hanging over her desk. "It's going well, just busy."

Xavier's grin broadened. "Yeah, King Wells is a slave-driver."

"I think I have the right to remain silent on that charge," she snickered with a wink.

The office door opened.

"If you have any more problems with getting the votes to pass it, let me know, Marcus. It's a worthwhile legislation. It needs to be law."

"Yes, sire. I'll keep you posted," Marcus replied as he stepped out of the office and briskly walked away.

"Hello, son. Alexandria, we are not to be disturbed for the next hour unless it's an emergency."

"Yes, sire."

"Talk to you later, Alexandria," Xavier told her with a wink.

Alexandria giggled. "Oh, Xavier, you are such a flirt!"

Xavier frowned at the comment as he entered his father's office. Flirt? Was that what he was doing?

"Did you have a good morning at school?" his father asked as he shut the door.

"Honestly? No. It kind of sucked," Xavier told him. "Dad, is it okay for a guy to talk to another girl when he has a girlfriend?"

Jeremiah's eyes jumped to meet his son's. "Yes, it's okay. What's going on, kiddo?"

Xavier shrugged. "Robbie is really mad at me. She says I'm flirting with Sara Jefferson, but I'm not. I think Sara's flirting with me. At first I thought she was just being nice to me because you're my dad, but after lunch today..." Xavier's words faded, and he looked up at the king. "What do I do to get Robbie to understand that I'm not interested in Sara, that she's the only girl for me?"

The king smiled. "Problems with the opposite sex can be very difficult and confusing, but if you told her what you just told me, I think that would go a long way to soothe any hurt that might be there."

Xavier nodded. "Yeah. All right. I'll talk to her then. Thanks."

"Any time, son. So, are you ready to get started on

telepathy training?"

"Yes, sir," he answered. For the first time, he was actually looking forward to the lesson, but that enthusiasm quickly dwindled.

The king's surge into his thoughts was strong and robust. Within seconds, Jeremiah skimmed past Xavier's memories like he was reading a picture book, leaving Xavier winded and scrambling to stop him. His father saw every thought and every memory. Xavier felt his entire body blush when the king stopped and studied the memory where he kissed Robbie and glowed pink in the process. He turned to Xavier and gave him a small smile before continuing deeper into the boy's emotions, thoughts, and memories. Xavier showed little ability in stopping or ejecting him from his mind.

By the end of the lesson, Xavier was left with a headache and the sinking feeling that he would never be able to block his father from his thoughts. But if he didn't learn impediment, the plan the prophet had for saving his father would be useless.

"Dad? What can I do to get better at this? Are there exercises or something?" Xavier questioned.

"I'm afraid not, son. The only way to get better at blocking telepathic advances is practice. You'll get there. Don't worry."

Xavier sighed heavily and hoped he would get there in time.

The rest of the afternoon, Xavier shadowed his father around. He learned that the kingdom's electricity, water, sewer, TV cable, and trash were all outsourced from a neighboring common community. His father paid these utility bills for the entire kingdom from taxes he collected from Warwood citizens. Xavier's jaw dropped at the bill amounts for the services.

Later that afternoon, Xavier followed his father down the

common corridor and into a large conference room. A large oblong table filled the room with about twenty-five chairs circling it. In front of each chair lay a manila folder. The king led him around the table and sat at the head of the table, patting the seat next to him.

"Here, son. Have a seat, and I'll fill you in on this process."

Xavier was excited to be able to sit in on a delegation meeting for a new legislation with the Delegates of Warwood. He found the idea fascinating and was curious about how it worked.

"Now this is the first phase of the law process, son. This is a proposed law that I've not seen yet. So at this point in the process, I listen to the proposal and provide suggestions and make sure it doesn't infringe on current laws."

"Can you... like... kill the proposal if it's a really bad idea?"

The king nodded. "Yes, I can. I've only done it twice in my reign. One of the proposals I vetoed was a knee-jerk idea following William LeMasters' assassination of my father and stepmother."

"What was the proposal?"

The king sighed. "The proposal would have banished all non-native citizens—those not born in Warwood. I understood that the people of Warwood were afraid, but I couldn't allow fear to be the catalyst for a law. I vetoed the proposal and managed to talk sense into the delegates."

Xavier nodded just as the door opened and a group of men and women filed into the room. They stopped to greet the king and prince before finding a seat at the table. Once everyone was present, Jeremiah motioned for the conference room door to be closed. He stood at his seat and simultaneously the group fell silent.

"Good afternoon, delegates. My son will be attending our

meetings in the foreseeable future. He's beginning his apprenticeship today."

"Good afternoon, Prince Wells," the group chimed.

"Hello," Xavier greeted bashfully.

Jeremiah smiled at the group. "Let's get down to business, shall we? Who's the spokesperson for this recommended legislation?" the king inquired.

"I am, sire," announced a heavy-set man with thinning hair and large eyes behind thick spectacles as he stood.

Jeremiah nodded. "The king recognizes George Force as speaker for the delegation. Delegate Force, are you prepared to present the legislation at this time?"

George paused, his eyes flickering nervously to another man sitting across the table. Finally, he answered, "Yes, sire. I am."

The king leaned back in his chair and settled in for the presentation.

"You have the floor, Delegate Force. You may proceed."

The beefy man cleared his throat and opened his folder. Then, after an uncomfortable glance at Xavier, he began, "King Wells and fellow delegates, the legislation I am presenting to you today on behalf of the Wellington Interest Group will have profound benefits and protection for all of Warwood citizens. As a result of the events that took place October 11th of last year, I make the following proposal."

King Wells stiffened, straightening slowly in his chair as a muscle in his jaw rolled. Something the man said had angered his father, but Xavier didn't understand what until George Force's next statement.

"We propose to organize a small group of powerful men to act as a task force for justice. The role of this group will be to subdue and control high officials who are found by this body to be a danger to Warwood and/or its citizens. In order to provide this task force with the appropriate abilities for combatting and subduing any person in question, we ask to be given the authority to grant the use of the King's Key at our discretion. The details of this proposal are outlined in the packets in front of each of you. I'll allow you a few minutes to skim through the contents before I open the floor for questions or suggestions."

Xavier's eyes darted back to his father, who was staring darkly at Delegate Force. After a moment, the king opened the folder in front of him to scan through the contents. Xavier craned his neck to look at the file, but his father leafed through it too quickly. After a couple minutes, the king tossed the folder onto the table in front of him, sighed bitterly, and irritably rubbed his face.

"Dad?" Xavier whispered.

But the king cut him off with a simple, jerky wave of his hand.

"Dad, is this because of me, because I attacked the kingdom?" Xavier questioned, using telepathy.

The king turned to him and whispered his response close to Xavier's ear. "I cannot discuss this here. I'll explain later. Please do not use telepathy again during these proceedings."

Xavier nodded, sat back in his seat and continued to study the group. Everyone was still shuffling through the file, except one man who was studying Xavier and the king. The all-knowing scrutiny of the man's gaze was uncomfortable, and he quickly looked away to the rest of the group. A few delegates had finished examining the details to the proposal and closed the file with disgust.

Once everyone had completed reviewing the file, George opened the floor for questions and suggestions.

"I don't understand the need for this... task force," a petite woman with red hair began tightly. "The people of Warwood already have means to prevent the problem you've presented here. King Wells himself proposed and lobbied for a change in the responsibilities of the High Council to include evaluating the king. Why would this be necessary?"

"Ms. Rowan, this proposal will expand the power of the people further in a way the High Council cannot. It will provide additional protection and means to handle tyrant leaders."

"By *handle* do you mean to overthrow?" another man asked.

"If necessary, yes. Look, ladies and gentlemen, this isn't a popular topic to consider. I understand that. But what if, God forbid, in the future we have a king who is powerfully endowed with abilities and wishes to oppress his people for his own gain and power. If we do not have this task force, a physical means of stopping him, we would be at his mercy."

Several of the group around the table nodded thoughtfully at Force's words.

Then Governor Bracus stood, his face scarlet with anger. "So, by passing this legislation, we will trade the possibility of one tyrant king for a group of tyrants on steroids! Delegate Force, explain to me who will be responsible for regulating this group? Who will rescue the people from this *task force* if they chose to take the power of the throne for themselves?"

The group began whispering feverishly at this question, and soon the whispering grew into heated discussions before exploding into a shouting match. Disconcerted, George glanced anxiously at the man across the table again. King Wells saw the exchange this time and stood.

"Order! Please, ladies and gentlemen, settle down!" the king announced, raising his hands consolingly. "I know this is a volatile, controversial issue that could change the course of our great kingdom. But shouting at one another isn't going to solve this amicably. Now, please, sit down and let's deal with this professionally."

The group slowly settled into their seats again and looked expectantly at their king. Jeremiah surveyed the group, checking for signs of dissention. Seeing none, he looked at the man who had sat silently through the verbal scuffle, the man who was truly behind the formation of the legislation.

"Delegate Force, you may sit. I have the floor," the king said without looking at George. "Delegate Grant?"

Slowly, the man stood, straightening his tie and jacket. "Yes, sire?"

"As this is your legislation, I think I'd rather address my concerns and questions to you if you don't mind."

The man's hand hesitated on his tie marginally before he responded evenly, "I don't know what you mean, sire. Clearly, Delegate Force is the speaker and therefore the driving force behind this proposal."

"No, George is a fall guy, a whipping boy. You are the driving force, Delegate Grant."

The man's eyes narrowed on the king, and his face twisted resentfully. "Sire, with all due respect, you know the use of telepathy during these sessions is forbidden. I don't appreciate..."

"I haven't engaged my telepathy, Lucas. Please don't make the mistake of assuming that without my telepathy I'm a bumbling oaf. One doesn't need telepathy to see the nonverbal exchanges between you and George," the king stated gruffly. His eyes moved to red-faced George, who was sitting very still with his eyes cast downwards. The king looked back to Lucas Grant and raised his brow as he nodded in affirmation toward the large man.

Lucas glared blatantly at Jeremiah for several long seconds before prompting confidently, "Sire?"

"I'd like to hear the answer to Governor Bracus's question, Delegate Grant. Who controls this task force?"

Grant shifted slightly under the king's penetrating stare. "The task force is an entity unto themselves. Therefore, they would govern and control themselves."

The king nodded pensively. "All right, that leads to the governor's second question. What recourse do the citizens of Warwood have if this task force goes rogue?"

"They will not go rogue, your highness. They will be hand-selected and trustworthy," Grant told him.

The king's brows rose at this. "Hand-selected? By whom? A delegation you and your lobbyists create? No, Delegate Grant. This will not happen. The citizens of Warwood have the control they need over the throne. This legislation smells suspiciously like an oligarchy. I will not allow this legislation to pass. It will never become a law."

Lucas Grant swelled in anger. "Sire! You boast to all who will listen that you've given power to your people, yet in the end, the power is ultimately yours and yours alone. The people of Warwood have no real power! The power of the people is an illusion, sire! You've misled your people! You're lying to us, King Wells."

"Now, wait a damn minute!" Governor Bracus shouted, jumping to his feet.

King Wells held up his hand and silenced the governor before turning back to Lucas. "I hear your frustration, Delegate Grant, but your presence here, presenting a proposal for a Code in the Laws of Warwood, contradicts your statement that the people have no power. How many codes and policies has this group presented and passed during my reign as king?"

Lucas Grant grew flustered and didn't respond, but Governor Bracus obliged. "Countless, sire. If your father was sitting there in your stead, Delegate Grant would be in the cell awaiting execution for blatantly questioning his king. I support King Wells' denial of this legislation. It sets up an opportunity for a coup. Not to mention, it's illegal for any citizen to obtain powers from the King's Key. After all, it is the key of the kings and therefore to be used only by kings."

The majority of the group murmured and nodded their assent. Again, King Wells held up his hand to silence the group as he regarded Delegate Grant. "I'm sorry, Lucas, but I hereby veto this proposal. It is my ultimate right to do so. I am the King of Warwood, and you'd do well to remember that. As long as I draw breath, Warwood will remain as it always has been—a monarchy."

Lucas Grant's head dropped marginally with submission. Jeremiah looked to the rest of the group.

"This meeting is now adjourned. Have a good afternoon," Jeremiah announced as he waved for Xavier to stand and follow him out of the room.

Father and son said nothing as they strode down the commons and into the king's office. With a frustrated sigh, Jeremiah paced behind his desk, rubbing his neck.

"Dad?"

The king held up a single finger before pressing a button on his intercom system. "Alexandria? Please contact General Hardcastle and General Jefferson and tell them to report to my office immediately."

Sighing loudly, the king sank into his chair and looked at his son. Giving him a small smile, he intoned, "Well, you just witnessed a not-so-subtle attempt to overthrow the king."

Xavier's eyes bulged. "What? Why didn't you arrest him?"

"He did it legally. I gave the delegates the right to question and challenge me," his father shrugged.

Xavier frowned. "It was because of me, wasn't it?"

Jeremiah shook his head as he answered, "No, son. It had little to do with your influx. There's a facet of people who wish to control the crown completely. The insurgency of your powers was only an excuse to attempt what they've been itching to do all along—overthrow me as their king."

Chapter 11

A n hour later, Xavier stood in the middle of the rugby pitch dressed in full combat gear with three royal guards standing across from him dressed similarly. Glancing into the stands, he saw his friends with what looked like popcorn and sodas.

"Glad I could be entertainment for them," Xavier muttered dryly.

But he couldn't stop the smile when he heard Garrett's voice call clearly from the stands, "Let's go, X. Kick some royal guard butt!" Then the other boys joined in with a chant, "X, X, he's our prince, watch out guard, he'll make you wince."

Xavier rolled his eyes at the rhyme and began preparing himself for the fight. His father had found three volunteers for his training. Xavier hadn't been happy to have new fighting opponents, but his father had insisted.

"Xavier, you need experience with a variety of fighting styles from a variety of soldiers," his father had told him.

Xavier understood his father's reasoning, heck, he even agreed with it to some extent, but that didn't mean he had to like it. So, here he stood in the middle of the coliseum facing three unknown men. To say he was nervous was an understatement. First, he had never fought three men at once before. Two yes, but not three. Secondly, he was given no information about the men's abilities. He wasn't sure what to prepare for, which his father had insisted was the point. Taking a deep breath and trying to calm his nerves so he could focus, Xavier unsheathed his sword and prepared.

"All right, men," Jeremiah's voice called out from the side of the field. "Anything goes, and remember, you won't be doing the prince any favors by going easy on him. General Hardcastle, General Jefferson, Lieutenant Davies and I will be on hand for injuries and maintaining blocks so that we can avoid serious injury. When you're ready, you may begin."

Xavier flipped his mask down to protect his face and stood ready.

The first attack happened immediately. The man on his left conjured and lazily launched an electro force at him. Xavier almost laughed at it, but instead of blocking it, he drew up a deflection shield and sent the force barreling back at the man. The man dove to the side as his own power whizzed inches over his head. The group of boys in the stands cheered and hooted. The man in the middle decided on a more direct, hands-on approach and charged Xavier with his sword raised. The boy smirked as the man drew within striking distance and swung his sword wildly. Did he really think Xavier would just stand there, unmoving in terror, and let him strike him down? Laughing, Xavier sidestepped the frontal assault and swung his sword as the man stumbled past, catching the man's underbelly with the blade of his sword. If the guard hadn't been wearing protective gear, he would have been cut down. Xavier's fans cheered loudly and began chanting his name.

"Lewis! You're out! That was a kill strike!" Loren shouted, disgusted that the soldier had attacked so carelessly.

The remaining man had watched both his comrades get

bested by a boy. It was obvious the boy was well trained after months of seclusion where he was taught to control his raging abilities for hours each day by General Hardcastle, General Jefferson, and King Wells. He wasn't a fool. He knew if they were to have a chance at defeating the boy, they would have to work together. He gave his remaining companion a hand signal as he slowly approached Xavier. Then he stopped a good fifteen feet from the prince and conjured a strong gust of wind that knocked the boy off his feet, sending him somersaulting backwards.

Xavier tried to grab the turf to slow the tumbling, but the gusts were too strong and simply ripped him from his hold. As the somersaults gained momentum, his body slammed hard into the turf, dislodging his sword from his hand. He was helpless! There was nothing he could do but hope the guard's empowerment would fizzle out or weaken. Finally, the power evaporated and released him. Xavier staggered to his feet, dizzy, disoriented, and vulnerable.

He felt the attack before he saw it. The second man was feet from him, his sword raised, poised to attack. With no sword to parry the attack, Xavier had only one course of defense—his abilities. Xavier dropped to his knees just as the sword whizzed past, inches from his head. Then, taking advantage of the man's extended, unstable stance, the prince punched him in the kidneys. The guard's body arched and he grunted loudly. Before the man could turn, Xavier jutted out his hand and sent him flying forty feet across the rugby pitch. Jeremiah slowed the man's fall and landed him gently on the ground.

"Jackson, you're out," Loren shouted.

Xavier thrust his hand out at his sword lying a good fifteen meters away, and the sword flew into his hand. He spun quickly and parried a strike from the remaining guard. Their swords clanged loudly and the jarring sensation that ran up Xavier's arm informed him that his opponent was quite strong. Groaning against the locked swords as the guard tried to outmuscle him, Xavier spun and swung his elbow up, striking the man in the neck. The guard staggered backwards, wheezing and coughing. In his vulnerable state, the man did nothing to prevent the kill strike of Xavier's sword.

Still gasping, the guard dropped his sword and held up his hands in surrender.

Xavier lowered his sword and stepped toward the choking man. "I can fix that," he told him and placed his hand gently on the guard's neck. "Hold still."

A bright white light flooded from his hand and engulfed the man's neck, face and chest. When it faded seconds later, the man stood and took a deep cleansing breath.

"Thank you, sire," he whispered, rubbing his neck.

"I'm sorry I did that," Xavier responded, but the royal guard was shaking his head.

"Don't be. You did what you should have done. I left myself open for that," he told the boy.

"Well done, son!" Jeremiah announced with pride as he ruffled Xavier's hair.

"Thanks, Dad."

"Oh, man! That was awesome!" Garrett whooped as he and the other boys raced over to him.

Xavier grinned and shrugged. "All in a day's work."

Loren burst into laughter. "Damn if that doesn't remind me of someone who will remain nameless, Sire *Wells*."

Jeremiah laughed lightly. "And here I was thinking it sounded a lot like you, and I was contemplating ceasing all contact you have with my son."

The group's laughter was cut short by Sir Blaire racing onto the rugby pitch, clearly alarmed.

"King Wells! Sire! Please, come quickly!" he called

urgently from the east entrance of the coliseum. "There's a problem at the lake!"

The group sprinted to follow Sir Blaire from the coliseum, across the field, and into the woods.

"What is it, Jack?" Jeremiah questioned as he walked beside the anima-lingua professor.

"I don't know exactly, sire, but a great deal of fish in the lake are dead. I have men testing the water for disease, but it's devastating."

"That doesn't make sense. Xavier and his friends were just here Saturday night," Jeremiah commented before turning to the prince. "Son, you didn't notice anything strange with the fish, did you?"

"No, sir. The lake, the water, the fish all seemed fine!" Xavier told him.

When they stepped into the clearing and Xavier got his first look at the lake, his jaw dropped. The surface of the lake was blanketed with floating fish corpses and a strong smell of dead fish clung to the air.

"Crikey! What happened to them?" Court gasped.

"That's what we're trying to determine, laddie," Sir Blaire remarked.

"Sire?" one of the men called to the king from the water's edge.

The king moved toward the man. "Did you find something?"

"Well, it's not contaminated water per se, but it appears that the fish suffocated, sire."

"Suffocated? Is that possible?" Xavier asked, sidling up next to his father.

"Prince Wells, fish need the oxygen in the water to breath. Now, in cool temperatures like we have this time of the year, there's usually plenty of oxygen in the water. Fish move more slowly in cold temperatures, you see and therefore they need less oxygen. But the water has unnaturally low levels of oxygen for its temperature, and it seems that the fish became highly agitated for some reason, requiring more oxygen," the man stated before looking back at the king. "If I didn't know better, I'd say the water had been flash-heated to temperatures in excess of ninety degrees."

Suddenly, Xavier's knees felt weak. He had done this! He had killed the fish by heating the lake so the girls would swim Saturday. He swallowed past the dread balling up in his throat.

"Ah, Dad," Xavier whispered. "I... Can I talk to you a second?"

"I'm sorry, son, I can't. Why don't you go on home and get cleaned up? I'll be home..." the king's voice faded when he saw the boy's expression. Without another word, the king took the boy's arm and led him to the edge of the woods away from the others.

"What is it, son?" he asked, studying Xavier with concern.

"Um," Xavier stammered, his eyes filling with tears. "I... I didn't know that it would hurt anything. I swear to you I didn't. I wouldn't have done it if I'd known."

"Xavier, what did you do?" his father demanded gently.

"I... I heated the water in the lake so the girls would go swimming with us," he admitted quietly.

The king closed his eyes in exasperation, the muscle in his jaw flexing. After a moment, he opened his eyes and sighed. "Thank you for telling me the truth and being forthcoming with this information, son. You know that I must tell Sir Blaire and his men this."

"Yes, sir," he mumbled, ducking his head guiltily.

"Come on, son. Let's do what we can to fix this," Jeremiah said, patting his shoulder and leading him back to the group. "Gentlemen, you can relax. I know the cause. Xavier has informed me that the water temperatures were indeed elevated while he and his friends swam here Saturday."

"They were elevated? How?" Sir Blaire questioned.

"I did it, sir. I didn't know it would hurt anything," Xavier blurted. "I wouldn't have done it if I'd known."

Sir Blaire glared at the prince. "Prince Wells, ignorance doesn't bring back the supply of fish we depend on selling at market to help fund supplies for the school!"

"I know, sir," Xavier mumbled as his shoulders and head sank lower with shame.

"Jack, Xavier and I will restock the lake with fish, and I will cover any losses the school has to its funding while the fish develop and mature. I'm assuming the money obtained helps care for the animals on campus?"

Sir Blaire nodded. "Yes, sire. I like to keep a variety of animals for the students to choose from and to become familiar with during their studies."

The king nodded. "I'll take care of it. Send me any bills for the animals. Plus, Xavier will stay with you to lend a hand in your clean-up efforts," the king told Sir Blaire before looking at Xavier and adding, "Without powers."

"Without powers?" Xavier gasped. "But, Dad, I told you it was an accident! I didn't mean to do it intentionally!"

The king nodded. "Yes, son, I know that, but maybe helping with the clean-up the old-fashioned way will help you use the head on your shoulders before showing off or altering nature from its natural state again."

Xavier sighed heavily and fought the urge to roll his eyes. Finally he muttered, "Yes, sir."

"Send him home when you're through with him," the king told Jack Blaire with a wink.

"Thank you, sire," Sir Blaire breathed out, shaking

Jeremiah's hand. "I appreciate it."

With a nod, King Wells waved at his son and left the lake with Loren, Ephraim and Xavier's friends following darting sympathetic looks in his direction.

The work was long, stinky, and gross. Xavier was given the task of cleaning the lake of the numerous corpses that polluted its waters, which meant that he had to swim out into the depths of the water to retrieve the floating dead fish. It wasn't a pleasant job with the fish bobbing and bumping against his head. It would have been so much easier to use telekinesis to remove the fish. While Xavier and another man cleared the lake, Sir Blaire and a third man built a bonfire to burn them.

A couple of hours later, the lake was finally cleared of the dead fish, and Sir Blaire gave Xavier the job of supervising the fire until the last of the fish had been burnt to ash. Sir Blaire and another man combed the lake's bottom for any missed fish before treating the water with some kind of chemical to balance the water's pH levels and aerating the water with an apparatus to increase the oxygen levels.

"Well, there's a handful of fish still alive near the rocks where it's cooler, and the oxygen levels weren't depleted. I would bet that over eighty percent of the fish were lost."

Xavier hung his head guiltily and avoided eye contact with the men as he watched the last of the fish crumble into ash in the glowing flames.

"Sir Blaire, all the fish are completely burned up now," Xavier announced as he stirred the ash with a long metal pole. All that remained were bits of the logs used to kindle the fire.

Sir Blaire approached him, took the pole, and stoked and poked at the fire. "Yes, they're all incinerated. Put out the fire, Prince Wells and then you can go home." He handed the boy a bucket.

Xavier stared at him. "But I could just use my abilities and have it out in..."

"Sire, King Wells said no empowerments. I do not disobey my king. Now, put out the fire with the bucket, young sire."

Sighing disgruntledly, Xavier took the bucket and trudged back and forth from the lake half a dozen times, but the flame still smoldered. Xavier glanced back at Sir Blaire and the other men to find them packing up the aerator machine and other equipment. With a wave of his hand over the fire, he extinguished the fire completely in a matter of seconds. After returning the bucket to Sir Blaire, he headed home.

When Xavier finally got back to the palace, it was nearly dark. He trudged moodily up the royal staircase dirty, exhausted, and smelling of fish. Loren stood next to the royal residence and grinned at his approach.

"Well, look what the cat dragged in! Get the lake sorted?"

"Yeah," Xavier mumbled as he walked past the general and into the royal residence. Mrs. Sommers looked up from dusting and clicked her tongue at him.

"My, you're a sight! I kept your dinner warm. It'll wait long enough for you to shower. Go get cleaned up, and I'll see to your dinner."

"Where's Dad?"

"He and Lana went for a walk. They should be back soon."

Nodding, Xavier climbed the steps to his room.

After he had washed away the smell of fish and felt human again, he made his way down the stairs. His father and Lana were sitting in the receiving room next to a small fire. The king was massaging Lana's feet as she talked about her day at work. The couple turned as the boy descended the last few steps.

"Hello, son," the king greeted.

"Hi," Xavier muttered and looked meekly at Lana. "Hi Lana."

"Hi, sweetie."

Xavier glanced at his father. "D... Dad? How angry are you?"

Jeremiah's brows rose and he stood. "What? Come here, son," he ordered gently.

Xavier sauntered to his father, his head hanging low.

"Xavier, I'm not angry."

"Disappointed?"

"No, son. I'm not even disappointed. I'm very proud of you, actually."

"Proud?" Xavier looked up at his father baffled. "But, Dad, I killed nearly an entire lake full of fish!"

"Yeah," the king sighed, dragging the boy into a bear hug. "That wasn't a smart move, but I don't hold that against you. You've worked your butt off to make amends, and I'm betting that you've learned to think things through before you use your powers to show off for a girl in the future. But what I'm proud of is that you took responsibility for your actions. You didn't run. You didn't hide. You didn't lie." His father hugged him closer. "That is why I'm so very proud of you!"

Chapter 12

Later that night, Xavier sat in his room finishing his homework when his father and Lana entered.

"It's getting late, son. You need to finish up and get to bed," his father announced.

"I know. I'm just about finished," Xavier told him, but then added with a sly smile directed towards Lana, "But if my *history* teacher would give me an extension on my assignment..."

Lana laughed. "Oh, no, I don't think she'll let that happen, Xavier! You know how stubborn that history teacher can get. She might be inclined to assign double the homework if you tried."

"Yeah, she's a real pain," Xavier admitted, laughing.

Laughing as well, the king ruffled his hair and kissed him noisily on the cheek. "Don't stay up too late, son."

"I won't," Xavier promised. "Good night, Dad."

"Night, sweetheart," Lana whispered, kissing his cheek and hugging him warmly.

"Good night, Lana," Xavier murmured.

He watched his father and Lana stroll out of his room hand in hand. Watching them made him miss Robbie. He wished she would just tell him what he did wrong. Since when was talking to another girl flirting? Okay, yeah, Sara kissed him, and he had to admit he enjoyed it, but that didn't make him a bad guy, did it? He didn't ask her to kiss him. Sighing heavily, Xavier decided he'd go to Robbie and make her see reason.

After he finished the last of his assignments, Xavier packed his books up in his satchel for the morning and crept quickly to his door. His father and Lana were sitting in the receiving room cuddling and talking softly. Deciding it was best to wait until after his father went to sleep, he closed the door and waited.

Nearly an hour later, his father's heavy footsteps trudged up the stairs, and Xavier darted to his bed and dove under the covers. The king's footsteps paused outside his door and the door slowly creaked open. Xavier froze and concentrated on breathing evenly and deeply and clearing his thoughts. After a moment, his door closed softly, and the king's footsteps retreated to his own room.

Thirty minutes later, Xavier quietly opened the door to the king's bedroom. Pausing in the doorway, he reached across the room with his telepathic powers, hoping to find his father asleep. The king was in fact asleep and dreaming of Lana and King's Mountain. Interesting. Xavier didn't linger in his father's dreams as he quickly entered the room and closed the door behind him. After giving his eyes time to adjust to the dark, he crept across the room and out onto the patio. Almost instantly, he teleported himself from the palace to Robbie's room and banged painfully into something large and unforgiving. With a strangled gasp, Robbie sat up in bed and flicked on her bedside lamp. Xavier blinked rapidly and saw he had nearly teleported into a large dresser.

"Ouch! Man, that hurts! When did you move your dresser next to the window?"

"Xavier! What are you doing here! You can't be in my room! You know what happened the last time!" Robbie blurted.

"I know. I just need to talk to you for a minute. Will you come with me so we can talk without waking your mom?"

Robbie just stared at him.

"Please, Robbie! I want to clear things up between us."

"Okay," she muttered grumpily, and Xavier grinned. "Well? Turn your back so I can put on pants! I'm only wearing a T-shirt!"

Smirking, Xavier turned his back as Robbie threw back the covers and pulled on a pair of jeans. "Okay, let's go," she announced, moving to stand beside him.

He turned, grasped her by the hips, smiled, and then teleported them to the field in front of the school. When he released her, Robbie moved to put some distance between them. Xavier kicked at a rock wedged in the dirt and looked at Robbie reticently.

Finally, he pulled in his courage and blurted, "Robbie, what did I do wrong? I don't understand why you're so mad at me!"

Robbie moaned in frustration and faced him. "You really don't get it, do you?" When he responded with a blank stare, she hissed something that sounded like a curse and continued matter-of-factly, "Let me put it this way, Prince Wells. Pretend that Beck came over and sat next to me at the picnic while you were getting us drinks, and when you returned, he refused to give back your seat next to me. What would you think or feel if you saw us sitting there laughing and joking, and he had his hand on me, but I didn't remove it? Then, the next day at school, he kisses me in the middle of the hall for everyone in the school to see, and by lunchtime you were getting pity looks because everyone *knew* Beck and I had been snogging?"

Xavier's self-righteous mood sank. He had been so sure he was innocent this time, but he wasn't. He hadn't stopped

Sara or, at the very least, backed up Robbie when she confronted Sara. "Wow, when you put it like that..." he whispered despondently. "I'm sorry, Robbie. I didn't think... I wasn't thinking. You're right. I should have stopped her, but I really didn't see any of what she did as important. Robbie," Xavier insisted, grasping her by the shoulders. "I love you! I don't see any other girl the way I see you. I'm sorry I was oblivious to her flirting."

He felt Robbie's forgiveness before she said it. "It's okay. Boys are stupid about that stuff," she added with a snicker.

"Gee, thanks," Xavier growled, tickling her.

Robbie giggled and tried to outmaneuver him, but he was faster, bigger and stronger. He pulled her to the ground and pinned her there while he tickled relentlessly until she was panting and cackling loudly.

"Xavier! Stop it!" she managed between breaths.

He stopped tickling and looked down at her in the moonlight. "All right, but on one condition."

"What?"

"You kiss and make up with me." He grinned down at her devilishly.

Robbie grabbed him by the back of the neck, pulled him to her, and planted a breath-stealing, intoxicating kiss that had his head spinning.

"Sara's kiss definitely didn't do that to me!" he murmured, sending Robbie into a fit of giggles.

"I love you, Xavier Wells," she announced, kissing him again.

The couple sat in the field kissing and teasing each other for nearly an hour when finally Robbie announced, "We really need to get back, Xavier."

"Yeah, I know," he responded wistfully. "So what happened with the headmaster?"

"He gave me detention for a week and called my mom. I

got an extra week added to my grounding."

"Geez, that means you're grounded for five weeks! I don't know if I can live without being with you for that long. I might have to sneak you out again tomorrow night," he informed her playfully and was rewarded with her giggles. "Are you still able to walk to school?"

"Yes, but I'm to go straight there and straight home. Mom has even given me a curfew to be home by, or she'll come searching for me," Robbie told him, rolling her eyes.

"That sucks. Well, if you're still allowed to walk, I'll meet you at your house, and we can walk the long way to school so we can have some time together."

"That sounds great!"

Xavier kissed her lightly before helping her to her feet and teleporting her back to her room.

"Home, sweet home," he announced, grinning.

Robbie kissed him suddenly, deeply and he felt his brain go to mush as the rest of his body rushed with heat. He moaned and squeezed her against him. When she pulled away, Xavier felt irritated. He wanted more! He was about to grab her and kiss her back, when she giggled.

"Xavier, your eyes are glowing again."

His hands dropped to his sides, and he pouted at Robbie. "You don't have to announce it every time it happens you know. I know when I'm glowing. How could I not be after that kiss you just gave me?"

She giggled again and hugged him. "I love that I and only I can do that to you. It makes me feel special, like I'm special to you."

"You *are* special, and you'll always be special to me, Robbie. I love you more than anything in the world," Xavier whispered in her ear, and he felt her shudder.

"Oh, Xavier. I... I..." she stammered, her voice breaking in a quiet sob.

"Robbie? Robbie, please, don't cry!"

"It's not that kind of crying. I... I just love you so much and you... overwhelmed me is all."

Xavier kissed her again, savoring the taste and the feel of her lips.

Robbie gently pushed him away. "Ah... Xavier, you better go. You don't want to get caught in my room again."

Xavier swayed slightly without Robbie in his arms; he felt off balance. "Yeah. You're right. I'll see you in the morning," he choked out thickly. Then after a quick kiss to Robbie's cheek, he teleported back to the patio outside his father's bedroom. He stood for several minutes in the chilly night air, cooling his body and regaining his senses. Finally, with an enormous grin, he crept back into the palace and into his room.

The next morning Xavier met Robbie in front of her house, and the pair walked the long way to school hand-in-hand. It would be the only time he would be alone with her for the next few weeks.

"You know, when you finish serving your time, I think we should go into Razorbill Cove and go to a movie and dinner. What do you say?"

"That sounds fantastic. I can't wait," Robbie answered, smiling and squeezing his hand. "How was your first day with your dad?"

"It was pretty interesting actually," he responded as they walked through the palace gates and started down the sidewalk that ran parallel to the palace walls. "I even got to attend a legislative meeting. This guy, Lucas Grant, tried to get a new law passed that would basically overthrow my dad. I didn't understand it completely, just that he wanted to have a group of men given more powers using the King's Key so they could attack the king if they thought he was a danger to the kingdom or something."

Robbie looked at him wide-eyed. "They actually presented that in front of the king? Did he have them arrested or something?"

"No. He said it was done legally, and he couldn't."

"Wow! You better watch out too, Xavier. They'll probably try it with you as well."

Xavier shrugged as they rounded the corner of the palace walls and began to cut across the field for a more direct path to the school. "I'm not worried about it. Dad will be king for years and years. By the time I become king, Grant will probably be dead. He's older than dad."

"Yeah, well, I think you should still watch your back."

"Why do you need to watch your back, mate?" Court asked as he and Erica fell into step with them having taken the secret passage.

"He needs to watch his back because there are people trying to overthrow King Wells from power, and he might be next," Robbie stated.

"Blimey! Who's trying to overthrow the king?" Court gasped.

"Delegate Lucas Grant," Xavier told him. "He presented dad with a law to pass that would have done it."

"Bloody hell! And Grant is still breathing?"

Xavier nodded. "I guess he did it legally, according to Dad."

"Come on, you guys. We'll be late for first class," Robbie told them, urging the boys to walk faster.

By lunchtime, Xavier hurried into the cafeteria with Garrett on his heels.

"Man, I'm starving," Xavier muttered, moving into line.

"Yeah, me too. Beck and Court are already through the line. How does Beck always manage to be one of the first people here?"

"Dunno," Xavier said absently as he picked up a lunch tray and carried it over to where the other boys sat.

"Hey, X," Beck greeted. "Hardcastle was just telling me about my-farts-don't-smell Grant conspiring to overthrow King Wells."

Xavier spooned a huge heap of mashed potato into his mouth and gurgled past it, "Yeah. He sure did try. Dad vetoed his idea though."

"Are you going to let that stuck-up, know-it-all, wanker get away with it?"

Xavier shrugged. "I don't want to, but what can I do?"

Beck grinned. "I've got a plan. What are you doing after training?"

"Nothing really."

Beck's grin widened. "Okay. We'll go after your training. Are you in, Hardcastle?"

Court met Beck's eyes and grimaced slightly. "Sure, why not? It's a good day to die."

Beck ignored the comment and looked at Garrett. "Bracus?"

"Mate, you know I'm in. I'm always in!"

Chapter 13

Later that afternoon, after combat training, where he lost, again, to Sir Blaire and two other men, Xavier started toward the stands where his friends sat waiting.

"Xavier?" the king called, and Xavier turned toward his father. "I've got a few things I need to deal with at the Governing Hall. I won't be home until late, so I'm afraid you'll be on your own for dinner tonight."

"That's okay," Xavier told him.

"Make sure you get to that homework after dinner, son," Jeremiah called as he and his entourage of guards left the coliseum.

Once the king was gone, Beck leaned toward the other boys conspiratorially. "Okay, I've got a plan on how we can teach that dodgy Grant a lesson. Garrett, do you still help out in the royal stables on the weekends?"

Garrett looked at his friend puzzled. "Yeah. What's that got to do with Grant?"

Beck grinned wickedly. "Do they still scoop the manure into barrels so that it can be used to fertilize the gardens?"

Garrett grinned. "Yes. Yes, they do! How are we going to get the manure where we need it?"

"Court will teleport it, of course," Beck announced.

"Me? Why me? Xavier knows how to teleport!"

Beck looked at the prince. "Do you know where Grant

lives, X?"

"Uh, no."

Beck looked back at Court triumphantly. "That's why."

Court groaned and asked, "Okay, how many barrels of horse shit will we need?"

"At least two. Though three would be better."

"Okay. See you all at Grant's house," Court grumbled before racing toward the stables.

Xavier smiled. "So, what are we doing with the manure?"

"You'll see."

The group arrived at Delegate Grant's house seconds before Court appeared with a barrel of manure. "I'll just pop back and get another one," he said before he disappeared again.

"Okay, mates! Here's what we do..."

"Wait a second!" Xavier blurted as his eyes fell on Grant's black Mercedes SLS AMG Roadster. The convertible top was down. "Oh, man! This is too good to ignore!"

Court reappeared, muscling a second barrel next to the first. "There. So, what's the plan?"

Beck started laughing. "Great idea, X! He'll think twice if he tries to overthrow the king again!" He turned to Court and Garrett. "We're dumping both barrels into the car. And," Beck continued, pulling a can of red spray paint from his bag, "we'll leave everyone a message that Grant is a traitor."

"I can take care of the manure so nobody has to touch it," Xavier told the group. "You guys can write messages on the car. When we're done, I'll teleport all of us back to the coliseum. We've got to be fast so no one sees us!"

The group nodded in agreement and then set to work. In less than a minute, manure filled the sports car with the words, "Grant is a traitor" painted on the hood and sides of the car.

"Time to go," Xavier said with smug satisfaction.

"Prince Wells?" Mr. Nottingham gasped, but the boy and his friends vanished a second later.

At the coliseum, the boys celebrated the victory, cheering and fist bumping one another, except Xavier. Dread gnawed at him. Jon Nottingham had seen him.

"Xavier? What's the matter?" Court asked.

"Mr. Nottingham saw me. I'm busted."

The group suddenly froze, and Beck summed up the group's thoughts with a simple, "Oh, shit!"

"Yeah, exactly. I've got to get home. Don't worry about it, guys. I'll take the fall for Delegate Grant's car."

"X, we can't let you do that, mate. This is going to bring trouble—huge, colossal trouble," Court protested.

"Yes, you can. Look, would you have done any of this if I hadn't told you about what Grant tried to do in the legislative meeting? I think I'd rather take the fall for the car than for Dad to find out that I blabbed about the meeting." Seeing Court's hesitant face, Xavier rushed to continue. "It's supposed to be a confidential meeting, Court. If you don't let me do this, colossal trouble wouldn't begin to cover it."

Xavier had no idea if the meetings were confidential or not, but he didn't want his friends getting in trouble for standing up for him and his dad. They deserved medals, not punishments.

Finally, Court nodded and stepped away. "All right, mate. If you're sure."

"I am."

"Good luck, X," the boys muttered regrettably.

"Thanks. See you at school tomorrow... if Dad doesn't murder me tonight," Xavier joked before teleporting to the palace.

He stared up at the palace with his heart in his throat. Inhaling deeply, he walked across the drive, through the entrance, and down the hall. Henrick stood guard outside the royal residence.

"Hello, Prince Xavier. How was your day?" he asked.

He shrugged. "It was all right. Dad home yet?"

"No. I don't expect him for another hour."

Nodding, Xavier opened the door to the residence. "Talk to you later, Henrick."

"Xavier, honey, is that you?" Mrs. Sommers called from the dining room.

"Yeah," he answered, shutting the door.

"There's pizza in the fridge. You can heat it up in the toaster oven if you want it hot."

"Okay. Thanks."

He stood in the middle of the room, not sure what to do. He flopped onto the couch in the receiving room fighting the panic rising inside him like a tsunami. He had really stepped in it this time. His father would go ballistic, but Xavier wouldn't hide this time. He wouldn't run. He would face his father and his punishment head on. Though he didn't have it in him to feel bad for doing what he did to Grant. He felt an enormous sense of satisfaction for getting even with Grant for treason because that is how Xavier saw Grant's actions in the legislative meeting. It didn't matter to him that the delegate had done it legally. In his mind, treason was treason no matter how you went about it, and Grant had gone about it in the most devious, cowardly way. He had enlisted another man to stick his neck out and present the legislation that would lead to the dethroning of the king. Yeah, the man definitely deserved every bit of what he and his friends had dished out. He couldn't feel sorry about having done it. He wouldn't be sorry!

A loud, firm knock on the residence door jolted Xavier to his feet and out of his thoughts. He walked toward the door, already knowing who was behind it. Squelching down the panic that suddenly rolled in his stomach, he shuffled to the door and opened it to greet Mr. Nottingham and Delegate Grant.

"YOU!" Grant spat, shoving an accusatory finger in his face. "You were seen vandalizing my property, and don't try to deny it!"

"I wasn't going to deny it, Delegate Grant," Xavier answered evenly and narrowed his eyes at the finger in his face. "Could you get that thing out of my face?"

Flustered by the nonchalant attitude the boy gave him, Grant dropped his hand and glared menacingly at the prince. "Where's your father? I want to talk to him."

Now, Xavier didn't plan to hide his indiscretion from his father, but he sure didn't want this yahoo getting to him first. "Uh, okay. Come on in, and I'll get him."

Henrick started to say something, but Xavier quickly closed the door.

"Have a seat," he told the men as he started up the steps that led to the bedrooms on the second floor.

Mr. Nottingham sat comfortably in the sofa, but Delegate Grant remained standing and peered interestedly around the room.

Xavier entered his father's bedroom and sighed. Now what? He had abilities! He could transfigure into his father's image and get rid of the men before the real thing came home. With his plan decided, he began meditating and breathing deeply. Then he pictured his father. Slowly, he felt the tingling heat build in his chest and spread throughout his body. He turned and watched with fascination as his body morphed into the spitting image of his father, ripping the clothes he wore. Xavier quickly scoured through his father's closet and pulled out a pair of kakis and a shirt. He dressed quickly, not bothering to tuck in the shirt tails. Finally, he exited his father's room and descended the steps to the men. Jon Nottingham stood and bowed slightly at him, but Grant elbowed past him.

"King Wells, your son was seen by Jon vandalizing my vehicle!"

"Really now?" Xavier asked, doing his best imitation of the king.

"Yes!" Grant shouted.

"Delegate Grant, do not shout at me. I'm your king," Xavier spat at the man, trying not to burst out laughing.

"Sorry, sire," Grant muttered before continuing, "but it's true. Jon caught him in the act before the boy teleported away from the scene of the crime."

"Hmm." Xavier nodded, trying to think of something his father would say to that. He finally looked at Jon. "Is this true, Mr. Nottingham?"

Jon hesitated, looking a bit shaken. "Uh, yes, sire. It's true. I saw the prince and a group of boys dumping manure and spray-painting the delegate's car."

Xavier nodded his head. "I see. Well, okay, I guess I'll deal with this. Thank you for coming to tell me."

"I demand to know what you will do! I deserve that much!" Grant argued.

"Mr. Grant, I'm going to deal with it. Xavier will be punished. Now, thanks for coming. Please leave."

Again, Jon looked hesitantly at the person he believed was the king.

Xavier all but pushed the men toward the door, but just as he reached for the doorknob, it swung open and the genuine King Wells and Ephraim stood in the doorway.

As Jeremiah took in the scene in front of him, from the two shocked, jaw-dropped men to his twin image, he battled a sudden, slightly delirious urge to laugh. Instead, he looked at his general, who was hiding a smirk behind his hand as he rubbed his jaw contemplatively.

"General Hardcastle, did my evil twin escape from the dungeons again?" he teased.

Ephraim gave up on hiding the smile. "It appears so, sire."

Jeremiah moved toward Xavier and studied him like an insect. "Hmm, interesting. I guess we better cuff him and lock him up again."

"Dad!" Xavier groaned in his father's body. "You know it's me."

"Yes, I do, and I'm sure you have a great explanation as to why you've transfigured into my image while you entertain two guests."

Grant finally recovered from his state of shock and looked accusingly at the twin image of the king before stepping up to the genuine article. "Sire, the prince has ruined my car! He filled the interior with manure and spray-painted derogatory lies all over the exterior!"

Slowly the king turned to his carbon copy. "He did what?" he whispered, temper gurgling into his words.

"He vandalized my car, sire."

"I'm afraid it's true, King Wells. I saw him myself," Mr. Nottingham commented softly.

The king glared at Xavier before barking, "Son, change back, now!"

"Yes, sir," Xavier muttered and instantly reverted to himself. His father's clothes hung on him, and he quickly grabbed the kakis to keep them from dropping to his ankles. "Father, I was going to tell you."

"Were you now? Is that why you transfigured yourself into my image?"

"No... I mean, yes. I did it because I wanted to be the one to tell you first. I thought... I..." Okay, so maybe transfiguring into his father wasn't the brightest idea. Finally, Xavier blurted, "Read my thoughts! Read my thoughts, and you'll know I'm telling you the truth!"

Jeremiah studied his son a moment and shook his head. "I don't need to do that. I can see you're telling the truth. I'm not sure how the transfiguration plays into your plan to tell me though." The king turned to the men. "Gentlemen, I need to discuss this situation with Prince Xavier. Rest assured, Lucas, he will be punished and he will put the car back to rights."

"What about my reputation? He destroyed my reputation, sire! How will he put that right?"

Jeremiah looked from Lucas Grant to Xavier and back again. "How did he damage your reputation, Lucas?"

"He wrote lies all over my car in spray paint. He wrote that I was a traitor!"

The king closed his eyes in exasperation. Slowly, he opened his eyes and met Grant's. "I'm sorry he did that. He doesn't fully understand our laws yet. I'll make sure that he does by the end of the week, where he'll make amends in church. He will apologize to you publicly and denounce the things he wrote on your car. Is there anything else?"

Grant's anger deflated and he shook his head. "No, sire. Thank you."

"No need. You didn't deserve this treatment. I will see to it that this is resolved," he reassured as he stepped with the men to the door and saw them out.

Once the door shut, Jeremiah pressed his head against it and sighed. Without looking at his son, he ordered, "Xavier, go upstairs and change. I'll be up in a few minutes."

"Yes, sir," Xavier muttered and shuffled to the stairs. Hesitantly, he turned to his father. "Dad? I wasn't going to lie to you or run. I planned to face what I did head on. I swear it."

The king turned and looked at the crestfallen boy. "I know. Go change, son."

140

J. Noel Clinton

Xavier changed out of his father's clothes and paced. Then he pulled out his math book from his duffle and sat at his desk. He opened the book to the page marked with his paper and stared unseeingly. He wouldn't be able to concentrate on his homework until he talked to his father. Nearly twenty minutes later, his father knocked on his door before opening it and entering. Xavier closed his book and stood.

"Dad, I'm sorry."

Jeremiah motioned for him to sit as he sat on the corner of his desk. "How about you start by telling me why you did what you did and then who helped you."

"No one helped me. I did it alone."

His father eyed him disbelievingly. "Well, I know that's a lie, but I won't push it. Why did you damage Delegate Grant's car and reputation?"

Xavier shrugged, but answered, "Because he tried to overthrow you. In my book, that's treason."

"Xavier, I told you that he had done so legally…"

"Yeah, I know, Dad, but to me, it doesn't matter how someone does it. If you try to overthrow the king, you're a traitor! He didn't even do it with any kind of honor! I mean, how big of a coward would you have to be to make some poor sucker do it for you?"

Jeremiah nodded and worked to suppress a grin. He couldn't let the boy know that he found the entire situation humorous. He agreed with the boy, but he had passed the law providing citizens the ability to question him and pass laws. He couldn't arrest a man exercising his given right no matter how he went about it or the subject of his proposal.

"Son, I understand how you feel, but if I were to arrest Delegate Grant just for proposing a new law, regardless of the subject matter of that law, how do you think our citizens

141

would perceive such an arrest?"

Xavier frowned. He didn't want to think about that! He didn't want to think about how anything Grant had done had been right. "I don't know," he mumbled, pouting slightly.

His father nodded and commented, "I think you do or you wouldn't be so disgruntled about it. Son, kings, great kings don't simply do what they want and punish whomever they please. We have laws to follow and rights to honor. Do you understand?"

Begrudgingly, Xavier nodded. "Yes, sir."

Jeremiah studied him a moment. "Now, after school and training tomorrow, you will report to Delegate Grant's house and clean up his car—without powers."

Xavier's jaw dropped. "But, Dad! That car is full of horse shit!"

The king didn't quite keep the smile from his face this time. "Yes, and you put it there. So you will clean it out."

"But without powers? Why? I could have that thing looking like new in less than a minute with my powers."

"Yes, son. However, cleaning up the car isn't only to put the car right. It's to teach you a lesson. How can you learn that lesson if you use your powers without fully understanding what Delegate Grant would have gone through if you hadn't been caught? He does not possess the ability of telekinesis, so he would have had to clean his car out by hand. In addition, you will publicly apologize to Delegate Grant in church Sunday and make it known to our citizens that he is *not* a traitor." The king patted his son's leg and stood. "Oh, and son? You're grounded for three weeks."

Xavier scowled. "You know? This is the worst punishment you've ever given me! Can't you just spank me instead?"

The king lost all will power and laughed.

Chapter 14

The next morning, Xavier entered the dining hall for breakfast to find his father and Ephraim there.

"I know, Ephraim. I'm not sure how they're getting in!" the king was telling him.

"How who is getting in?" Xavier questioned, flopping into his chair and scooping a spoonful of egg into his mouth.

The men looked uneasily at the boy and said nothing.

Xavier looked from his father to the general. "Oh, come on! How am I supposed to learn about being king and the problems of a king if you don't share things with me? What's going on?"

The king sighed and glanced at Ephraim before answering. "Son, a few dark soldiers penetrated the kingdom's security. They made it as far as the palace gates before they were stopped."

Xavier frowned. "How are they getting into the kingdom and past the gatehouse security?"

"That, young sire, is what we're trying to determine," Ephraim told him.

"So this morning I will be interviewing the guards on duty. Then I will send the royal guards out to walk the kingdom's security wall and see if we can determine where they penetrated our defenses," the king told him. "When you arrive this afternoon, we'll go through the reports of the security check and interviews. Do you have a particular power you'd like to work on today during combat training?"

Xavier shook his head. "Not really."

"Okay, I'll find some men to help us out. Now, after your training, you're expected to report to Delegate Grant's home and clean up his vehicle."

Xavier made a face. "Are you sure I can't use my powers?"

The king pinned him with an unwavering stare. "No powers, son."

With a disgruntled sigh, Xavier finished his eggs.

After breakfast, Xavier met Robbie at the usual spot so that they could walk to school together. Xavier told her about the break-in.

"Wow! This is serious, Xavier. If dark soldiers are getting into the kingdom, you're not safe," she concluded, her eyes wide with worry.

"Robbie, I'm not in danger," Xavier dismissed with a snicker. "I can take care of myself."

Robbie didn't look convinced.

"Hey, X!" Beck shouted as he and Garrett raced across the field in front of the school.

Once the boys fell into step with Xavier and Robbie, Garrett asked, "So? What's the verdict?"

"What are they talking about?" Robbie asked.

"We taught that traitor Grant a lesson yesterday for trying to overthrow the king," Beck answered.

"Oh no!" Robbie groaned and looked at Xavier. "What did you do?"

Before Xavier could answer, Beck grinned and responded wickedly, "We filled his sports car with manure."

Robbie's jaw dropped.

"Yeah, but unfortunately, Xavier was seen at the scene of the crime," Garrett added.

Robbie's eyes darted back to her boyfriend. "And you're still walking? I'm surprised King Wells didn't murder you for that."

"Well, I have to clean out Grant's car, and I'm grounded. Oh, and I have to publicly apologize in church Sunday and swear in front of everyone that Grant isn't a traitor. I'm a little worried about that part of the punishment. I mean, what if God strikes me dead for lying in a church?"

The boys expelled a sympathetic groan.

"Man, I'm so sorry, X. We'll help you with the car," Beck promised.

"No. You can't. If you do, Grant will know you were in on it," he told him.

"But, X, it's not right that you're taking the fall for us! Just let us..."

"No, Garrett. Seriously, guys, it's okay. I'll be fine."

Begrudgingly, the boys agreed to stay away from Grant's residence, and the group entered the school uncharacteristically quiet.

After lunch, Xavier sat under a large tree in the courtyard with Robbie, holding her hand.

"Awe, looky here, Bill. The Prince of Pipsqueaks has a girlfriend. How much did you have to pay her to be with you?"

Jonas McKnight cackled, fist bumping his thuggish-looking friend, who commented, "Good one, Jonas."

Xavier rolled his eyes and stood. He was very nearly as tall as Jonas. He smiled placidly at the older boy.

"I'm not a pipsqueak that you can torment anymore, Jonas. I don't give a crap what you think or say. Everyone knows you're nothing more than a thug and a bully," he growled at Jonas before turning to Robbie and holding out his hand. "Come on Robbie. Let's go."

Xavier pulled Robbie to her feet just as Jonas gave him a hard shove in the back. He slammed into Robbie and the couple fell. Xavier managed to twist Robbie in mid-fall so that he wouldn't land on top of her. Then with inches between their bodies, he caught her with his telekinesis. As Robbie hovered above him, a collective moan of appreciation surrounded them, and Xavier gently lifted Robbie to her feet. Then he climbed to his feet, dusted himself off, and flashed Jonas a pompous grin.

"Nice try, Joney." Xavier turned and approached Robbie. "Are you all right?"

Robbie nodded just as a warning flashed into his thoughts, and he spun just in time to block Jonas's electro force. Jonas's face was twisted and reddened with anger. Xavier stood at the ready, studying the older boy and waiting for another attack. The older boy's obscene thoughts punched into his mind.

"Jonas! You're mental!" Drew called out from the crowd. "Prince Wells could turn you inside out! You should have seen..."

Suddenly, Jonas attacked again. Xavier deflected it and with a wave of his hand, he slammed Jonas to the ground, pinning him there. Jonas struggled in vain to get loose.

"I tried to warn you," Drew stated. "You're in completely over your head."

"All right, what's going on?" Spencer shouted, pushing through the crowd that had formed around them.

Xavier released Jonas, and the boy scrambled to his feet, jostling his way through the crowd.

When Michael Spencer made his way out of the crowd, he could smell the charged air. His eyes fixed on Xavier. From what he gathered from the other students' thoughts, there had been a confrontation between the prince and Jonas McKnight, but the prince had not been the instigator and had only protected himself.

"All right. I want everyone to clear out and get to class. Prince Wells, isn't the king expecting you?"

"Yes, sir." Xavier looked back at Robbie. "Are you sure you're all right?"

Robbie nodded.

"Well, I better get over to the Governing Hall. See you tomorrow," he told her, kissing her quickly before teleporting out of the school courtyard to the Governing Hall.

When Xavier entered his father's office, he found him at a long table with both Loren and Ephraim studying papers skewed across the table. The three men looked up as Xavier approached them. His father beckoned him with a finger.

"So there's no evidence of the defenses being compromised?" the king asked the generals.

"No, sir," Loren stated perplexed. "The wall is intact. The gatehouse was not infiltrated this time. There's absolutely no sign of where the dark soldiers gained access."

Jeremiah nodded gravely and looked at Xavier. "Okay, son. Let's see what you make of this. The dark soldiers who infiltrated the kingdom last night refused to be taken alive. Unfortunately, we cannot interrogate them or penetrate their minds to determine how they got in. So we are left with using our own detective work to determine the answer. What we know about the situation is this: the men quietly and without raising alarms gained access into Warwood; it wasn't until they reached the palace gates that they met opposition, and there is absolutely no evidence that the men breached the palace wall or gatehouse."

Xavier frowned. "Maybe they flew over?"

His father shook his head. "No. If they had, an alarm would have sounded. We have motion sensors to detect an aerial invasion such as that."

Xavier's brow furrowed. "The tunnels?"

"No. The tunnels are a well-kept secret. Only those of us that reside in the palace know about them," Ephraim rebutted.

The three men watched the prince as he worked through what they had already determined to be the case. Finally, Xavier's face blanched and he looked up at his father, appalled. "Someone is helping them."

The king nodded. "It appears so."

"It could be Delegate Grant, Dad. He was so keen on overthrowing you..."

"No, Xavier. It's not Lucas."

"But, it *could* be!"

"No, son. Lucas Grant wants the throne for himself. He wouldn't support the Dark Army or LeMasters."

"Oh," Xavier muttered. "Then I guess that means I still have to clean out his car and take back calling him a traitor, huh?"

The king laughed. "Yes, son. That's exactly what it means."

Both generals stifled smiles and snickers.

Later that afternoon, Xavier entered the coliseum for his combat training and found that his cheering section had grown exponentially. There were twenty to thirty students sitting in the bleachers with drinks and popcorn that Beck was passing out from a large plastic bag. As soon as they saw Xavier, they erupted into cheers and chants, and he waved shyly at the group.

"Keep your head in the exercise, son," his father whispered.

With a nod, he took his position in center field and busily tightened his protective gear. He was swinging his sword experimentally, loosening his arm and shoulder muscles when he saw his opponents and his jaw dropped. Standing across from him were about a dozen royal guards. His head jerked in alarm to his father, sending a panicked message.

"I have to fight all of them? At once?"

"Xavier, you need a challenge. Aside from Sir Blaire, the guards you've faced thus far haven't been much of a challenge. The sheer number of opponents should prove to be a good exercise of your abilities."

"A good exercise of my abilities? You've got to be kidding me! There's no way I'll ever have to fight a mob of dark soldiers at once."

"Son, we don't know that. I'd rather you be overly prepared than not prepared well enough," his father scolded.

With a bitter, indignant sigh, Xavier hissed, "Fine."

Scanning the group across from him, his mind raced with the best strategy. He needed to cut the number of men at least in half with his first attack to stand any chance of succeeding. To do that, he would have to send a powerful electro force down the center of the group. Then he'd simply deal with whoever was left standing. Simple. *Yeah, right!*

Taking a deep breath, Xavier stood at the ready and waited for the exercise to begin.

The king's voice called out over the field, "Everyone ready? Gentlemen, don't hesitate and don't go easy on the prince. He won't go easy on you. Most importantly, don't make the assumption that since you outnumber the boy twelve to one that he will be an easy mark." The king paused, glanced at his son and back to the group of soldiers. More than likely, Xavier would be overwhelmed by the sheer number of opponents and would fail in this exercise, but that would provide him something to strive to accomplish. He needed this challenge. The boy couldn't become too complacent. Complacency was a sure path to carelessness and laziness. "All right, gentlemen. Begin the exercise."

Suddenly the group of men charged him, and Xavier felt a strong urge to flee. Instead, he lowered his sword a fraction, produced an electro force in the palm of his hand and propelled it toward the center of the group rushing him. The force hit dead center and took out nearly half the group. Cheers erupted loudly from the stands, and the chanting grew louder.

"Prince Xavier! Prince Xavier!"

But he had no time to bask in the cheers and celebration, for the men that remained were answering his attack with forces of their own. He barely managed to conjure a blocking force in time, and the guards' electro forces bounced harmlessly away.

His cheering section released a loud collective moan.

"Come on, mate! You can do it!" Court's voice rang out above the others.

"Yeah, X. Kick some butt!" Beck shouted.

Xavier looked back at the remaining men. Seven men were still too many to fight at once. He needed to decrease their numbers again and fast because they were closing in on him. He noticed the group to his right had spread out strategically in their approach, but the left group remained close together, making them an easy target. With a swirling motion of his hand, a blazing ring of fire encircled the men, reaching at least ten feet into the sky, trapping them.

Another loud burst of rambunctious support exploded from his cheering section, and Xavier smiled. Feeling confident and a bit cocky, he lifted his sword and faced the three remaining men. They attacked at once from different sides. Just as their swords were inches from him, Xavier teleported ten feet from his opponents and watched as they ran into each other before collapsing in a heap. Xavier grinned as the crowd roared with laughter and shouts.

"Missed me!" Xavier boasted.

The men scrambled to their feet and charged at the boy with swords raised. Again, Xavier teleported and stood behind the men, watching smugly as they swung at empty air.

"Woohoo! Go Xavier!" a girl shouted, elated and laughing.

This time he struck the men as they turned to face him with a force that sent them airborne thirty feet backwards before they fell hard to the ground. One man screamed out in pain as he awkwardly landed on his shoulder. He managed to climb to his feet and stagger to the sideline, where Loren stood mending injured guards from Xavier's initial attack.

Only two men remained.

Ha! Easy! Xavier thought with a smirk as he raised his sword and cheekily beckoned the men with his hand.

A groan of appreciation came from his friends.

This time the guards didn't openly attack. Instead, the men began circling the boy, looking for a weakness or an opening. The boy appeared overly confident and that could be used against him. The higher-ranking guard made eye contact with his subordinate and gave him a hand signal that only guards knew. The younger guard nodded his understanding and the pair continued to circle Xavier.

Suddenly the younger man lunged at the prince, and Xavier turned to meet the attack. Then the hair on the back of his neck stood at attention as he felt a second attack coming from behind him. Xavier dropped to the ground and rolled, tripping and knocking the higher-ranking guard off his feet. The guard fell heavily on top of him, and he grunted as an elbow or knee, something hard and pointy jabbed painfully into his groin. Coughing and feeling close to vomiting, Xavier curled up into a fetal position, trying to remember how to breathe. Slowly the man stood and pressed his blade against his neck.

"You are dead, your highness," he whispered, panting.

Xavier eyed the man resentfully. The guard had done it on purpose, he realized. He had intentionally hit him in the nuts to gain the upper hand. Xavier opened his mouth to tell the man off but only managed a wheezing sound followed by a bone-racking cough.

"Well done, Sergeant Hensley, Private Jones," the king praised as he brushed past them and knelt next to Xavier. "Are you all right, son?"

Xavier hissed in a breath and shook his head. "N... no," he managed before coughing.

Without a word, the king nodded and held his hands over Xavier. A bright white light engulfed father and son, and when it disappeared, the pain was gone. Not quite trusting that the pain was truly gone, Xavier gingerly got to his feet. The king smiled and clamped him on the back.

"Better?"

Xavier nodded and glared up at Sergeant Hensley. "That was a low, rotten thing to do, man."

The sergeant shrugged indifferently. "Young sire, this is combat. There's no such thing as a low or rotten strategy if it gets the job done."

Xavier stepped angrily toward the guard, but his father intervened.

"Son, Sergeant Hensley is right. You do whatever you can to survive and win the fight. With that being said," the king grinned, "you did a spectacular job! You took on a dozen soldiers and wiped out ten of them! I think you may have gotten a little cocky with Sergeant Hensley and Private Jones though. If you hadn't toyed with them and simply gone for a kill strike, you wouldn't have lost."

His father was right. He had allowed his success to go to his head and it had cost him. It wouldn't happen again.

Chapter 15

Weeks drifted by at a snail's pace, and a couple of days before the royal wedding, Xavier's grounding came to an end. The pending marriage had the entire kingdom alive with excitement and gossip. The academy closed early for the weekend so that every citizen could participate in the preparations.

On the last day of school two days before the wedding, the king canceled Xavier's training until after the wedding.

"I don't want you injured. How can you be my best man if you're too hurt to attend?"

"I can... what? Your best man? Me? What about Loren or Ephraim?"

"They'll be there as my groomsmen, of course, but my best man can only be you, son."

He stared at his father's smiling face before smiling back shyly. "Thanks, Dad. That means a lot."

The king yanked him into a breath-smothering hug. Then, kissing the boy's crown, he whispered, "Are you sure you're okay with this?"

He smiled slyly at his father. "Why? What's the matter, getting cold feet?"

Jeremiah's laugh boomed out, and he trapped his son in another bear hug. "No. No cold feet."

Xavier hugged his father tight and said in earnest,

"Really, Dad. I'm okay with it. I'm more than okay with it. I'd give anything to have mom here with us, but... she can't so..." His voice faded as his thoughts lingered on his mother. He still missed her—every day. When he first came to live with his father, he used to daydream what his life would have been like if his mother had lived. She would have come to live with them in Warwood. She was a common, but that wouldn't have mattered. She was the Queen of Warwood, and the people would have loved her! Grudgingly, he pulled away from his father's warmth.

"Your mother was a beautiful bride," Jeremiah whispered.

"Did you love her?" Xavier blurted. Where had that come from? And why did he suddenly feel close to tears? Blinking rapidly, he turned away from his father and his all-knowing eyes and busily fidgeted with a vase of flowers on the long conference table.

"Xavier, son, look at me," the king ordered softly.

Quickly wiping his eyes, he reluctantly faced the king. Jeremiah studied the boy's face a moment before standing, approaching him, and placing his hands on the boy's shoulders.

"Xavier, I loved your mother very much; I still do. Nothing will ever change that. I am a very lucky man to have found that kind of love again. Lana is not your mother. The love I feel for her isn't the same as what I felt for Julia, but it's just as strong, just as powerful. Do you understand what I'm saying?"

Xavier nodded and whispered, "Yes, Dad. I understand."

"And," the king added, placing his hands on either side of the boy's face to ensure he had his complete attention. "It's okay for you to love Lana. It's okay to feel happy to have a mother again. She'll never take your mother's place in your heart, but your heart is more than big enough to love two mothers."

Xavier couldn't stop the tears from flooding his eyes this time. "Really? I... I'm not betraying mom?"

The king's grip tightened in earnest, and he said stoutly, "No, you are not betraying your mother's memory at all."

The tears spilled down his cheeks, and he tried to speak, to thank his father for easing his guilty conscious for wanting Lana to be his new mother, for wanting his father to marry her, for wanting a complete family. He couldn't speak, so he simply buried his face into his father chest and tried to stop the continuous stream of tears from flowing.

The king's arms wrapped around him, and he simply held him until the tears ended. Finally, Jeremiah held his son at arm's length and wiped the tears from his cheeks.

"Let's take the rest of the day off. What do you think?"

Xavier gave a watery grin. "That would be great."

* * * * *

Xavier knocked on his father's bedroom door. "Dad?"

The door flew open suddenly, and Loren stood grinning broadly down at him. "Your father is having a bit of a panic attack," he chuckled as he stepped aside to let Xavier into the room. "He swears I've hidden his royalty sash." Loren rolled his eyes and leaned in to whisper, "It's draped over the patio door, where he put it ten minutes ago. Henrick and I are holding a wager on how long it will take him to remember. Want in?"

Xavier snickered, shaking his head as he entered the room.

"Now where's my goddamned tie?" Jeremiah spat, stomping out of the bathroom to where an amused Henrick and Ephraim stood.

"Sire, it's draped around your neck," Ephraim stated matter-of-factly, which sent both Loren and Henrick sputtering into laughter.

The king swelled with a retort, but Ephraim interrupted him with a stern reprimand. "Loren, Henrick, get out! You're only making him worse by needling his already raw nerves!"

The pair tried to hide their smirks as they gave a mocking bow and exited the room after patting Xavier on the head.

"Jer, stop a moment and sit down," Ephraim ordered gently, and the king immediately obliged as he sank into an armchair next to the hearth. "Good, now take slow deep breaths and get ahold of yourself."

Jeremiah nodded as he closed his eyes and inhaled deeply before releasing the breath with a sigh. After repeating this several times, his eyes opened and they met the general's with calm and clarity. "Thank you, Ephraim. I'm good now."

"Are you sure?"

"Yes, thank you, my friend," he snickered embarrassedly. "I can't believe how nervous I feel right now. Blimey! I've fought battles, addressed entire kingdoms, but the thought of..."

"Yes, I know. Nothing is more frightening than to open yourself to love and the pain it can bring with it. But, sire, there's no alternative to living, to really living. It's what makes us different from the dark followers: our willingness to open our hearts to hope and love." Ephraim clapped the king's back and grinned. "Oh, and sire? Your royalty sash is on the patio door, where you placed it during your last rant when you raked Mrs. Sommers over the coals for misplacing your black belt."

"Well how the hell was I supposed to know she placed the belt on the hanger of my tuxedo suit?"

Ephraim winked at Xavier, who stifled a snicker before remarking in earnest, "You're one lucky man, Jeremiah. God only knows what Lana sees in you."

The king cleared his throat uncomfortably before standing and continuing to dress.

"Now, what can I do for you, little sire?" Ephraim asked Xavier.

"Uh, I need help with my tie," Xavier remarked, holding up the tie he clutched in his hand.

Ephraim gestured for the prince to stand and follow him to the full-length mirror. Turning Xavier to face the mirror, the general positioned himself behind him. "I can't do it unless I'm looking in the mirror," Ephraim remarked with a smile.

As the general knotted the tie at his neck with deft fingers, Xavier took note that he stood less than half a head shorter than Ephraim. His father still stood a good head taller, and Loren a good head and half, but he was no longer the scrawny little boy who had stood in this room getting his tie tied two years before. Not only had he grown taller, but his shoulders were broader, and his arms had filled in with lean muscle. His face still had the softness of a child, but the rest of him was growing into a man. This thought brought a smile to Xavier's lips, and he straightened proudly.

"There you go!" Ephraim announced patting his shoulders. "What's the grin for?"

Xavier grinned even larger. "I was just noticing that I'm nearly as tall as you, Mr. Hardcastle."

Ephraim laughed. "Don't get ahead of yourself, laddie. It takes more than height to make you a man."

"Yes, sir."

The groom's party left the castle and headed to the church in the king's limo. Jeremiah's previous anxiety was long forgotten, and he seemed to be happily anticipating his marriage. As they entered the church, Xavier lingered by the entrance as his father spoke to the priest about the ceremony. A door opened to the left of the vestibule, and

Robbie exited wearing a deep plum, satin dress. It fell off her shoulders with a feminine flair and stooped low in the back, revealing her bare back to below her shoulder blades. She wore matching plum gloves that reached her elbows. The skirt of the dress fell to just above her knee, leaving her shapely legs open to his appreciation. His eyes skimmed up her womanly frame, feeling heat ignite inside him at the view. She turned and saw him and her jaw dropped open as she shuffled toward him.

"Xavier? Oh. My. Gosh! You look... great!" she whispered.

"Me? Have you looked in a mirror? You're gorgeous, Robbie. I... I can hardly breathe looking at you! I... I..." Xavier reached for her, pulled her toward him, and kissed her. He felt Robbie melt into him, and her arms slid around him as she sighed against his lips. Slowly, he pulled away from her and looked into her large brown eyes, feeling slightly dizzy.

"Wow!" Robbie muttered before giggling.

It was the cutest sound Xavier had ever heard, Robbie's giggle. He couldn't help but smile at her.

"Son, we need to get ready and leave the ladies to do the same," his father called from the pulpit.

Xavier nodded to the king before quickly brushing his lips against Robbie's and finally releasing her. He strutted down the aisle toward his father well aware that Robbie's eyes followed him. He grinned as her thoughts chased after him, too strong to be denied and left unheard.

"My, my, Sergeant Davies. The boy looks a bit cocky, wouldn't you agree?" Loren muttered.

"Why, yes, General Jefferson. I think you're right. He looks so smug he's practically glowing," he responded.

Xavier shook his head and continued past the men to follow his father into a small room off to the right of the pulpit.

"Xavier, come here, son," Jeremiah called from the couch where he sat. "We've got thirty minutes before the ceremony begins."

Xavier smiled and flopped onto the couch next to his father, who hugged him close.

"Are you nervous?" he asked.

"Nope. Not at all," the king answered with a broad smile. "Robbie looked beautiful in her gown."

"Yeah," Xavier responded wistfully. "She really did!"

"Well, try to keep yourself under control, son. We don't need anyone glowing in public," his father recommended.

"Ha! You're so funny!"

"Am I? I thought I was simply stating a fact," his father said meaningfully.

Xavier gaped at his father. "Wha... you mean..." He jumped to his feet and raced to the nearest shiny object and inspected his reflection as Loren and Henrick snickered behind him. Sure enough, his eyes were aglow. "Oh. My. God!" He blinked hard and looked back at his reflection. Yep, still there. He spun to face his father. "How do I make it stop?"

The king smiled sympathetically and patted the seat next to him. Xavier moved toward his father as he shot Loren and Henrick a hard glare, which only seemed to increase their mirth.

"Loren, Henrick, leave us!" Jeremiah barked irritably.

With smirks still playing across their faces, the men saluted and left the office. "Those two are driving me up the wall today!" his father muttered as Xavier sat next to him.

"How do I keep from glowing?" he practically begged.

"You can't. You can only control your thoughts so that it doesn't occur in public."

"What? You mean... I'm always going to glow?"

"Around Robbie? I hope so, son," his father responded gently.

"What?" he gasped, looking at his father desperately.

"Son, the glow signifies your deep feelings for Robbie. If you didn't glow around her, I'd worry. But the point of this conversation is to manage your feelings so that it doesn't occur in public. That can be very embarrassing."

Xavier frowned in thought. "Okay. So how do I do that?"

"Well, you'll have to have a focal point."

"Another one?" Xavier spat. "Geesh! How many focal points am I gonna need?"

Jeremiah smiled down at his son. "You need a focal point that douses your strong feelings, son."

Xavier nodded. "Like what?"

"I can't tell you what would work for you, son. That will be up to you."

"Do you have one?"

"Yes."

"What's yours?"

"My father."

"Oh," Xavier muttered. It made sense. Thinking of his father would surely calm the heated sensations that Robbie generated in him.

"It needs to be a focal point that provides strong adverse feelings to what Robbie creates. My father was a very harsh man. He instilled fear, dread, and resentment most of the time. So, for me, he was perfect."

"Hmm." Okay, so maybe his father wouldn't be effective enough. After all, his eyes were still glowing in his father's company. "Grandmother! She'd definitely do it for me!"

His father nodded. "Well, let's give it a try. Follow me."

Father and son stood and entered an adjoining bathroom to stand in front of a mirror.

"Okay. Close your eyes and think of Robbie."

Xavier closed his eyes but found it hard to concentrate with his father standing directly behind him. He opened one eye and looked at his father. "Dad? Could you maybe... step back please? This is weird enough without you standing over me like that."

"Yeah, sure," he responded, backing towards the door.

Xavier closed his eyes again and pictured Robbie. He sighed as he relived their kiss and a smile split across his face. Slowly he opened his eyes and found that both his face and his eyes were glowing with a faint, shimmering pink hue. His father stepped forward.

"Okay, now think of your grandmother. Think specifically of an incident where you were angry, fearful, or resentful. Those are strong feelings that can battle... what you're feeling in Robbie's presence."

Xavier nodded and thought. There were so many memories that would work, but one memory in particular came to mind—the day he had inquired about his father. His mother had been visibly upset, and he had felt bad about hurting her. His grandmother had come unglued and slapped him across the face as she called him names and insulted his father. He looked at his reflection and saw no sign of glowing. He looked up at his father's reflection and grinned.

"It worked! Who knew my grandmother would actually help me one day!"

Jeremiah laughed and clapped him on the back. "I'm glad, but remember, using this technique is much more difficult and requires more concentration when you're face to face with Robbie. Keep practicing until the ceremony. Hopefully you can minimize Robbie's effects on you at the reception." His father winked at him and left the bathroom.

Chapter 16

"Would all rise for your king, King Jeremiah Xavier Wells IV," the priest called as the door opened next to the pulpit and Jeremiah and Xavier exited the office. Once they were settled by the altar, the priest announced to the crowded church, "Please remain standing for the bridal party."

The church organ began to play as the groomsmen escorted the bridesmaids up the aisle. Xavier looked up at his father who stood tall and straight. By all exterior cues, the king was calm and collected, but his demeanor refuted the strong feelings Xavier felt radiating off his father. He was nervous, scared to death, and second-guessing putting Lana in any kind of danger by marrying her. Xavier slid his hand into his father's, who looked down at him questioningly.

"You deserve this, Dad. You deserve Lana and happiness. Don't be nervous. It'll be okay," he told him silently.

Tears filled his father's eyes and spilled down his cheeks before he could swipe them away. Then he squeezed Xavier's hand thankfully, winked, and turned back to the wedding party marching down the aisle.

Once the groomsmen and bridesmaids were in place, the music changed abruptly to the bridal march. Then Lana was there, standing at the end of the aisle on the arm of Governor Bracus. The king's breath hitched at the sight of her. Slowly she crept toward them at the altar. As she moved past the patrons in the church, row by row bowed in honor of her, signifying her change in status to queen. Unlike the king, Lana's thoughts were nowhere near as panicky. Her smile revealed the excitement and happiness ballooning inside her. When she finally reached them, Xavier felt his father's anxiety and fear drop away the moment he took Lana's hand. Love rolled off the king, and Xavier's eyes widened at how easily his father's thoughts came to him.

"Are you getting that?" Loren whispered.

Xavier glanced at the general and nodded. The king was projecting his thoughts unwittingly. The general cleared his throat uncomfortably as the king's thoughts over the beauty of his bride continued.

Xavier wondered how to deal with this. If Loren was hearing his father's thoughts, then it was possible others in the church could hear them as well. Before he could determine what to do, Lana cleared her throat, leaned in toward the king and kissed his cheek.

"Sweetheart? Your thoughts are projecting," she whispered softly.

His father's embarrassment flooded Xavier's thoughts before he cut the connection completely. Xavier looked up at Loren, who had bowed his head to hide his amusement, but his shaking shoulders gave him away. After a glare from the king, Loren's laughter escaped, and Xavier couldn't stop his own laughter from joining in.

Father Reinhart announced that the congregation be seated.

"In the name of the Father, and of the Son, and of the Holy Spirit, the grace of our Lord Jesus Christ and the love of God and the fellowship of the Holy Spirit be with you all," the priest announced.

"And also with you," the crowd recited.

"Welcome! We are gathered here today for one of the happiest occasions in human life, to celebrate before God the marriage of our beloved king to our beloved queen. Marriage is a most honorable estate, created and instituted by God, signifying unto us the mystical union, which also exists between Christ and the Church; so to may this marriage be adorned by true and abiding love. Who brings this woman to this man?"

"I do," Governor Bracus stated before bowing to the king and Lana and turning to sit in the front pew.

Xavier stood next to his father as the priest continued with the marriage ritual as his eyes slid and met Robbie's. God, she was beautiful! She grinned at him, and he couldn't help the goofy grin that split across his face. He winked playfully, his smile broadening as her face ignited red.

Both Loren and Ephraim read passages in honor of the king and his bride. The passages spoke of love and God's love for man. Ephraim's passage resonated with Xavier, and he could feel his father's resolve cement in place as Ephraim read.

"*If I have the gift of prophecy and can fathom all mysteries and all knowledge, and if I have a faith that can move mountains, but have not loved, I am nothing,*" Ephraim continued to recite the verse as Xavier's mind roamed. The verse reminded Xavier of the words Ephraim had used to calm the king just this morning that love is what made the king different from their enemy. Love was worth preserving.

After both the king and Lana exchanged vows, and the priest blessed their rings, Jeremiah slid Lana's ring onto her finger and smiled, "With this ring, I thee wed."

Once Jeremiah and Lana exchanged rings, they lit the

unity candle as the priest proclaimed, "The separate candles symbolize that the groom and bride entered as individuals. They now light the unity candle to show recognition of their commitment to share a future, a vision, a dream under the watchful eye of God. They light the unity candle to symbolize their love from this day forward."

No one told Xavier how extensive a Catholic wedding could be and he shifted impatiently from foot to foot until he felt a soft jab to his ribs.

"We're nearly there, little king. Hang in there," Loren's voice hissed in his ear.

He sighed with relief when he realized Loren was right as the priest announced, "King Wells, Queen Wells, in so much as the two of you have agreed to live together in matrimony, have promised your love for each other by these vows, the giving of these rings, and the joining of your hands, I now declare you to be husband and wife. May the Lord bless you and keep you. May the Lord make his face shine upon you, and be gracious unto you. May the Lord lift up his countenance unto you and give you peace. Congratulations, Sire Wells, you may kiss your bride."

With a boyish grin, King Wells lifted Lana's veil, pulled her into his arms, and dipped her before kissing her. The church erupted in laughter and cheers. Finally, the king set Lana to rights and lovingly stroked her cheek.

"I present to you, King and Queen Jeremiah Xavier Wells IV!" the priest announced and the cheers erupted into a thunderous roar.

Xavier grinned up at his father and Lana. He had a mother again! Laughter burst from him when his father grabbed Lana and gave her another passionate kiss as the congregation roared and laughed louder. Finally, the king took the queen's hand and led her down the aisle as bows waved them past.

The crowd made their way past the newlyweds, congratulating the king and kissing the queen's ring as a sign of her sovereignty. Once the last of the guests had passed, Ephraim turned and grinned at Jeremiah. "Congratulations, Jeremiah, Lana. Loren and I will walk ahead with the lad to the Reception Hall. Come when you're ready."

"Thanks, Ephraim. I appreciate it," Jeremiah stated, shaking his general's hand firmly before clapping Xavier's back. "It's customary for the bride and groom to arrive last at the reception. Plus, we have a photographer who needs to take our wedding picture. We'll see you over there, okay?"

"Sure, Dad. See you there," Xavier answered before following Loren and Ephraim out of the church.

When they arrived at the Reception Hall, it sounded as if the party had already begun. Music poured out of the building as well as conversations and laughter. When they entered the Reception Hall, there was a brief hush from the crowd before they all started cheering and applauding. Many pounded Xavier's back, congratulating him on his new mother. It was a bit weird. He turned to Ephraim.

"Why are they congratulating me? I didn't marry Lana!"

"The addition to the royal family by marriage or birth is a rare occasion. So as a result, it is cause for celebration for the entire kingdom. It's an exciting event."

"Oh," Xavier muttered before scanning the crowd for his friends.

When his eyes settled on Robbie, he found himself struggling for breath. She was drop-dead gorgeous. Slowly he moved toward her, his smiling face unable to form a coherent thought beyond, *Mine!*

"Hi," she whispered when he stumbled to a stop in front of her.

"H... hi. Wow! Have I told you how beautiful you are?"

Robbie giggled and kissed his cheek.

"You've already told me that, but thanks! You look fantastic yourself," she commented, stroking the lapel of his jacket flat.

Suddenly, the crowd burst into thunderous cheers and applause, and the king escorted his new bride through the throngs of people crowding closer to get a good look at the royal couple. As his father approached Xavier, he grinned. "There you are, kiddo. We have the front table."

"Can I sit with Robbie, Dad? It's yours and Lana's day, not mine. You're who everyone wants to see. Please?"

Jeremiah hesitated, but Lana answered quickly, "I don't see why not, honey. Go and sit with your friends and enjoy yourself."

Xavier grinned up at his stepmother before looking to his father for confirmation.

The king laughed. "Far be it from me to disagree with my bride before we've been married for more than an hour."

"Thanks!" he chirped as he took Robbie's hand, and the pair scurried through the crowd to a table their friends had confiscated for themselves.

"Hey, X! Great wedding! Boy, did your dad lay it on Mrs. Applegate in the end!" Garrett laughed.

"Yeah. He sure did," Beck commented cordially before adding, "Hope the queen didn't get knocked up from it."

Xavier laughed uncomfortably before shoving his friend. "Shut up, Beck."

"What? I'm just saying that I wouldn't want be anywhere near the palace tonight. I doubt anyone will get much sleep with those two going at it," he remarked crudely, nodding toward the king and queen.

"Ew... stop Beck! Geesh. There's something seriously wrong with you, mate. Why would you even bring up my... my... parents having sex tonight?"

"What? I'm just saying what everyone in this room is

thinking," he responded innocently.

"Yeah, well, would you want to hear it if you were in my shoes?"

Beck shrugged. "Fine. I'm just saying you might want to stay with Hardcastle tonight, but I'll stop talking about it."

Xavier eyed his friend dubiously. "Okay... thanks."

The group settled around the table.

"Hey, Xavier. You can stay at my place if you want," Court whispered to him.

"Okay. Thanks, Court."

After a full-course meal, a few tables were quickly cleared and the lights lowered for dancing. Several couples had already made their way onto the dance floor when Xavier looked at Robbie.

"You wanna dance?"

"I'd love to," she answered, smiling.

Taking her hand, Xavier led her onto the dance floor. His heart pounded loudly in his chest, and he ached to hold her. Then he turned and she slid into his arms. She felt perfect there. He nuzzled against her, trailing small kisses up her neck. He felt her shiver against him, and he squeezed her tighter. She pulled back just enough so he could kiss her properly.

When the kiss ended, Robbie's large dark eyes looked up at him and he lost his breath.

"Do you ever think about what it would be like when we get married someday?" Robbie asked.

"All the time," he whispered.

She smiled. "I can't wait until that day. I'm ready to marry you. I'd marry you tomorrow if our parents would allow it."

"Me too," Xavier whispered, kissing her lightly on the lips.

"Hey, X!" Beck's voice interrupted their kiss, and begrudgingly, Xavier withdrew from Robbie's sweet, soft lips.

"What?" he asked grumpily.

"Check it out, man," he answered, gesturing to the king and queen dancing on the dance floor, completely oblivious to the people around them for they were kissing, really kissing. "Good thing they're wearing clothes."

"Beckley Wilson! How dare you say such crude things about the king and queen! Shame on you!" Robbie spat impatiently.

Beck had the common sense to look embarrassed before muttering, "Sorry."

He drifted off to dance with Melissa, and Xavier hugged Robbie close again.

"Thanks. Beck is a great guy and friend, but he goes overboard trying to be funny sometimes."

"Yeah, I know. I think it's because he doesn't have a mom. She died in childbirth. It's just his dad and him."

Xavier knew this of course, and it was one of the reasons he felt close to Beck. "Yeah. I know," he sighed, leaning back to look down at Robbie. "I love you, Robbie Minnows," he whispered, kissing her. Then he pulled her into his arms and they continued to dance.

Several couples had joined them on the dance floor, but everyone else sat at tables watching the king and queen dance. Every now and again, people would glance at the prince before whispering to those at their table. Some looked at him in reverence, whereas others looked at him apprehensively, as if he would explode at any moment. Sighing at the unnerving attention, Xavier concentrated on the girl in his arms. She felt good there, and she smelled so good too. He kissed her neck and smiled as she shivered in response. Still smiling, he looked over her shoulder at his father and Lana dancing and kissing, oblivious to everyone around them. Xavier sighed contently. Beck may have gone over the top in saying it, but he was right. Xavier needed to find somewhere else to sleep tonight.

Chapter 17

"Are you sure about this, Xavier?" Robbie asked.
"Yeah, man. The king will kill us if he finds out!" Court responded.

"Don't be such babies," Erica spat, rolling her eyes. "I think it's a brilliant plan!"

Court eyed his girlfriend before looking at his friend meaningfully. "You do realize that if your only ally in this hair-brained idea is Erica, we're totally screwed. Right?"

"Besides, you don't even know how to drive!" Robbie spat.

"Dad let me drive once on the moor between the kingdom and Razorbill Cove. Come on, guys! Won't it be fun to get away from all the stares and whispers and just spend some time alone? I don't know about you, but I'm sick of all the whispering behind my back. Half the kingdom looks at me like... like I'm a god or something, while the other half looks at me like I'm going to explode and kill everyone at any second."

Robbie took his hand and gave him a reassuring smile.

Court groaned in defeat. "Okay, mate. We'll go. What's the plan?"

Xavier grinned.

That evening as the king entered the residence, Xavier

raced to take his briefcase as he peeled off his jacket. Lana smiled warmly at the king and the couple embraced in a welcome-home kiss.

"Dad," Xavier prompted, waiting impatiently for the couple to come up for air. "Daaaad!" Yes, he whined like a three-year-old, but he couldn't help it.

Finally, the king looked down at his son with his wife held tightly in his arms. "What is it, son?"

"Well, I was wondering... well, actually Robbie, Court, Erica, and I were wondering if we could have a picnic in the woods for dinner tonight."

"Son, I'm not sure that's a good idea. With recent attacks and infiltration in the kingdom, I don't like the idea of anyone being out after dark."

"We weren't planning on being out late. I promise. I... I just need to get away from everyone staring at me... judging me. I need some time with my friends. Please? We're only going to be gone for a couple of hours or so."

The king sighed and looked at Lana. "What do you think about this?"

"If he and the other children are back before dark, I don't see the problem. The attacks have always occurred after dark." Lana turned to Xavier. "You are to be home by seven o'clock. Understood?"

"Yes, ma'am!" Xavier exclaimed, hugging his parents before racing up the stairs and grabbing a bag he had already packed for the picnic. Seconds later, he was thundering down the steps with the backpack over his shoulder and barreling out the door.

"See ya!" he chirped, shutting the door behind him.

The king and queen stared after the boy in amusement.

Xavier waited outside the palace door next to the guard on duty, who kept throwing him nervous glances. Xavier did his best to ignore the tension and uneasy thoughts radiating off the guard. He didn't have to wait long before Robbie could be seen hurrying up the palace drive. She let out a giggle of excitement as she threw herself into Xavier's arms and kissed him, sending a humming sensation all the way down to his toes.

"Come up for air already!" Erica's snide comment announced her and Court's arrival as the palace door slammed shut behind them.

Xavier grinned sheepishly at his friends before motioning them to follow him. "Come on. The garage door is on the other side of the palace."

The group slipped into the garage, shutting the door firmly behind them. Xavier flicked the light switch, revealing the rows of pristine vehicles.

"Sweet!" Court announced. "Are these all your dad's?"

Xavier puffed up with pride. "Yep. Which one should we take?"

Court jogged down the rows of cars before skidding to a halt in front of the black Ashton Martin Vanquish. "This! This one!"

Grinning, Xavier turned to a locked black box mounted next to the light switch. With a flick of his finger, the lock clicked loudly and the door popped open. "What's the parking number on the wall behind the car?"

"Twenty-five!" Court shouted.

Xavier quickly swiped the keys from the corresponding hook and raced to where his friends stood staring at the sleek, shiny sports car. He pressed the unlock button on the keychain and the car's headlights flashed with a quick chirp. "Well, are you going to stare at it or are we going to take this bad boy for a spin?"

They climbed into the car and fastened their seatbelts. The group's excitement and giddiness was so contagious that Xavier couldn't contain his grin as he started the car and the engine roared to life.

"Yes!" Court yelled, pumping his fist into the air.

Laughing, Xavier shifted the car into drive and slowly crept forward toward the garage door.

"Okay, here's the tricky part. Robbie, you'll need to hit the garage door button when I tell you. Then, when you see the garage start to disappear, you'll need to press the button again."

"I don't understand," Court responded from the back seat. "I thought you were going to teleport us out of the kingdom."

Xavier looked at his friend in the rearview mirror. "I can't unless the door opens. The garage, like the entire palace, is encased in lead paint and materials. So Robbie will open the door and then close it once we start to teleport."

"Oh. Are you sure this will work?" Court asked.

Xavier glanced at him in the mirror again before looking at Robbie. "In theory, it should."

"In theory? Oh, great! And what if it doesn't work in theory? We won't end up stuck in the garage door or anything, will we?"

Xavier shrugged. "I don't think so, but we definitely won't be able to go for a picnic next to the sea."

The last thing he saw was Robbie's nervous smile as he closed his eyes to concentrate. "Erica, Court, just stay quiet. I need to concentrate. I've never moved anything this big before."

"Great! Now he tells us!" Court muttered before falling silent.

Xavier slowly breathed in through his nose and out through his mouth for several long seconds before whispering to Robbie. "Now, Robbie."

He heard the moan of metal on metal as the door began

to slide up. He felt his senses opening up, and he could visualize the streets of Warwood until he could see the road just outside the kingdom gates clearly. His hands pulsed with power as he felt its warmth spread through his body and beyond. He heard Robbie press the garage door button a second time, and knew his power was working. Finally, the car bounced as its tires settled back onto solid ground. His friends gasped, and he opened his eyes to see nothing but empty road in front of them. He turned and looked behind them. Sure enough, several hundred meters away the kingdom gates loomed.

"Holy shit! You... you actually did it! Dude! You did it," Court exclaimed loudly, thumping Xavier's shoulders happily and letting out a loud whoop.

Grinning from ear to ear, Xavier rolled the windows down and slammed the gear into drive again, punching the accelerator. The car roared forward, kicking gravel and dust up behind it as they sped forward.

"Woohoo!" Court yelled out the open window as the car neared one hundred miles per hour. "This is awesome, X!"

Robbie's hand slipped around Xavier's and he glanced at her elated, smiling face. His heart danced in his chest, and he flattened the accelerator to the floor. Robbie's squeal was reward enough as laughter erupted from her. The car ate up distance, and in no time, they neared the road that would take them toward the shoreline for their picnic. Xavier slowed the car to the legal speed limit and within a half a mile turned right on Shore Road.

"Nearly there," he announced over his friends' excited voices.

"Cool! We still have nearly three hours before we're due home. This is going to be a blast!" Court exclaimed and then planted a long kiss on Erica, who reacted atypically with a giggle.

When the group arrived at the pebbled beach, Xavier barely shifted into park before Court was thumping on the back of his chair.

"Come on, mate. Let me out! Let's go! Let's go!"

Laughing, Xavier held his hands up in surrender. "Okay, okay. Is it okay if I turn off the car first?"

Soon the group tumbled out of the car, laughing and grabbing their gear. As they approached the beach, Robbie grabbed Xavier's hand and pulled him to a halt as Court and Erica continued to the beach to find an ideal place to set up for the picnic. He looked down at her questioningly, finding her grinning at him. Her eyes glistened like melted chocolate, and her cheeks were flushed with excitement. Xavier dropped his bag and the blanket he had brought for them to sit on, pulled her to him, and kissed her. It wasn't a chaste, delicate kiss either. Nope. It was a real, honest, deep, grown-up kiss that had his toes curling and his head buzzing.

"Crikey! Xavier, mate, you're glowing pink!" Court blared loudly.

With a groan, Xavier separated from Robbie and glared at his friend. "Not a word, Hardcastle, or your big toe will become your nose. Got it?"

Court opened his mouth for a rebuttal, but he turned to Erica instead. "That's not possible, is it? I mean, he can't actually do that, can he?"

Erica giggled and shrugged. "Who knows?"

"Come on, Court. Let's see if we can find some wood for a fire."

"Sure thing."

The boys wandered inland, picking up anything that would burn. There were scarce pickings.

"This won't make much of a fire," Xavier remarked.

Court frowned. "Nope. I remember a fallen, old tree next

to the road when we turned off to come here."

"Sounds like a plan. Beat you there!" Xavier remarked before disappearing before Court's eyes.

"Show off," Court muttered as he closed his eyes to concentrate on the log he had seen. When he arrived, Xavier already had a pile of dried wood started and was trying to snap another limb off the fallen tree.

"Come on! Help me," he groaned with exertion.

Once the boys had an armful of wood each, they teleported back to the shore where the girls sat on blankets, unloading food from a basket Robbie had brought.

"About time!" Erica called out. "We were about to start eating this without you. Hurry up and start the fire. I want to eat—I'm starving!"

"Sorry for the inconvenience, *sweetheart*. You try and find wood on a moor that has nothing but weeds, dead flowers and rocks!"

Rolling her eyes, Erica continued to help Robbie dish out the food on four separate plates while the boys dumped the pile of wood onto the rocky shore before stacking it for the fire. Once the wood was arranged, the boys stepped back and looked at one another.

"Well? Do you want to do the honors?" Xavier asked, gesturing to the kindling.

Shrugging, Court stepped toward the firewood. "Sure."

In no time, the warmth of the fire washed over them, and the boys settled on the blanket next to their girlfriends. Xavier gave Robbie a quick, innocent kiss on the cheek. "Thanks for dinner."

Robbie grinned at him. "Anytime! Here," she remarked, handing him his plate. Cold roast beef sandwich, some sort of potato salad, fruit salad, and cheese.

"Looks great!" he responded and took a deep bite of his sandwich. It was fantastic! He could taste the rich beefy flavor with onion and cheddar cheese. He groaned appreciatively as he took a second bite.

"It's hard to believe Christmas will be here in a couple of months," Robbie commented with a shiver.

"Are you cold?" Xavier asked, grabbing his bag and pulling out a spare blanket. He wrapped it around her shoulders before kissing her briefly.

"Thanks. You're so thoughtful," she whispered with a shy grin.

"Are you two planning any mummering pranks?" Erica asked with a sly, knowing grin.

"Nooooooo," Court exclaimed, shaking his head adamantly. "We learned our lesson the year before last."

Xavier nodded his agreement. "Isn't that the truth! Did the rest of the guys stay out of trouble last year while I was a prisoner at King's Mountain?"

"Yeah. We just hung out at Garrett's house, watching movies and playing video games all night long. Nothing too exciting."

With a sigh, Xavier muttered, "I hate that I missed it though."

The group finished the sandwiches, packed up the food containers and cuddled around the fire. Xavier scooted closer to Robbie and slid his arm around her.

"Here," she whispered as she opened the blanket, silently inviting him to share with her.

Xavier moved even closer to her so that their hips touched, and he snaked his arm around her back, resting it on her opposite hip. Her heat radiated through his body, setting it afire with a sweet aching feeling. He needed to kiss her! He nuzzled against her neck, kissing it lightly and feeling her shiver before she giggled.

"Xavier!" she hissed, pushing him lightly. "Stop! That tickles!"

Xavier grinned up at her before grabbing her by the hips, pulling her back against him, and nuzzling into her neck again. She squirmed in his hold, giggling. Xavier kissed a trail from her neck up to her earlobe.

"Ahhh! Xavier! Stop... I... I can't... can't breathe!"

He released her, grinning triumphantly. Then the pair looked at their friends to find them snogging. Xavier's grin grew, and he pulled Robbie against him and nodded at Erica and Court before whispering, "If they were snogging any more than that, I'd be worried they'd swallow each other's face!"

Robbie giggled hysterically at his joke, and he felt his confidence soar.

"Shut it before I have to embarrass you in front of your girlfriend, tadpole," came Court's muffled voice behind Erica's lips.

"Hey, I'm bigger than you now, pipsqueak!" Xavier refuted, throwing a pebble at his mate.

"Yeah? Well, I can still kick your butt!" Court challenged jovially.

"Oh, yeah? Well, *big man*, I'm ready when you are!" Xavier remarked, standing.

Court mirrored his actions, "Let's do this, but there's one rule: no powers!"

"Deal," Xavier responded, holding out his hand to shake on their agreement.

Court shook his hand before immediately yanking him towards him, throwing him off balance and tackling him to the ground.

Caught by surprise, Xavier tried to buck the other boy off him, as he was attempting to put him in a headlock. With his adrenaline pounding in his head, Xavier rolled suddenly to his left, knocking Court off him and jumping to his feet.

"Cheat!" Xavier spat.

Court gave him a devil-may-care smile. "All is fair in love and war."

"Right. Which is why you don't want me using my powers because you know I'd kick your ass."

Court mocked a shocked, disgusted expression. "Prince Wells! Is that the kind of language becoming of our future king?"

Xavier snickered, shaking his head. He should have never told Court about his father's reprimand, but at the time, he really needed to vent. He didn't think it was fair that his father reprimanded him about his language when he had overheard worse from him!

Court suddenly lunged at Xavier's legs, trying to take him to the ground, but Xavier was ready and simply jumped over his friend, who went sprawling past. Robbie's loud giggling made his smile broaden at his friend.

"Want to try that again?" he teased.

Court got to his feet and dusted himself off. His face was flushed, and he glanced at Erica, who rolled on the ground, laughing. Xavier felt Court's embarrassment and humiliation. He had looked like a fool in front of his girlfriend. Sighing, Xavier's grin dropped, and he beckoned Court with a wave of his hand.

"Come on, mate. Bring it!" he encouraged, knowing Court couldn't turn down a direct challenge, but he felt his friend's hesitation. Then he barreled towards Xavier, and Xavier spun to avoid being tackled, or so it would appear to Court and those watching. It wasn't a fair fight. Xavier knew that it wasn't just because he was now taller than Court; height really didn't make much of a difference. What made it an unfair fight was that Xavier was trained in hand-to-hand combat whereas Court was not. Even without his potent powers, Xavier was superior. So, as a result of timing his spin a second too late, he felt Court's shoulder burrow into his rib cage, his feet flip out from under him, and Court's body slam him to the rocky ground. It hurt. It hurt a lot, and it knocked the breath from him.

Wheezing for breath, he held his hands up in surrender as Court sat up and gave him a surprised but triumphant look.

"Okay, mate. You won. Could you get off me?"

Court stood and helped Xavier to his feet. "You all right?"

"Yeah, just got the breath knocked out of me."

Court walked a little taller back to Erica and grinned down at her. "Yeah? What do you think of me now? You didn't think I'd win, huh?"

Erica batted her eyes coyly before punching him in the gut and running. Court tore off after her fleeing, giggling figure spouting words of revenge.

Xavier shook his head, chuckling as he sat next to Robbie and poked at the fire with a stick.

"You let him win."

Xavier looked at her quickly. "What do you mean?"

Robbie glanced over her shoulder at where Court had Erica cornered, backing her towards the rolling tide, thrashing against the pebbled shore before giving him a knowing look. "You let Courtney win."

Xavier shrugged. "Maybe not. It's possible I misjudged the timing of his attack."

"No," Robbie cooed as she snuggled against him, entwining her arm with his and taking his hand. "You didn't misjudge, but I'm very proud to be your girlfriend. You knew you had the advantage because of all the training you had at the mountain, but you let him keep his pride in front of Erica, who would have teased him to no end if he lost. You're a good friend." She kissed him on the cheek.

"Wait. I do a good deed for a friend, and all I get is a measly kiss on the cheek?"

She grinned and gave him a proper kiss that made his heart race in his chest. The couple leaned against one another, enjoying the time alone together.

Chapter 18

It was nearly an hour later when Erica and Court returned. "Where've you two been?" Xavier asked, smirking at his best mate.

Court swelled as he boasted, "A gentleman never speaks of such matters. Hasn't the king taught you that?"

Erica guffawed. "What matters? That you fell asleep in the grass?"

Robbie and Xavier tried to hide their snickers.

"Only after I snogged you into oblivion!"

Erica laughed loudly. "Into oblivion? How do you figure that? I think it was the other way around since *you* were the one who fell asleep!"

Robbie and Xavier couldn't help but laugh at their friends' antics. One thing was certain; Court would never have a dull moment with Erica as a girlfriend.

"We'd better start back," Robbie announced, standing and gathering her belongings.

"Yeah, it's getting close to curfew time," Xavier responded as he stood, summoned a ball of water and dumped it on the fire to extinguish it.

The group made their way back to the car, teasing one another and laughing.

"Oh, crikey!" Court exclaimed, ducking and gesturing the others to do the same.

Xavier slowly rose to peer above the rocky outcrop that hid their presence. A man in police uniform slowly got out of a patrol car, staring intently at their car.

Straightening his tie, the officer walked slowly up to the car, examining it appreciatively as he approached the driver's side door. Leaning toward the car, he peered inside before trying the door.

"Man! What are we going to do?" Court whispered.

"We need a distraction. I'll go back towards the shore and see if I can get him away from the car. As soon as he clears the area, you guys get to the car. Then I'll teleport into the car." Xavier pulled out the keys to the car. "Do you think you can start it?" he asked Courtney.

"Yeah, of course, but how are you going to get him away from the car?"

Xavier glanced above the rocks again before answering. "Don't worry about that. Leave it to me."

The officer strolled back to his patrol car to radio in the issue. Xavier disappeared from his friends and reappeared behind the officer.

"Dispatch, this is Sergeant Mullens. I'm off Bay Road and came across a 2016 Ashton Martin..."

"Hey! What are you doing to my car? You'd better not scratch it!"

The officer turned. "Your car? Aren't you a little young to drive, young man? What's your name, son?"

"Well, it's my dad's car. We came to the shore to do a little fishing. I just came back to get my tackle box. My dad's on the beach. Do you need to talk to him?" *Please, please say no and go away*, Xavier thought.

The officer replaced his radio in the console of the patrol car, straightened, and closed the car door. "I think that would be best."

Just great! Xavier forced a smile and turned to lead the

officer away from the car toward the beach. "He's just up the beach a ways," he commented throwing the officer an innocent look over his shoulder. He guided the officer past a large rock before descending down a rocky embankment toward the shore. The vehicles were out of sight and Xavier reached out to his friends to find that they were already piled in the car. *"Court, you need to drive. Start the car. I'll be there in seconds."*

"But, I don't know how to drive!"

"Court! Just do it! Leave the passenger seat free for me."

"The beach is empty kid. Time to tell me what's really going on. Did you steal that car?"

Xavier turned to face the officer. "No, sir. It really is my dad's car. Sorry, but I have to go, or I'll be late for my curfew."

"Son, you have a lot more to worry about right now than being late for your curfew. I think you should come with me."

"Ah, well, I was afraid you might say that. That's a problem, Officer, because I can't go with you."

"Can't?" the officer repeated stonily.

"Right, I mean, I *won't* go with you. Have a good day, sir!"

The last image Xavier had of the officer was a gaping, shocked expression as he teleported from the beach to join his friends in the car.

"Let's get out of here! Now!" Xavier barked at Court.

Court slammed the car into drive and fishtailed as he tried to turn around, slamming the rear fender of the car into the patrol car.

"Shit!" he exclaimed as he righted the car and accelerated down Shore Road. Xavier looked over his shoulder to see the officer racing up the embankment and towards his patrol car.

"Faster, he's getting into his car. We've got to lose him!"

"What about the dent in the car. The king will kill me!"

"I can fix it, Court. Just drive!"

Sirens erupted from behind them, and the group turned to look at the patrol car, which was now in pursuit of them.

"He's gaining on us!" Erica shouted. "Grow a pair, Hardcastle, and floor it!"

Court accepted his girlfriend's challenge and pressed the accelerator to the floor. The car growled as it leaped forward, accelerating to nearly a hundred miles per hour.

"He's still gaining on us! What are we going to do?" Robbie shouted.

Xavier glanced over his shoulder. *What kind of engine does he have in that car!* "Don't worry. We'll lose him. Everyone sit tight and stay quiet. I need to concentrate!"

He closed his eyes and meditated. Hoping his teleporting power didn't fail him when he needed it most. He pictured the car disappearing and reappearing in front of the palace gates. What he didn't take into consideration was the fact that the car and the people in it were traveling at speeds in excess of one hundred miles per hour. In the next second, Xavier opened his eyes to screams. The gatehouse loomed in front of them and the car was barreling toward it like a missile. With no time to think, let alone meditate, Xavier teleported all of them out of the car. They hit the ground violently at a hundred miles per hour. Instinctively, he extended his powers to slow the group to a gentler stop as the car collided with the palace gate in a thunderous crash.

The beautiful car was mangled beyond recognition. Xavier immediately looked around for Robbie. She lay twenty feet or so away from him, not moving.

"Robbie!" he crawled toward her, his heart thumping loudly in his ears. "Robbie? Are you okay?" he asked as he reached her and gently rolled her over.

She blinked and inhaled a shuddering breath. "I... I don't know. I... I think so."

"Can you sit up?" he asked, helping her to sit up.

Slowly she rose, blinked and looked down at her torn and battered jacket. Gingerly she began to move her arms and legs before looking at him. "I'm okay. I'm okay." Her eyes widened as she looked down at his left arm. "You're not! Oh my God, Xavier! Your arm!"

Xavier looked down at his arm, which had taken the brunt of the initial impact. It appeared to be dislocated at the elbow. Funny, it didn't hurt at all!

"It'll be okay. I'll heal it after I check to make sure the others are okay." He glanced around and found Erica slowly getting to her feet.

"All right?" he asked.

Erica looked at him with a stunned, shocked expression and slowly nodded.

"Where's Court?"

"Here!" Court's voice called from the side of the road. "I'm here. I think my leg's broken. Is Erica okay?"

"Yeah, she's fine!" Xavier reported, staggering to his feet and going to his friend. Sure enough, his leg was indeed broken. The tibia protruded just beneath the skin in a compound fracture.

"Mate! Your arm! That's sick!"

"You're the one to talk. You have two knees, dude," Xavier responded before both boys burst out laughing.

Robbie and Erica rolled their eyes. "Boys," they muttered together.

"Prince Wells? What in the hell are you doing out here? Are you responsible for the attack on the front gate?" a harsh voice shouted behind them.

The group turned and saw Henrick Davies and a couple dozen royal guards behind him, all combat ready. Xavier slowly stood and faced the lieutenant. The reprieve from pain ended at that moment, and Xavier clutched his broken arm with a hiss.

"Move!" the king's hard voice ordered as he jostled through the ranks of soldiers. Jeremiah stomped toward Xavier, his eyes hard and unforgiving. He looked at each child in turn before turning to Ephraim and Loren. "Loren, take the girls home since they are uninjured."

"My pleasure, sire," he muttered, glancing furiously at Court and Xavier. Crap! Last time he saw Loren this pissed, heads rolled. Well, maybe not heads, but definitely butts burned.

"Ephraim, get the boys to medical. I'll be there as soon as I check the integrity of the gate and speak to the men on duty."

Ephraim nodded and went to his son, lifted him like he weighed nothing more than a feather and looked pointedly at Xavier. "Prince Wells? Can you teleport?"

Xavier had an urge to laugh at the question. If only they knew how well he could teleport. "Yes, sir."

Without a word, the king turned and marched back toward the gatehouse while dread gnawed into Xavier's gut. He was in so much trouble!

"I can set my own arm, you know," Xavier growled as the healer prodded and positioned his arm for the healing.

"I'm well aware you have healing capabilities, sire, but a healer should never heal himself if he has the option of another healer," the slight man intoned nasally.

Xavier rolled his eyes just as his father entered the examine room.

"Sire, if you would please not move!"

"I didn't!" he protested, hissing past the nauseating pain as the healer repositioned his arm.

"Prince Wells," the healer sighed impatiently, "you tensed your muscles, which moved your arm. As a healer, you should know how important it is to remain still during the process."

The king briskly stepped forward. "Here, allow me," he announced hoarsely as he firmly grasped Xavier's arm to hold it in place.

Xavier yelped at the sudden pressure as pain raced up his arm. "Ow! Watch it, Dad. That hurts like a mother!"

Jeremiah gave his son a quick hard glance before nodding to the healer to perform the procedure. The healer's power lit up the room, and Xavier felt the heat seep into his arm. The power was soothing at first, but then suddenly there was a small cracking sound and a flash of pain in his arm as the power set the bone in place. Xavier yelped before clamping his eyes shut against the pain. The bones broken at the mountain didn't hurt like this when healed. Maybe the healer was doing it wrong!

"No, he's doing his job correctly, son. At the mountain, Ephraim administered apothecary."

He wanted to ask why he didn't get apothecary in the hospital but bit back the words. He was already in enough trouble; he didn't need to add whining to it. Five minutes later, the healer straightened.

"That should do it, sire. Don't lift anything heavy for 48 hours while the healing is still fresh."

Xavier nodded as he stood and rolled down his sleeve. "Thanks, Healer Thomas."

"Yes, thank you, Paul," Jeremiah said, shaking the healer's hand before placing it on Xavier shoulder, turning him, and leading him out of the hospital.

"Dad..." Xavier started, but the king squeezed his shoulder, silencing him.

"We'll talk about this when we get home. I don't think it's

a good idea to have it out about your poor choices in public. Do you, son?"

Xavier's throat constricted and he could only shake his head.

When they entered the palace, Loren was on duty at the residence door. The general's eyes narrowed on Xavier. "You are either the stupidest boy alive or you have a death wish! What in the hell were you thinking, stealing your father's car and joyriding across the moor?"

Xavier felt his legs stiffen as a sudden desire to run from the general entered his brain, but his father's constant guidance prevented the thought from becoming reality.

"You not only endangered yourself, my daughter, Robbie, and Courtney, you endangered your destiny and all hope of defeating the Dark King! Damn it, kid. Use your head for something other than snogging Robbie!"

When Xavier reached the threshold, Loren loomed over him, and his eyes flashed angrily down at him. Xavier couldn't meet the man's eyes, and he stared at Loren's shoes, feeling overwhelmed with shame and guilt.

His father opened the door. "Inside, son. We have a lot to discuss." His father's whisper, although soft, promised to be anything but soft during that discussion.

His head hanging low, Xavier walked past Loren to enter the residence, but Loren surprised him with a swift and hard wallop on the butt. He winced and his eyes watered.

Trying not to rub his butt to ease the stinging pain, he glanced up at the general and muttered, "I'm sorry."

With a bitter huff, Loren turned and resumed his guard. The king nudged Xavier into the residence and closed the door firmly behind them.

"Sit down, son," Jeremiah ordered, gesturing toward the receiving room.

Sighing, he shuffled into the room and flopped onto the sofa, still looking at the ground in front of him. His father settled into the armchair to his left and sighed. For several long seconds he said nothing, and Xavier couldn't help but take a quick peek at his father, who was sitting back in the chair with both hands covering his face.

"Jeremy? Is he okay?" Lana asked as she flowed into the room wearing her nightgown and robe.

His father sat up. "Yes, sweetheart. Luckily, he only had a broken arm that could be healed quickly."

"Oh, thank God! Xavier Wells, if I weren't so relieved that you're okay, I'd skin you alive, boy!" Lana exclaimed grabbing him and pulling him into a tight hug.

Xavier relished in the warmth she provided, but his father's next words sent a chill through his body.

"Courtney didn't fare as well. He had multiple compound fractures in his leg. It will take some time to heal, and the healers will have to heal it in stages. He'll be in the hospital for a couple of days. By the looks of the car, they're all lucky to be alive. If they hadn't teleported out of the car when they did, they'd all be dead. No one could have survived that kind of impact."

Lana's arms tightened around Xavier. "Oh my God! Xavier Wells!" she gasped pushing him to arm's length. "Look at me, young man!"

Slowly he raised his eyes to meet Lana's wide, worrisome eyes.

"What on earth were you thinking? Why did you take your father's car? Why were you speeding all over the moor?"

"Sire, there's a phone call for you," Mrs. Sommers announced.

"Take a message, Emma."

"I think you should take this. It's the Razorbill Cove

Police Department. They believe your car was stolen, and there was an incident involving the car."

Xavier's eyes widened. *Shit! It just gets better and better.*

His father's eyes hardened on him. "I'll take it in the library, Emma."

"Yes, sire." Emma nodded and walked toward the kitchen.

"Do you want to tell me what I should expect from this call before I take it, son?"

Xavier gulped. "Ah, well, we got scared cuz a police officer was sniffing around the car. I... uh... I tricked the officer to follow me while the others got in the car. Then... I... I teleported into the car and w... we took off... Only..."

"Only?"

"Uh... well, we might have accidentally fishtailed right into the police car."

"Bloody hell, Xavier!" the king exploded, jumping to his feet. "Stay put! Don't move a single muscle until I come back!"

Xavier watched with blurred vision as his father stomped into the library. "I really screwed up, Lana. I... I don't... I don't know how to make this right."

Lana hugged him again. "Sweetheart, sometimes making something right takes time and patience. You've broken your father's trust. All you can do now is own up to your mistakes, apologize, make amends, and learn from your mistakes."

Xavier nodded as he steeled his courage to face this. He had to man-up and make it right, no matter how long it took, no matter what he would need to do. Lana kissed his forehead gently.

"Do you need me to stay to keep your father calm?"

"No. I deserve his anger. I was thoughtless, reckless, and

endangered my friends," he answered, his thoughts wandering to Robbie. "I could have killed them," he finished with a whisper.

"Yes. That is true, but you didn't." She kissed his forehead again. "Good luck, sweetie. I'm going on up to bed. Tell your dad for me, okay?"

"Yeah. Good night, Lana," he answered as she stood and walked toward the staircase.

Five minutes later, the king exited the library, rubbing the back of his neck. "Well that was fun," he commented sarcastically. "You and I will go into Razorbill Cove tomorrow and pay for the damages for the patrol car. They agreed not to press charges."

Xavier expelled a relieved sigh.

The king's hardened eyes nailed him to the sofa. "Oh, so you're relieved by that? You could have killed yourself, but you're relieved that you will not face criminal charges from the Commoners?"

"No, sir. I just... It's just one less thing to worry about. I'm sorry, Dad. I am! I was stupid and I... I lied to you."

"Oh, yes, you don't need to remind me that you lied to me. Picnic in the woods? In the course of three short hours, you've all but pulverized my trust in you! Damn it, Xavier! I don't even know what to say to you!"

"I know, Dad, I messed up. I... I wasn't lying when I said I wanted to get away from prying eyes and whispers. I wanted to be away from..." he gestured widely, "all of this and just be a teenager, an ordinary teenager who has nothing more to worry about than if his hands were sweating when he holds his girlfriend's hand! If I could go back in time and change it, I would, but I can't. I'm not Abraham! I'm not a time bender! God, I wish I were!" Xavier continued to rant and pour out every pent-up thought that festered in his mind. "Actually, I wish I could just be normal, but it's stupid to wish for something that's impossible. God, Dad! I just want to go out with Robbie and not have my every move monitored and watched. I wanted to be alone with her to ..."

"Alone? Why did you take Erica and Court with you?"

"I didn't think Robbie would come if I didn't include Erica to talk her into doing it."

"I see, but I don't think your excuse warrants the theft of a car..."

"Dad, it was your car! Why does everyone keep saying I stole it?"

"Because you *did*!" his father shouted the last word. "It was not *your* car, son. Therefore you stole *my* car!"

"All right! Geesh, you don't have to yell!" Oops, he shouldn't have said that! He watched as the king swelled with fury.

"How dare you tell me I don't have to yell? Do you really think I have no cause to be upset, son?" Xavier guessed his father's questions were rhetorical because he never paused for a response between them as he continued, "Do you realize you could have *died* today? You could have killed Robbie, Court, or Erica? *And* do you realize that you teleported in front of a commoner, who's now asking all kinds of questions?"

Xavier's jaw dropped at the last question. Double crap! He had forgotten about teleporting in front of the officer.

"I... God! Dad, I... I... just tell me what to do! I don't know what to do to make this right! I'm sorry. I really am! I ... what do I do?"

The king's anger seemed to abate. With a noisy sigh, he rubbed his face vigorously.

"First, we go to bed. I'm too tired to make a decision about your punishment tonight," the king announced.

Xavier couldn't believe he had heard correctly. "What?

Go to bed? How am I going to sleep with all of this unsettled?"

His father looked down at him knowingly. "I guess you won't." With that, the king left the room.

Chapter 19

Xavier tossed and turned that night. He kept seeing his father's disappointed, angry eyes glaring at him. He almost wished his dad had spanked him, caned him even, if it meant he didn't have to look at him like the enemy again. His eyes filled, and he abruptly swiped the tears away. It did no good to feel sorry for himself; it didn't change anything.

Sighing, he flopped onto his stomach, closed his eyes, and tried to get comfortable. However, it seemed that no matter how he flopped or what position he lay in, some part of his body always felt pinched, twisted, or numb. Groaning loudly, Xavier sat up in bed and climbed to his feet, only to topple to the floor with a loud thud. His covers were twisted around his legs like a great python.

"Argh!" he muttered, exasperated. As he struggled to free his legs, he felt like crying again. Expelling a shuddering breath, he stood, walked to the bathroom, and splashed warm water on his face. He felt horrible. He had really, really messed up this time. God! He wished he could talk to Robbie. She had a knack for always making him feel better.

Looking at his reflection in the mirror, he whispered, "You must be a total idiot for even considering sneaking out to Robbie's." He flicked the bathroom light off as he walked toward his dresser muttering, "But I'm still going to do it. Seriously, how much worse can this possibly get?"

The words, "much worse," popped into his head as he stripped off his pajamas and pulled on jeans, a hoodie, and sneakers. He crept out of his room and tiptoed down the hall to his father's room. His hand hesitated on the doorknob as he suddenly realized it wasn't just his father's room. Lana slept beyond this door now. The king was a heavy sleeper most the time, but was Lana? What would he say to her if she woke up and caught him? A string of likely and unlikely excuses raced through his mind.

With a deep breath, he slowly opened the door and stepped into the room, closing the door softly behind him. He froze and waited for his eyes to adjust to the darkness. Suddenly, the room was no longer pitch black as a greenish hue faintly illuminated the room. His thoughts went directly to the comment Beck made at the wedding reception. Oh God! He didn't need to see *that*! Panicked and slightly appalled that he might see his father in an intimate moment with Lana, he snapped his eyes closed, anxiously reaching for the doorknob to escape. But when he peeked out of one eye to find the doorknob, the room was pitch black again. He frowned and listened. His father's even, rhythmic breathing indicated that he was asleep and not engaged with Lana in any way. Then he heard Lana's softer, quieter breathing, and knew they were both asleep.

Then what was the greenish hue that he saw? He nearly yelped when it suddenly returned. Then it occurred to him that he could make out the layout of the room and could see every object in the room. His father and Lana slept side by side; his father's arm draped protectively over Lana's waist. It wasn't his father glowing! Xavier had night vision! It was just like on TV when they showed the view of someone wearing military night googles. He could see in the dark! How cool was that? He grinned widely as he slowly made his way through the dark room to the patio door. Once outside, the intensity of the greenish hue lessened with a full moon night. He really didn't need help seeing things.

He didn't need to meditate to teleport to Robbie. His need for her was so strong that he simply disappeared from the patio and reappeared in the middle of her room without doing more than thinking about her.

Her room was dark, but with his night vision, he could see her burrowed deep under her covers so that only her closed eyes could be seen. Smiling, he tiptoed toward her, knelt by her bed, and softly stroked her hair from her face. She moaned sleepily and snuggled deep into her covers. Xavier leaned over her and kissed her forehead lightly. No response. He kissed both eyes. She rolled onto her back but continued to sleep.

Xavier crawled onto the bed, straddled her body with his, and looked down at her with a large grin. Slowly, gently, he nibbled on her bottom lip before kissing her awake.

Suddenly, Robbie jerked, drawing up both legs, and kneeing him in the privates. A breath left his lungs in a yelp, and he quickly rolled away from her. He tried to breathe and ended up coughing so hard he was sure his testicles might come out of his mouth. The light flipped on, and Robbie looked down at him on the floor. He cradled himself, tears streaming from his eyes as he coughed so much he was dangerously close to throwing up.

"Xavier?" she hissed, trying to keep her voice down.

"Y... y... yeah?" he managed, his voice tight with pain.

"Are you okay? Oh God! I'm sorry. I didn't know it was you!" she exclaimed quietly, rushing to his side. "I didn't mean to... to... hit you... *there.*"

"I... I h... hope not!" he coughed out.

"Are you okay?"

"No. God, I think I'm permanently damaged."

"Well, you shouldn't sneak up on me in the middle of the

night doing... What were you doing?"

Still cradling himself, he slowly straightened his legs, wincing. He took several deep breaths and was relieved to find the coughing had subsided. Man, did he hurt though. "I was just trying to kiss you awake."

"Oh. I'm sorry. Do you need me to do something...?"

Xavier couldn't have kept the ornery grin from his face if he tried.

"Don't you dare say kiss it to make it feel better!" she scolded, trying not to laugh.

Shrugging, he slowly sat up. "Naw. I'll be okay... in a few... years," he answered with a wink and a grin. Xavier leaned against Robbie's bed, still trying to regain his breath. Robbie copied his actions, sitting beside him.

"Why did you come?"

Xavier's grin dropped. "I... I just... I needed to see you. Are you sure you're okay? You didn't get hurt at all in the accident?"

"I'm fine, Xavier, aside from a couple of scratches. You and Court got the worst of it."

He nodded. "Yeah. Court will be the hospital for a couple of days. His leg was broken so badly that they need to heal it in stages."

"Yeah, I heard."

Xavier exhaled heavily. "I don't know what to do to make this right with my dad. He's so mad, so disappointed. I screwed up. I screwed up big. I worry he'll never look at me the same again."

"Xavier, your dad's mad and maybe a little scared because of what could have happened to you, to all of us, but he'll get over it. It'll be okay. You've messed up before and he's forgiven you."

Xavier eyed her disgruntledly. "Thanks," he hissed sarcastically, and Robbie giggled.

"I'm sorry, but you know I'm right. You're very creative at finding trouble. I find it attractive, but I can understand why it drives him up the wall."

Xavier nodded. "Yeah. I'm just worried. He refused to punish me tonight. He said he needed a clearer head and we'd discuss it in the morning. I think he did that on purpose to mess with me. I can't sleep. All I can do is wait and worry."

"Aw, my poor abused boyfriend," she commented as she patted his leg and kissed his cheek. "You know, it might help if you suggested a punishment to your dad. The bigger the punishment, the more respect he'll have for you."

Xavier paused in thought before answering, "That's a great idea, Robbie! No wonder I love you so much! You're brilliant!"

Robbie's huge grin took his breath away.

"I know what you can do for me," Xavier whispered, his smile dropping into a somber expression.

Robbie looked up at him, her eyes widening. "What?"

Xavier leaned toward her, tilted her chin up with his index finger, and covered her mouth with his. When she responded by kissing him back, he couldn't think straight, and he kissed deeper. Soon, Robbie was wrapping her arms around him and snuggling closer. Xavier's breath quickened. This was heaven, absolute bliss. His hands ran up and down her back. He just needed to touch her!

Robbie pulled away suddenly and pressed her head against his chest, out of breath and flushed. "We better stop. You better go home, Xavier."

Xavier was confused. What had he done wrong? "Robbie?"

She looked up at him. "Xavier, you're glowing so brightly I could turn out my light and we'd still be able to see each other clearly. You are a *very* good kisser, which is why we

200

need to stop before…"

Xavier blushed as he realized what she meant. Wow! Um… what could he say to that? Thank you? No, that didn't seem appropriate. "It's your fault," he stated with a grin. "You're so hot that I can't keep my hands… uh… lips off you. But you're right. I should go. Can I have one more kiss for the road?"

Robbie snickered. "Road? It will take you literally a fraction of a millisecond to get home!"

He grinned mischievously. "Come on. Just one more?"

Giggling, Robbie leaned toward him until she was inches from him and whispered, "Just one more." Then she gave him a heart-thumping, inferno-igniting kiss. Xavier whimpered, actually whimpered!

Suddenly he jerked to his feet, ending the kiss. He stood, awkwardly, looking down at her, and muttered in a rush, "I better go," before disappearing from her room. He stood for nearly ten minutes out on the patio, trying to calm his pulse and cool the blood pumping through his veins. He knew if anyone could see him now, they would be astounded at how brightly he glowed. He couldn't go into the palace glowing. It could wake his father, or worse Lana. How would he explain glowing pink as he crept through their room? Closing his eyes, he focused on his grandmother, her shrieking voice, her hateful eyes, and her cruel words. When he opened his eyes, the pink glow was gone, and he breathed out gratefully. Then he crept back to his room.

To Xavier, it felt as if he no sooner closed his eyes and began to drift off to sleep when his father was shaking him awake. Xavier looked at his bedside clock. He had gotten back into his room around four, and it was now seven. Three hours! Three freaking hours of sleep! He looked grumpily up at his father.

"Why are you waking me up at this hour? I don't have school! I want to sleep in!"

The king straightened, his face turning from impassive to hard. "I don't really have much regard for what you *want*, son. Doing what you *want* is why I'm waking you at *this hour*. Get dressed! We have a meeting with the Razorbill Cove Police Department at eight-thirty." Without another word, his father turned and treaded heavily out of the room.

"Great!" Xavier moaned, flopping back into his bed. It was going to be a long freaking day. He moved slowly, but he took a shower and dressed.

As he sleepily climbed down the staircase, his father called out, "Here!" as he tossed him a granola bar and an apple. Xavier juggled the apple, which ended up hitting the ground and rolling the remaining distance down the steps. He looked up questioningly at his father.

"You missed breakfast moving like the walking dead. We've got to go. So pick up the pace, young man," he elaborated.

He scrambled down the remaining steps, picked up the now bruised apple, and hurried after his father, who was already out the door. Henrick stood at guard duty.

"Sire," he bowed toward the king before his eyes settled on Xavier. A spark of humor lit up his eyes, and he gave the boy a slight bow as he whispered, "Good morning, dead-man-walking."

Xavier gave the lieutenant a glare as he hurried to catch up with his father. If his father was already taking him to the police station to discuss his punishment, he must have an idea in mind on what his punishment would be. They exited the palace where one of his father's cars waited for them—a sapphire blue Dodge Viper. A guard stood next to the vehicle, holding the driver's door open for the king. Xavier climbed into the passenger seat and buckled his seatbelt.

His father folded his long frame into the car, fastened his seatbelt, shifted the vehicle into drive and modestly pulled away from the palace.

Xavier stared out the window as they passed through the palace gates and idled down the residential streets. He watched the houses creep by, wondering about the people who lived in each house. What was their biggest worry, their greatest hope? What did they think of him? Did they think he would make a good king, like his father? Or did they believe he would destroy their homes? Then he remembered Robbie's suggestion to offer an idea for his punishment to his father so that he would realize that he was truly sorry for his actions and took them seriously. But what could he suggest? It would have to be big, a fantastic idea. When he finally had an idea in mind, he realized that they had already left the kingdom, and it was fading into the distance behind them.

"How long will it take us to get there?" Xavier asked, wondering if he would have enough time to make his proposal.

"About an hour," his father answered.

Nodding, Xavier inhaled a deep breath. "Dad? I want to talk to you about what I did. I know I keep saying it, but I really am sorry. I could have killed my friends... Robbie... myself. It was a very bad idea to take the car in the first place. Plus, I was dishonest with you about where we were having our picnic. I deserve whatever punishment you decide on, but... I wanted to make a suggestion. I want to show you that I'm disappointed in myself and that I really am sorry for my actions. So I think I should be grounded and I should volunteer to help fix the gatehouse, and maybe I should volunteer community service for Razorbill Cove as well. Like, maybe I can clean up the beaches by picking up trash and that sort of thing. And if you can think of something else I need to do, I'll do it. I'm so sorry!"

Xavier peered up at his father's profile, waiting for his response. The king sighed weightily and pulled the car to a stop on the side of the road. When his father's eyes met his, Xavier's gaze dropped submissively.

"I know you're sorry. I know you regret your actions. I will consider your suggestions, but first I need to smooth things over with the Razorbill Cove Police Department. So when we arrive, I want you to keep your temper in check and express nothing but regret and humility. Understand?"

"Yes, sir."

With a nod, the king shifted the car into drive and continued the drive to Razorbill Cove. When they arrived at the police station, Xavier followed his father into the station while butterflies tap-danced in his stomach. The king stopped at the front desk and greeted the receptionist with a smile.

"Hello. I'm Jeremiah Wells, and I have an appointment with Chief Jackson."

After glancing briefly at her appointment book, the woman smiled back. "Yes, he's expecting you, King Wells. One minute while I notify him that you've arrived."

Xavier's brow rose at the greeting, surprised that a commoner would address his father by his official title. The receptionist hung up the phone and smiled again.

"You can go on back. Just go past the squad room and down the hall on the left. He's the last door on the right."

"Thank you." Jeremiah gave the woman a nod, turned, grasped Xavier's shoulder and led him past the squad room.

Xavier's eyes wandered from person to person in the very busy and active room. Police officers, some in uniform, others in plain clothes working on reports, interviewing suspects or witnesses, or huddled together in what Xavier could assume was important official police business.

"Well, well! It's a pleasure to see you again, kid. I assume this is your father, the true owner of the car?" the police officer from the previous night teased.

Jeremiah regarded the man briefly before holding out his hand. "Jeremiah Wells, Officer...?"

"Sergeant Mullens. It's good to meet you finally. You've got... a very interesting, clever boy there."

Jeremiah glanced down at Xavier with exasperation.

Xavier gulped.

Jeremiah looked back at the sergeant. "We are here to meet with Chief Jackson. Would you please join us?"

When they entered the roomy office, Chief Jackson stood, came around his desk and greeted Jeremiah like a long lost friend. "King Wells! It's wonderful to see you again! I hear you recently got remarried! Congratulations!"

"Thank you, Gary, but really, it isn't necessary for you to address me so formally. We've known each other for years. Surely you can call me 'Jeremiah'?"

Gary laughed heartily, shaking the king's hand. "Yes, I can, Jeremiah. It's been a while since we've seen one another. I had hoped you were staying out of trouble, but it appears this youngster has taken up the family tradition."

"Unfortunately," his father muttered, glancing briefly at Xavier. "I've come to make amends and pay for any damage done to the car. I've asked Sergeant Mullens in on our meeting since he was the officer on the scene."

Chief Jackson acknowledged the sergeant with a nod. "Mullens, I need to emphasize that whatever is discussed in this room is confidential and must never be repeated."

"Sir?" Mullens questioned, clearly puzzled by the secrecy.

The chief stood, walked to the door, and shut it securely, before turning and meeting the sergeant's eyes soberly. "What you're about to learn is a highly protected secret that few know. The President of the United States and the Prime Minister of Canada are both aware of what I'm about to tell you, and both have deemed this information classified. I don't need to tell you the penalty for revealing classified information. Do I?"

Sergeant Mullens was taken aback. He glanced briefly at the boy and his father sitting near him before looking to his chief. "No, sir, but I'm confused."

The chief moved to sit behind his desk again. "I'll let King Wells elaborate," he remarked, nodding to Jeremiah.

"Sergeant Mullens, I'm Jeremiah Wells, and I am king of a neighboring society called Warwood. I know that what I'm about to tell you sounds outlandish, but if you consider what you witnessed with my son, it may provide you with an explanation. The people of my kingdom are not ordinary men, women, and children. We are empowered humans who are simply developed into the next stage of human development. My people are what you'd call gifted with supernatural abilities."

The sergeant stared, dumbfounded, at the man in front of him before grinning broadly and laughing. When no one joined him, his eyes darted from face to face before settling on the chief's. "He's serious?"

"Yes, Sergeant. It's true. Surely seeing the boy disappear before your eyes supports this information."

"Well," the sergeant began, studying the fresh-faced boy thoughtfully. "I... I just... I thought maybe I was overworked... or the kid was some magician. Wait, are you saying he can literally... disappear?"

The king looked briefly at Xavier before answering, "Yes, but more than likely, he teleported in front of you to get back to his friends, who were already in the car."

"Teleport?" the sergeant's eyes ignited with excitement. "Are you serious?"

"Yes, it's true, Mullens, and this fact is not to leave this room. Understood?"

Nodding, he answered quickly, "Of course, of course. I understand. It's just so unbelievable. How is this possible?"

The king shrugged. "We were born this way. Our scientists have determined that our brains are physically different, with more connective tissue between the hemispheres. We can access multiple parts of our brain simultaneously."

"It must be amazing living in your city surrounded by people with superpowers. What I wouldn't give to visit! My kid would shit himself to know that superheroes exits."

"Superheroes?" Xavier blurted with a dry snicker. "We're not superheroes. We're... just... people."

The officer looked up with an awestruck expression. "You are far from just people, kid. You're... amazing."

"Sergeant Mullens," Jeremiah interrupted. "You're more than welcome to visit Warwood. When you determine a date you'd like to come with your family, give me a call, and I'll make arrangements for you to stay at the palace," he told him, handing the officer his business card. "How old is your boy?"

Mullens took the card with a large smile. "Thank you! My Ryan is fifteen. My daughter, Jasmine, is twelve. And don't you worry, King Wells, your secrets are safe with me."

"Mullens, you need to sign this confidentiality form before you leave this office," Chief Jackson remarked, shoving a form and pen in the sergeant's direction.

He signed the form quickly before standing, nodding respectfully to Jeremiah, and exiting the room.

The chief let out a long breath.

"Can I trust him?" Jeremiah asked.

Chief Jackson considered his question in earnest before remarking, "Yes. Mullens is a straight-laced cop. He'll honor his word." After inhaling a cleansing breath, the chief's eyes settled on Xavier. "Now, you must by Prince Wells."

"Yes, sir," Xavier answered quietly as the man's jovial expression turned stern.

"You've certainly caused your father and this police district a lot of headaches, boy."

"Yes, sir. I'm sorry about that. I'd like to make amends for what I've done." Xavier took a deep breath. "I broke the law by driving without a license, I damaged police property, I took my father's car without permission, I crashed the car into the gatehouse, damaging the gatehouse and totaling the car, I hurt my best friend, and nearly killed all of us in that car. I'll do whatever you and my father find reasonable."

The chief looked at Jeremiah and snickered. "Are you sure he's your son? It wasn't that long ago you sat across from me, but you were singing a much different tune if I recall."

Jeremiah nodded as he smiled sheepishly at the man across from him. "Xavier is more mature than I was as a teen."

Nodding, the chief looked back at Xavier. "You will serve community service on weekends for the next six months."

Xavier's eyes widened. "Six months?" he whispered.

"Yes, sire. I will not accept your father's money to fix the damaged cruiser. You will pay for it with sweat and sore muscles, young man."

"Chief Jackson, normally I would whole-heartedly agree with you, however, Xavier cannot be out of the kingdom without a full detailed guard flanking him. We are in the throes of preparing for war."

"War?" the chief exclaimed, his eyes widening. "What's going on, Jeremiah? As chief of public safety in your closest neighboring city, I must insist on being briefed."

Jeremiah shifted in his seat. "There's a faction of my kind

who wish to overthrow me and take control of not only Warwood, but eventually, the world. If they succeed, it will mean commoners will be enslaved or killed. It will be the darkest days in humanity's history. It will be hell on earth."

The chief released a long, low whistle. "What do you need from me? Do you need more men? Would you like me to contact our friends in Washington and Ottawa?"

Jeremiah began shaking his head at the first sentence. "I'm afraid the presence of commoners, even highly trained fighters, would only mean more deaths. Your men are no match for an empowered warrior."

• The chief gave him a doubtful look. "Surely more men would only help."

"No, Gary. I assure you it would not."

"Jesus, Jeremy! You're asking me to sit on my hands while you go to battle in my backyard. What if the fighting extends beyond your borders? Do you really expect me to do nothing?"

"Yes, I do!" Jeremiah barked and the men sat stonily, glaring at one another. Finally, the king looked down at his son, who sat quietly watching the tense exchange. "Look Gary, how about you come for a visit this week, and we'll show you what one empowered warrior can do. If you still think your men can help, I won't talk you out of it. Deal?" He extended his hand to the older man.

The chief gave him a curt nod before taking his hand. "Deal." He leaned back in his chair and regarded Xavier a moment before looking back at Jeremiah. "What of the boy?"

"Oh, he will see punishment, but I can't have him out of the palace unprotected right now. If you believe six months of community service will pay off the debt, then I will pay the debt, and he can repay me with six months of community service to Warwood."

The chief nodded thoughtfully. "Well, in that case, I think we have deal. I have time in my schedule to visit tomorrow afternoon. Will that work for you?"

Jeremiah stood. "We look forward to seeing you tomorrow. I'd like to extend the invitation to your lovely wife. Lana and I would be honored if you'd join us for dinner afterwards."

"Oh, Sally would love that! She's always had a soft spot for you. She'll be very pleased to see you again and to meet your youngster."

Jeremiah smiled genuinely. "I look forward to it. We'll see you then. Goodbye, Gary." He shook the man's hand one last time before he steered Xavier from the precinct.

Chapter 20

"So, how did it go with your dad yesterday?" Robbie greeted him as she slid her hand into his and they began their walk to school together.

Xavier sighed. "Well, I'm grounded for a month, and I have community service every weekend for six months," he answered. "Not to mention, he still looks at me like I'm defective or something. I don't mind the punishments. I deserve them, but I just wish he'd look at me normally. You know? Not like I'm a huge disappointment."

"I'm sorry, Xavier. I'm sure he'll get over it in a day or two," she responded, hugging him to her side as they walked.

They walked this way for most of the way to school only to separate when they reached the school's drive. As they climbed the steps and walked past Spencer, he gave Xavier a knowing grin. "Ah! I see Evel Knievel is on time today!"

Xavier rolled his eyes as he brushed past his uncle and led Robbie to their first period class. When they entered the classroom, eager students surrounded them.

"Hey, Xavier!" one boy said grinning ear to ear. "Word is that you went for a joyride in your dad's sport's car. Is it true?"

Dumbfounded, Xavier looked down at Robbie, who turned to hide her smile. He turned back to the waiting group. "Ah, yeah. I guess it's true."

"Whoa! I heard Drew talking about it, but I thought he was lying! Did the cops chase you too?"

Xavier looked from one fervent face to another. He could feel their awe and excitement. He could see their admiration in their eyes. He stood a little taller and smiled at the group. "Yep. The cops chased us for at least a mile on Route 10, but it was no match for my dad's Aston Martin. But I didn't want the guy following us all the way back to Warwood, so I teleported us, car and all, to the kingdom's gates. I just miscalculated the distance we needed to come to a stop since we were traveling over 130 miles per hour."

"Shit, man!" another boy stated. "How did you guys survive? I hear the gatehouse door was nearly destroyed from the impact."

"Yeah, it was. After I teleported us, I saw that there was no stopping the impact. So I did the first thing that came to mind; I teleported us out of the car."

"You were lucky you weren't all killed," one girl piped up.

Xavier shook off the comment. "Naw, I slowed us down before impact. Yeah, we got banged up, but nothing life-threatening."

The group all burst out at once with more questions.

"Excuse me," Lana announced her presence and the children quickly bowed before scrambling to their seats.

Xavier turned to face his stepmother with chagrin. "Lana... I..."

"It's 'Mrs. Wells' at school, Xavier. We'll discuss this later. Have a seat."

"Yes, ma'am."

At the end of class, as children scrambled from the room, Xavier stayed seated.

"Aren't you coming, Xavier?" Robbie asked, standing next to him.

"No, you go ahead. I need to talk to Lana."

As Robbie left the room, he stood and approached Lana anxiously. "Mrs. Wells?" he prompted as he stopped in front of her desk. She looked up from the papers she was grading. "Ah, I'm sorry about what I said... about the accident. I didn't mean it really. I... I..."

"You were showing off," she finished.

He bowed his head with embarrassment. "Yes, ma'am. They were so enthusiastic about... what happened. I guess I just got a little... cocky."

"Mm hm. I see. So you are not proud of the chaos you caused by stealing your father's car and starting a high-speed car chase with Razorbill Cove's police department?"

Xavier blushed, feeling ashamed. "No, ma'am. I'm not. I hate that Dad looks at me with disappointment and shame."

"Then maybe you should show that in your actions and words when he's not looking. Do you realize that he gets reports about your behavior, progress, and work from your teachers weekly? And after your latest shenanigans, I imagine he'll be requesting reports more often."

"Seriously? Doesn't he trust me?" Xavier blurted, feeling defensive and betrayed. "He has teachers spying on me and reporting my every move to him?"

Lana gave him a severe look before responding firmly, "He's your father, Xavier. He's monitoring your schooling as any parent should. However, since you are the future king of our great kingdom *and* have been known to struggle with control over your abilities, don't you think he has good reason to want to keep track of you?"

Xavier bit back his retort. She was right. He knew she was, but it didn't mean it didn't hurt that his father was going behind his back. Trying to keep his irritation out of his voice, he asked, "Are you reporting what happened before class today?"

He must have failed at keeping his emotions out of his tone because Lana frowned at him and arched her brow. "You don't think I should?"

"Lana, if you do that, he'll be even more pissed at me! I was stupid to brag about it! I know that, but it's not how I really feel about what happened. It eats me up knowing Dad is disappointed in me! I can't stand the way he looks at me now. If you tell him, he'll hate me!"

"Xavier," she began softly as she walked around her desk and placed her hands on his shoulders. "Your father could never hate you. He loves you." She hugged him briefly before drawing him back at arm's length. "I cannot lie to your father. If he asks me how you did in my class, I must tell him. He's not just your father and has a right to know, but he's my husband, and I will not lie to him."

"Fine," Xavier sighed, turned, and stomped out of the room.

After lunch, Xavier teleported to the Governing Hall and entered his father's office with trepidation. Had his father gotten his report on his *progress* at school for the day already? The king looked up as he continued his conversation on the phone.

"Yes, Marcus, Chief Jackson has permission to enter the kingdom. Allow them to pass and direct him to the Governing Hall. I'll call the palace gatehouse guards and let them know to watch for him. Thanks."

Hanging up the phone, he looked back at Xavier. "How was your morning at school?" he prompted.

Xavier knew a set up when he heard one. Lana had told him about his lapse in judgment. "Well, okay, but I did something stupid this morning."

Jeremiah raised a brow. "Oh, do tell."

Sighing, Xavier looked at his father's tie to avoid the dark emotions he knew he would see in his eyes as he told him. "Well, when I got to my first class, a bunch of kids where really anxious to hear about the police chase. I... I kinda boasted about it... Lana overheard me. I don't know why I did it. I... I guess I wanted them to think I was cool instead of some kind of freak."

When his father didn't respond right away, he ventured a glance at his face to see his father staring at him.

"Dad. Please, say something! I can't stand the silence while you stare at me."

"What would you have me say?"

"Anything! That I'm a disappointment as a son and as a king. That I'm grounded longer. That I have to apologize publicly to all those kids. That you hate me! Just... something!"

"Hate you? Son, I could never hate you."

"Well, the way you've been looking at me... it feels like you do."

"Son, I hate what you did. I hate your choices recently, but I could never hate you." His father stepped around the desk and pulled Xavier into a bear hug, squeezing him tightly.

Xavier felt tears spring into his eyes as he muttered against his father's shoulder. "I hate that I could have killed my friends. I hate that I caused more damage to the gatehouse when we are constantly under watch for an attack. I hate that I lied to you and destroyed your trust in me. I hate that I was selfish and that my decisions didn't take any of this into consideration. I hate that I disappointed you, *again*."

The king pulled him back to look down at him. Xavier felt more tears fill his eyes before rolling down his cheeks as he looked into his father's eyes, which showed nothing but acceptance and love for him. He felt unworthy.

"You are worthy," his father whispered. "I am angry because I love you more than my next breath, son. I'm angry because the crash could have been much, much worse. If anything were to happen to you, I'd never recover from it." He wiped the plump tears from Xavier's cheeks as he smiled. "Nothing will ever change the fact that you are my son, and I love you. However, you cannot expect me *not* to be disappointed and angry when you do things that are ill thought out."

Xavier nodded, his eyes dropping from his father's.

"Now, go and wash your face. We have company arriving in a couple of minutes, and we must demonstrate the power of our people. We cannot allow commoners to become part of this war. It will only mean certain death for them and distract our people who will try to protect them."

Nodding, Xavier entered the lavatory through a door to the right of his father's office. Closing the door, he stared at his reflection with a grimace. No more stupid decisions! He couldn't take the guilt he was feeling. "Time to be a king," he muttered to himself as he splashed cool water over his face several times before drying off and joining his father in his office.

When he opened the door, he found Chief Jackson and a frail woman standing next to him. She reminded Xavier of his mother, and he couldn't take his eyes off her.

"Son, come. I'd like to introduce you to Mrs. Jackson," his father announced, waving Xavier toward him.

Slowly, he shuffled toward the adults, his eyes never leaving Mrs. Jackson, who had turned to look at him.

"You... you..." he looked at his father with shock.

The king smiled gently. "Yes. She does, doesn't she?"

Chief Jackson frowned, his eyes darting between father and son. "What is it?"

"Xavier is taken aback by your wife. She looks a great

deal like my first wife—Xavier's mother."

"Oh, where is his mother?" Mrs. Jackson questioned with a warm smile. "I would love to meet my *twin*."

The king shifted awkwardly and glanced down at Xavier's distraught, bowed head before answering, "She was killed a little over two years ago."

Mrs. Jackson's smile dropped and her eyes moved from the king to the downcast head of the prince. "Oh! I'm so sorry," she whispered and pulled Xavier into a warm hug.

Xavier accepted the hug and relished her warmth. A part of him allowed him to pretend she was his mother. He blinked back the tears before withdrawing and smiled feebly up at the woman.

"It's okay. It was a long time ago."

"Losing one's mother is never okay, but you learn to cherish the memories and keep her alive in here," she whispered as she tapped his chest above his heart.

He nodded and his smile widened slightly. "Thank you, Mrs. Jackson."

Jeremiah cleared his throat and looked at the chief. "What do you say you observe my son's battle training, Gary? I think it will give you an idea of what our people are capable of."

"You're training the boy?" the chief asked, shocked.

Jeremiah had the sense to look awkward before answering. "Yes. I know you won't understand this, but the boy is... a target of our enemy." He glanced at Xavier before continuing, "Xavier must be able to protect himself."

Chief Jackson looked down sympathetically at Xavier. "Why would your enemy target a boy?"

"I accidently killed his father," Xavier muttered, looking at the floor.

"What?" the chief's eyes darted to Jeremiah.

"It was self-defense. William LeMasters had invaded

Warwood and killed many people. He was an evil man who would have faced the death penalty for his crimes. Xavier didn't realize his actions would kill the man."

"What..."

"It's complicated, Gary."

The older man nodded. He had long ago come to understand that the people of Warwood were a secretive bunch, and although he knew they possessed powers, he was certain that what he knew about them was just one small piece to the puzzle.

"Well, let me get my men organized for the training and we'll head over to the coliseum," Jeremiah stated as he picked up the phone.

A half hour later, Xavier stood in the center of the rugby pitch tightening his protective gear. He glanced into the stands before he remembered that his training wasn't occurring at its normal time and his friends would not be there. Sighing, he looked across the field at the twenty men huddled together planning their strategy. He glanced at his father, who was talking to the chief and his wife. Sighing again, he picked up his sword and readied himself. The men across the field spread out from each other and stood at the ready.

"All right, gentlemen. You know the rules. Anything goes! We've increased safety measures for this exercise so that our guests will not be injured by a stray empowerment. Give them a show of what our people are capable of. You may start when you're ready."

No sooner had his father said the words when five men left their positions to race toward him with loud battle cries. Instantly, Xavier raised his hand with an electro force blazing brightly. He started to strike but paused when he felt the hair on the back of his neck rise. He hit the turf just before a blade whizzed overhead. The charging men had been a diversion.

He quickly rolled onto his back and swept his hand at the two men who were staggering after their failed assault. The men were propelled a hundred feet across the field. A gasp of surprise came from the sideline where his father stood with the Jacksons. Jumping to his feet, Xavier surveyed the men, who had slowed their attack. Suddenly, half the men disappeared. Xavier spun to find them reappearing behind him. So plan B seemed to be to surround him in hopes that when they attacked, he wouldn't be able to defend from every direction. His mind raced for a defense for the situation. The men were too far away to attack them with any accuracy. He would need to wait until they were within twenty-five or thirty feet to have high success with his attack. He spun back to face the men on the other side.

The guards slowly, cautiously stalked him. He tracked them with his eyes, his body remaining at the ready and still. He allowed his senses to reach out to the men. Their thoughts crowded into his mind. The problem was he couldn't tell whose thoughts were whose. A thought came as a warning, and Xavier spun to find his attacker. He raised his sword just in time to parry the attack and the sound of metal scraping metal echoed around the coliseum. The man continued to bear down on his sword in an effort to outmuscle him. Xavier dropped suddenly to the ground, rolled into the man's legs, and knocked the man to the ground with a loud grunt. Swinging his sword, Xavier struck the man in the back of the head. While he busied himself with the lone attack, half a dozen men took the opportunity to advance on the vulnerable boy!

Feeling panicked, Xavier sent out a powerful force towards the nearest men, and they were launched backwards, landing awkwardly. He jumped to his feet and lifted his sword as one guard arched his sword in attack. The impact sent Xavier's sword to the ground. Unarmed and helpless, he ducked as the guard swung again and someone grabbed him from behind. Struggling in the man's strong grasp, the second guard rose and pointed his sword at Xavier's heart. When the man lunged his sword forward, Xavier heard Chief Jackson shout in alarm just before he teleported to the side of the field next to his father.

The king rose a brow as he regarded the boy next to him. Panting and stooping over with his hands on his knees, Xavier worked to catch his breath as they watched the men in center field collide. The guard holding him was impaled in the gut with the sword.

Jeremiah nodded to Ephraim, who ran onto the field to administer first aid and access the severity of the damage. The remaining guard scanned the field. Xavier, needing a few more minutes of rest, stepped behind his father to hide.

"What are you doing, son?"

"Resting," he said simply, his voice breaking.

The king smiled at the chief and his wife before turning and exposing Xavier to the guards who were frantically searching for him. "Would you please stop messing about and finish this exercise? I realize this is not much of a challenge, but I'll soon fix that."

Xavier rose and regarded his father. "What does that mean?"

"It means you need a challenge to help you grow into your role. It means you need an added complication."

The guards had spotted him and rushed towards them to attack. Xavier looked at them irritably before flicking his finger and sending the men to the ground. Not a single one got up off the ground, but they were not unconscious. Their miserable moans floated in the air toward them.

Xavier focused on his father. "What kind of complication?"

"We'll discuss it tonight," his father responded and looked at his downed men. "Son, release them. You are causing them undue pain."

Xavier released his empowerment and the men slowly got to their feet.

"That was amazing!" Chief Jackson announced, ogling the prince and king. "What did you do to them?"

"I just increased gravitational pull," Xavier answered with an innocent smile.

"Yes, the boy is a very powerful member of our society. Unfortunately, he tends to let it go to his head and make careless decisions. Case in point, a joyride with his girlfriend in his father's stolen car."

While the chief snickered and winked at his wife, Xavier protested with a whine.

"Geesh, Dad, I said I was sorry a billion times! I'm grounded for a month and have community service for half a year. What else do you want from me?"

Jeremiah delivered a stinging smack to Xavier's backside as he answered, "Think through your ideas before acting! That is what I want from you!"

"I did. I just didn't count on the Razorbill Cove Police showing up," Xavier answered, rubbing his backside and giving his father a huge, mischievous grin.

Chief Jackson's chuckling exploded into a deep, belly-rumbling laugh. "Oh, dear God in heaven. You've met your match, Jeremiah. The boy is the spitting image of you!"

Still laughing, the chief draped an arm over Xavier's shoulder and led him out of the coliseum. "Did your dad ever tell you how we met?"

Giving his father a triumphant grin over his shoulder, Xavier answered, "No sir! He hasn't, but I'd love to hear all about it."

Loren moved into step with the king. "Oh, boy! I doubt

that story will help teach Xavier to stay out of trouble."

"My thoughts exactly, but it doesn't look like I have a choice in the matter," the king grumbled as they followed a now giggling Xavier and chuckling chief of police.

Chapter 21

A royal guard walked by the palace gates toward the small sentry house at the right of the entrance. Laughter filtered through the night air from the additional palace security strategically placed near the entrance. A group of men, clad in black, hid in the shadows outside the palace gate watching for an opening to slip inside and infiltrate the castle. A young guard exited the sentry house to make his rounds around the palace walls.

After an abrupt nod from their commander, two young dark soldiers immediately set off after the young guard, quickly killing him and dragging his body into the dark shadows behind shrubbery. The remaining men quickly slipped inside the palace walls, keeping to the shadows and darting toward the palace.

Loren exited his residence, straightening his cloak and glancing up the royal staircase at Henrick on duty.

"All quiet?" he asked his subordinate and friend.

"As a mouse," Henrick responded. "Or as quiet as you get when Lucy lays down the law and scares you."

"Ha! I'm not afraid of my wife! I just didn't have anything more to say on the matter."

Henrick's bellowing laugh echoed around the atrium as Loren strolled down the hall to exit the palace and check with all the guards on duty. Since the recent infiltrations, it was necessary that he and Ephraim monitor all forces around the palace to ensure the safety of the royal family.

Xavier jerked upright in bed, panting and sweating. He shakily wiped his brow as he swung his legs over the side of the bed. The feelings of terror and danger lingered, but the dream itself remained elusive. Whatever it had been, Xavier knew it had been much more than a dream. Why couldn't he remember it? He stood, stumbled to the bathroom and splashed cool water on his face. Staring at his reflection, he concluded he wouldn't be able to return to sleep until he assured himself all was quiet in the kingdom and that his people were in no danger. Without further thought, he quickly returned to his bedroom and pulled on jeans and a hoodie.

He quietly crept down the steps toward the door. Knowing Henrick was on duty, maybe he could get reports from the guard stations and determine if there were any threats. However, when his hand clutched the doorknob, part of his dream slammed into his memory. He saw a dark soldier attack an unsuspecting Loren and standing over his body as he took his last breath.

Throwing open the door, Xavier hurried out of the residency.

"Prince Wells? What in the bloody hell are you doing up at this hour?"

"Henrick! Is Loren on duty tonight?"

"Xavier, I must insist that you go back inside..."

"Is Loren on duty!" he shouted, grabbing the lieutenant by the robe.

Henrick's brows rose and he stammered. "Y... yes, he just left to do his rounds and check in with each security point in the kingdom."

"Shit!" Xavier exclaimed as he raced down the steps.

"Wake my father! Something is about to happen!" he shouted over his shoulder as he ran down the stairs toward the palace entrance.

When he reached the door, he paused and slowly cracked open the door. Peering out, he saw Loren a few feet away talking to a guard on duty by the door.

"What do you mean you're alone? Who's supposed to be on duty here with you? It's mandatory that three guards be on guard at the palace entrance!" Loren spat.

A shadow to Loren's right moved slowly toward him. Surely the guard could see him! But then why wasn't he alerting the general? Suddenly, it made sense. The guard was a traitor! The dark soldier was ten feet, eight feet, six feet from Loren!

Xavier slammed open the door with a bang. Then with an ease he no longer found shocking, he blasted the dark soldier with a force that sent him twenty feet into the air before he dropped to the ground with a crack. The dark soldier was most certainly dead. Without hesitation, Xavier marched toward the traitor, and with one quick movement of his hand, slammed the man to the ground at Loren's feet.

"What the hell?" Loren gasped, his eyes darting from the royal guard to the dead soldier in the middle of the drive before resting on Xavier. "Xavier?"

"He's a traitor. He was distracting you so the dark soldier could kill you!"

The door behind them slammed open a second time, and the king stood in the doorway, his eyes quickly assessing the situation before he hurried toward his son.

"Loren, secure the prisoner and lock him up until we can interrogate him. I'm ordering all guards to do a sweep of the area. I doubt there's a sole invader." Jeremiah rubbed Xavier's head affectionately. "Come, son. You need to get to safety."

"No, Dad. You're right. There are more dark soldiers, but I'm not going to run and hide while our people are in danger! I will help with the sweep of the area."

"Son..."

"Dad! You can't keep me from this war. You can't protect me! It's coming. I can feel it. It's coming soon! This is what my training has been for! It's my destiny!"

"You're not ready..."

"Who is ever ready for war? Ready or not, it's happening and I cannot hide. I must do this. You know what I say is true!"

The king stared down at his young son, just shy of fifteen. The prophecy was such an unfair burden for the boy to bear, but he was right. He couldn't be protected from it. He was the only protection the world had against the darkness that was rising.

"Okay, son. We'll do the sweep together."

Xavier gave his father a quick nod. If he was with his father, he could protect him from unforeseen attacks. He could prevent his death. He had to prevent it!

The king motioned for him to follow, and father and son began to sweep the perimeter of the palace. Slowly, they made their way around the palace to the side lawn. There were very few places for soldiers to hide here, as there were no obstructions or bushes. However, the back garden was a different story. The king stopped short of the row of pines that served as a privacy fence for the back garden.

"Okay. Listen, I will go in first..."

"No," Xavier hissed. "We go together. We watch each other's backs."

"Xavier..."

"Dad, we're wasting time," he whispered irritably and slipped into the pines.

His father followed behind him, pivoting often to make

sure they weren't being followed. Just as Xavier started to step from the pine foliage, a thought slammed into him and sent him staggering backward into his father.

"Wait!" he warned his father wordlessly. *"There are half a dozen dark soldiers lying in wait in the garden."*

"Yes, I hear them now. Two are behind the raised garden wall, one behind the dogwood, and the other three are crouched on the lawn at the west and south parts of the garden," his father responded quickly. *"I will race out first and take cover behind the garden wall. My presence will create a diversion. The soldiers will be too busy trying to kill me to pay you any attention. Now, I want you to slide to the west along the pines using the foliage as cover. When you hear the fighting begin, you can pick off the men at the west part of the garden. Once that area is secure, you can emerge and take cover behind the garden wall at that end. If the men are still unaware of you, you can pick off more. And, son. Kill them. Do not try to keep them alive for information. Your life is too valuable to risk it. Understand?"*

"Yes, sir."

"Okay, go now. Quiet as a mouse."

Xavier crept quietly west, parallel to the garden just beyond the foliage. One soldier was very close. He could hear his pants and anxious thoughts. It seemed the man didn't agree with his commander to remain at the palace in the hopes of completing their mission of killing the king. Any misgivings Xavier may have had about killing these men evaporated the moment he learned the men's sole purpose.

Shaking with anger and fear, Xavier extended his hand toward the heavy breather, closed his eyes and twisted. The unmistakable cracking sound and a soft thud that followed sent relief and satisfaction through Xavier, and he opened his eyes to see a still, dark heap on the ground in front of him. When his father emerged from the pines, this man would have been the first to see him. His proximity was too close for comfort to ensure success with their plan. With a shudder and pushing away the fact that he had killed yet another man, Xavier continued to creep along the pines until he was about six feet from the fifteen-foot palace wall, where he stopped and waited.

"Ready?"

"Yes, sir. I'm in position."

The king rushed into the garden, and immediately the dark soldiers shouted out urgently.

"To the right!"

"Attack, men!"

"It's the king!"

"Kill him, kill him!"

Flashes of electro forces and other powers erupted in the night around him. Whistles, cracks, and pops filled the air, but Xavier stayed the course of the plan. He continued to monitor his father's thoughts and status. Plan or not, if any of the dark men's empowerments hit their mark, he would attack immediately.

"Move forward, men! We've got him pinned down by the north wall."

Still, Xavier waited.

"Give it one more minute, son. They're moving very slowly. You'd think they were afraid of me or something," his father jested with a silent chuckle that had Xavier smiling. *"Okay. In three, two, one. Now!"*

Xavier scrambled from behind the shrubbery just as his father stood from his hiding point. Xavier felt the hair on the back of his neck stand on end as the air pressure around them converged toward the king. Then, with one sweep of his hand, two thirds of the dark soldiers were thrown backwards twenty feet, several knocked unconscious. Xavier watched in awe as his father knelt, spun on his knee and took out another soldier. The unmistakable crack made it clear that the solider wouldn't be getting up, ever.

A stinging jolt jerked the prince from his state of awe, and he spun to find a man advancing on him confidently. He saw him only as a boy—the poor fool.

Xavier smiled sweetly at the man before hitting him with a force so potent the man dropped like a stone with an expression of shock on his face. Xavier turned away from the dead man and saw his father take down the last of the soldiers by slamming the man to the ground so violently that his skull burst like a grape. With a grimace, Xavier looked away from the lifeless body and up at his father.

The king scanned the garden, and once satisfied that the threat had passed, he turned toward Xavier and frowned.

"You're bleeding," he commented and approached him to examine the wound.

"Yeah. I got too caught up in watching you kick butt, and I got zapped a little."

The king tore Xavier's hoodie at the shoulder to expose the wound. "This needs to be cleaned, and then it can be healed. Come. Let's get back to the palace entrance."

When father and son made their way back to the front of the palace, it was alive with activity.

"Sergeant Michaels, what's the report from the exterior perimeter?" Loren barked.

"All clear, sir. It appears there was just the one intruder, sir."

"I wouldn't be so confident of that, Sergeant," King Wells announced briskly before addressing Loren. "Loren, send a group to the rear garden of the palace. There are a dozen soldiers there. No survivors. Then meet me in the residence. I'm getting Xavier out of this commotion."

"Yes, Sire," Loren nodded, before turning to give the order.

"Come on, son. It's over for now. Let's get inside," Jeremiah said softly, placing a hand on his shoulder and guiding him into the palace and up into the residence.

Lana greeted the pair at the door.

"Jeremy? What's going on? The door guard said there was an intruder."

"All is well now, sweetheart," he answered, hugging his wife and kissing her tenderly. "Do you think you could fix us some coffee and Xavier some hot chocolate? Loren and Ephraim will be here soon for debriefing."

"Of course. It won't take but a couple of minutes," she answered with a small smile and hurried into the kitchen, leaving father and son alone.

"Are you all right?"

Xavier nodded.

"Xavier, it's okay to feel... upset about... I know seeing men die can be shocking regardless of the circumstances."

"I've seen men die before, Dad," he whispered, unable to keep his voice from cracking.

Tears filled the king's eyes just before he grabbed his son by the nape of the neck and hauled him against him in a tight hug.

Xavier couldn't stop the tears then. They flowed silently down his cheeks, and he closed his eyes, trying to fight the unwanted feelings of guilt and despair.

"It's not something a father would ever want for his son. I wish to God I could take this burden from you. It kills me that I can't," the king muttered.

His father's arms felt warm, safe. Xavier wished his father could take away the burden of his destiny, and they could just be... a family—a normal family. Well, as normal as they could be considering they possessed powers.

Chapter 22

The next morning, Xavier walked with Robbie to school. "You're quiet. Are you okay?"

Xavier nodded. No, he wasn't okay, but what could Robbie do about the nightmares? What could she do to help him come to terms with what he was forced to do because he was somehow prophesized to be a great savior? Nothing. There was absolutely nothing she or his father could do to lessen the burden. His father had tried to talk him into sleeping in his room, but it felt awkward sleeping in the bed with Lana there. Plus, wasn't he getting too big for that kind of thing?

"Are you sure?"

"Yeah. I'm okay. It was just a really long night."

"I heard. Mom was talking about it with Aunt Rebecca on the phone. If you hadn't come along when you did, Loren would have been killed. I'm really proud of you, Xavier," she told him, taking his hand and squeezing it.

Xavier gave her a small smile. "Thanks."

Robbie pulled him to a stop and smiled broadly up at him. "No, I mean it. I'm very proud to be your girlfriend. You are a great empowered, but I'm proud of you because you use your abilities to help others when some people would use them to help themselves."

As Xavier pondered her words, suddenly she was kissing

him. His heart lurched in his chest as her mouth moved against his. He dropped his books to the ground and grabbed her like she was a lifeline. Wrapping his arms around her, he took control of the kiss and kissed her back fiercely. They were too wrapped up in each other to hear the car honk behind them, and it wasn't until the driver laid on the horn that the pair jerked apart. Blushing and embarrassed, Xavier scrambled to pick up his books and scurry to the side of the road. The driver slowly pulled past, grinning and shaking his head.

"Come on. We better get to school, or we'll be late," he muttered, grabbing Robbie's hand and pulling her along.

The school morning went on as normal, but Xavier felt disconnected. One thought kept coming to mind. What would his life be like once the war was over? Would his father still be alive? Who else would die in this senseless war?

"Earth to Xavier!" Court announced, tapping him smartly on the head.

"Ouch! What?" he snapped, rubbing the top of his head.

"It's lunchtime, mate! Come on," Court responded.

With a sigh, Xavier gathered his books and followed his best friend out of the classroom and into the crowded hall when suddenly a loud pulsating alarm blared throughout the school. There was a brief moment of inaction from the students as they looked around at each other in confusion. Then Michael Spencer's voice came over the intercom system.

"All students report directly to the auditorium, immediately. This is not a drill!"

No sooner had the announcement been made than the crowded hallway erupted into a panic. Students pushed and shoved their way toward the auditorium.

"What's wrong with everyone? Why are they panicking?"

Xavier asked Court as a boy jostled him into his friend as he hurried by.

"They're afraid. After the attack on the palace last night, most kids are saying their parents reckon it's just a matter of time before another all-out invasion."

They were probably right, but panicking didn't make it better. It only made it worse.

"Ouch! Hey!" Daniel shouted when a larger boy shoved his way past and knocked the smaller boy to the ground. With this level of panic, Daniel was in danger of getting trampled. Xavier immediately shot his hand toward the smaller boy just as he cried out again as someone in the crowd stepped on him. Xavier lifted him into the air above the other students. Daniel's shocked face would have been comical if the situation hadn't been so serious.

"Hey! Everybody, stop it!" Xavier shouted, but no one was listening to him. He had to get their attention before someone got seriously hurt! He took a deep breath and shouted out, "Stop it, now!"

This time his voice came out as though he was speaking through a megaphone. The crowded hallway instantly stilled and quieted. "Stop acting like a panicked mob! No matter what's happening, behaving like this will only help the enemy! So everyone take a deep breath, *walk* to the auditorium and watch out for the smaller students before someone gets hurt!"

Slowly the students began to move again, silently and slowly toward the auditorium. Xavier lowered Daniel to the floor, and the small boy nodded his thanks before following the crowd.

"Nicely done, mate," Court muttered.

"Thanks. You better get going. I need to go and find my father and see if I can help."

"Wait! Xavier, Spencer said to report to the auditorium."

"I know, but if there's an invasion, I need to help. You *know* I have to go, Court!"

Court gave his friend a dubious look before responding. "Well, okay, but at least find out what's going on from Spencer before you leave. Right now, you don't even know what's going on or where to go!"

He had a good point. "Okay. You're right. Let's go. There's no time to waste."

As they entered the auditorium, Spencer was on the stage having a heated conversation with Sir Blaire. Xavier moved toward the men, working his way through the crowded room. Just as he reached the stage stairs, Spencer's voice came over the speakers.

"Quickly find a seat and settle down so you can hear my directions."

As the students quickly found their seats and grew quiet, Xavier hurried onto the stage and approached his uncle.

"Prince Wells, you need to take a seat," he stated firmly, his voice echoing around the auditorium.

"No, sir," he responded. "You need to tell me what's going on."

"I will, sire. I will tell everyone once you're seated."

Xavier glanced at the other students seated in the auditorium watching their exchange in rapt silence. "Tell us now," he responded, looking back at his uncle.

Spencer glanced briefly to the children and back to Xavier. He gave him a slight nod before turning and facing the students.

"The Dark Army has been detected less than a mile from the kingdom, and they are heading this way. There's no need to question their intentions. They seek to attack Warwood. The guard and other citizens are preparing to defend our city now. They will fight better if they are sure their children are safe. Therefore, every child under the age of sixteen will follow the teachers to the right of the stage through the escape passages and out of the kingdom to safety until the danger has past. Students sixteen and older who wish to fight may do so. You will follow Sir Blaire to the palace walls. You will work with the royal guard to protect the palace as the last line of defense."

Xavier looked at his uncle with disbelief. He intended to send him to safety while war raged within the kingdom. Xavier turned on his heel and started for the door.

"Xavier Wells!" his voiced boomed loudly. "Stop right there, young man! You are not sixteen or older! You're going with the younger students to safety."

Xavier spun and gave his uncle a hard look. "I can't do that, Uncle. You *know* I can't! I need to find my father and help defend my kingdom."

Red rushed up his uncle's neck and spread over his face. "You will do as you are told, boy!" he shouted, stomping toward him and grabbing him by the arms.

"No!" Xavier shouted back before getting control of his emotions and continuing more calmly, "I'm sorry, Uncle. I'm not trying to be disrespectful, but I *have* to go! You know it's... it's my destiny."

Stubbornness filled his uncle's eyes. "Your destiny isn't to go to battle at fourteen!"

He was nearly fifteen, but that wasn't the point, so Xavier let the comment slide. "Uncle, my age doesn't matter. All that matters is that I must go. Please, you must let me go!" he pleaded, trying to pull his arms free, but the man's grip was like a vice.

"I will not allow you to go and get yourself killed!" he shouted, fear spiking his voice.

"I have to go!" Xavier shouted. "You *know* I do. Our world will fall if I don't. My father will d... It's my destiny!"

"No, it's not! You're only a boy! Those are trained killers

preparing to attack! If you're killed, your destiny is moot! Now, you will come with me even if I have to carry you kicking and screaming!" Michael Spencer growled, lifting him into a bear hug and carrying him across the stage. "Mr. Underwood, organize the other children."

"NO! Uncle Mike! You've got to let me go!" Xavier struggled in vain against Spencer's clutches. There was no way he could get free through physical means. Closing his eyes so he could concentrate on keeping the ability under control and restrain it from surging, he summoned his electro force so that it radiated from his body and in turn gave his uncle a sharp electric shock. Michael dropped him and shouted a string of curses before glaring down at the prince.

"If I must, I will knock you unconscious, but one way or another, you are coming with me!"

"Uncle Mike, please just listen to me..."

"No, you listen to me, young man..."

"I'm the *Chosen*!" Xavier shouted in desperation and the entire auditorium stilled.

Quickly glancing around at the shocked faces of those around him, Xavier cleared his throat and repeated more calmly. "You know that I'm the Chosen, Uncle. You can't hide me away from this! If I don't fight, if I don't fulfill my destiny, there's no place on earth I can hide from the darkness that will infect every inch of the globe. I can't let the Dark King win."

The students erupted in low murmurs, but Xavier's eyes never left his uncle's.

"I have to fight!" he said barely above a whisper. "I'm the only one who can stop him! I must fight Fox. If I don't fight, we'll lose, and we'll lose a hell of a lot more than this kingdom. Please! Let me go! Please."

As Spencer looked down at him in anguish, Sir Blaire

uttered the words that everyone in the auditorium thought. "You... you're the... *Chosen*?"

Xavier looked at the shocked face of his anima-lingua instructor and nodded. "Yes, I am." He turned back to his uncle. "I've got to go," he begged. "Please, Mike. I *have* to. Follow your orders and save the rest of the kids, but you've got to let me go."

Spencer and Xavier stood staring at one another. Finally, Spencer broke the silence that had spread throughout the auditorium.

"For God's sake be careful, Xavier! Your father will not survive if something were to happen to you."

With a nod, Xavier ran off the stage and into the crowd of children, who parted like the red sea, many bowing to him. Others whispered words of encouragement.

"Xavier! Xavier, wait!" Robbie's desperate voice stopped him in his tracks. He turned just as Robbie threw herself into his arms. He caught her and squeezed her tight, suddenly very afraid of what he had to do, but he could do it, he would do it, if only to keep her safe.

"Robbie, you've got to go with them. I can't..." his voice broke, and he swallowed the lump in his throat. "I can't do what I've got to do if I have to worry about you. You... you are my weakness, and my feelings for you are too strong to hide. Fox would use you against me."

Robbie pulled away to look at him, tears streaming down her cheeks. "I... I know. I'll go with them. You just have to promise me that you'll come and get me when this is all done."

"Robbie..."

"Promise me. Promise me you'll be here after the smoke clears!"

He stared down at the tear-soaked face of the girl he loved. He couldn't deny her of this comfort. He smiled down at her and kissed her firmly as the crowd of children around them looked on in eerie silence. Finally, he looked down at her and grinned broadly. "If I can get a kiss like that when I see you again, I'd promise you anything!"

Robbie burst into laughter, and the couple clung to each other desperately.

"I have to go now," he whispered. "I love you!"

Xavier kissed her quickly on the lips and turned to leave.

"Hey, X!" Beck's voice called, and he turned to look at all his friends crowding in behind Robbie. "Kick some ass for us, okay?"

Xavier's smile couldn't be denied as the auditorium of children erupted into cheers. With a nod, he raced from the auditorium and out of the academy, where he immediately teleported away to find his father.

Chapter 23

Xavier appeared at the teleport location near the palace on a run. Dozens of Warwood guards were standing at attention as the king addressed the group from the palace steps with Loren at his side.

"The time is now, men! We've been preparing for this attack for months! We are ready! There will be no retreat this time! We are the last line between freedom and oppression for all mankind! We cannot fail! We cannot give in! We cannot surrender! This is the moment to show what we're made of: are we lesser men or greater men? This is war for the light and goodness in the world! We will not be defeated for we are on the side of righteousness. We must fight through this night of hell, so that the morning will be a glorious day in the light! We will not go gently into the dark! Rage against the dark so that light may prevail! The time is now, my brethren! Who will fight with wild abandon for our kingdom?"

The soldiers let out a loud chorus, "I, my king!"

"Who will stand in the way of evil and fight?"

Again the crowd shouted, louder this time, "I, my king!"

"Who will fight by my side to protect what is right and honorable?"

"I, my king," they shouted even louder.

"The time is now, brothers! War is here! Today we make

war, so that tomorrow we will have everlasting peace!"

The crowd of guards erupted in cheers and began to clang their sword sheaths against the stone drive.

"Dad!" Xavier blurted, shuffling through the crowded drive towards his father.

"Let the prince through!" his father barked savagely and the men parted. The king clapped Xavier affectionately on the shoulder before addressing the guard again.

"Gentlemen! There's no need to fear. As I said, we fight so that light will prevail! A piece of that light is among us! He is indeed the most powerful empowered I've ever known. He's worked tirelessly to prepare himself to tip the balance of justice. We will succeed, for the Chosen is among us!"

The men suddenly burst into murmurs and feverous whispers, many reaching Xavier's ears.

"The Chosen exists!"

"Who is he?"

"The prince! It's the prince! Have you not seen that boy fight? He took out a dozen royal guard members on his own!"

"You're kidding! But how? He's just a boy!"

"The king has been training him since he went to the mountain nine months ago. The boy is wickedly fast with his empowerments. They say he can kill a man without ever touching him!"

"Gentlemen! Please! I will lay to rest the rumors of the Chosen's identity now." After a quick nod to Loren, the men suddenly hoisted Xavier into the air and onto their shoulders so that he could easily be seen by the guard. "May I present to you, Prince Xavier Wells V, your future king and the Chosen One."

The guards stared up at Xavier in awe, and Xavier could feel the heat of embarrassment rush up his neck and over his face.

Then a group of men to the left began to chant his name. Xavier stared at the men in shock. It was one thing for his friends to chant his name and cheer him on, but members of the guard? He recognized several of the men as guardsmen who had assisted him in his combat training. The guard who had hit him in the privates led the chant, grinning broadly. It wasn't long before the entire guard joined in. He didn't know what to say or do, but pride and humility swelled up inside him. He waved to the men, who simply burst into cheers and shouts of encouragement!

Slowly, Loren and the king lowered him to his feet. Jeremiah grinned down at him before rubbing his head affectionately. Then he turned to the cheering men.

"Okay, men! It's time! It's time to kick some ass! Report to your stations. Dismissed!"

The soldiers gave a final shout, "Yes, my king!" before racing off in formation out of the palace gates, leaving a fraction of the group behind to guard the palace.

"Come, Xavier. I had Ephraim organize our combat gear in the atrium. Let's suit up," his father announced and led him into the palace.

Ephraim was standing in the atrium waiting on them, already fully clothed in combat gear.

"Young, sire," he greeted with a quick nod before turning to the king. "Sire, the blacksmith was able to complete the armor for the boy based on his school uniform measurements. It should fit like a glove."

Jeremiah gave him a satisfied smile as he looked down at the shiny metal armor. "It will do perfectly. What do you think, son?"

Xavier stepped forward and looked at the breastplate and arm and leg shields. It was beautiful! Next to the armor lay a beautiful sword with his initial engraved in the hilt. Kneeling, he ran his hand along the blade.

"Careful, the edge is razor sharp!" his father warned.

Xavier looked up at the men. "It's fantastic!"

The three men smiled down at him. "Well suit up, gentlemen," Ephraim suggested.

Within minutes, they were adorned with shiny, polished armor.

"Okay, Xavier, I must ask you to stay behind us when we attack the Dark Army…"

"No, Dad! I won't. I want to fight by your side. I'm not hiding behind you like a little boy!"

"Xavier, please. We don't have time for this! You will not be hiding, son. You'll be in the thick of battle! I'm asking you to stay behind us because we have worked together in battle before. We have trained together and have fighting method and rhythm. Please, son, let us initiate the battle."

Xavier looked from man to man before sighing. "Okay. I get it. I don't want to throw a monkey wrench in your attack plan. I'll stay behind you, but if one of you is hit, I'm going in!"

"Deal," the men answered together.

"Let's just hope they don't mess with this pretty face," Loren teased, gesturing at the king's face.

Jeremiah frowned. "Me? I'm not pretty!" he responded indignant.

Both Loren and Xavier snorted, "Yeah, you are."

Jeremiah looked at Ephraim.

"Don't look at me to dispel the claim, sire. It's no secret that most women in the kingdom have their eyes on you. I doubt it was just about the money."

"You're kidding me!"

"No, Dad. My first few days here I was attacked by a group of women hoping to get a glimpse of you."

"No, they attacked you because you're their prince and they were excited to see you."

"No, Dad," Xavier laughed, shaking his head. "They were spying on the castle with binoculars, hoping to see you! They were stalking you!"

The king's face went crimson as the group attempted a not so subtle snicker. The king huffed indignantly before barking, "Let's go." Then he spun and led them out of the palace.

As they exited, a loud blast from the kingdom's gatehouse shook the ground.

"Damn it! We're too late!" Loren hissed.

"Let's go!" the king announced, grabbing Loren and teleporting away.

"Give them a second, laddie," Ephraim responded. "We should teleport together. Do you want to do the honors or shall I?"

"I will," Xavier answered, grabbing hold of the general and teleporting them to Center Square.

His father and Loren were already racing toward the swarm of dark soldiers fighting their way through the guards, who fought to keep the invading army at bay.

"Ephraim! Now!" Jeremiah shouted over his shoulder.

"Watch your back, boy, and stay behind us," Ephraim told Xavier before sprinting towards the men.

Xavier followed, or at least started to follow, but a scream to his left drew his attention to a small group of vendors huddled in fear and surrounded by dark soldiers. How they had gotten past the line of battle Xavier didn't know, but the merchants didn't stand a chance. Without a second thought, he raced toward the soldiers closing in, menacingly, on the civilians.

"Mercy!" cried an old woman, holding up a hand in defense of the large man towering over her.

He drew back his sword with a smirk. "There is no mercy in war!"

He wasn't going to make it in time, and he couldn't use an empowerment, as the group of innocents was too close. He might strike one of them! He did the only thing he could do.

"Hey, numb nuts! Why don't you pick on someone your own size?" he shouted, never breaking stride to reach them.

The furious soldier turned toward him, ready to fight, but when his eyes fell on Xavier, he saw only a boy, and he grinned cheekily. "It would take three of you to be my size, *boy*."

Xavier stopped within feet of the dark soldier. A subordinate soldier took a step toward Xavier but stopped when the large man held up his hand.

"Yeah, I guess it would," Xavier commented, looking the man over. "Maybe you should eat less pork rinds, dude. You're starting to resemble a rhino."

The soldier straightened with anger, his hands clenching at his sides. Xavier studied the man closely, waiting for the move he knew was coming. The moment the man's hand twitched into action, Xavier threw a shield around the civilians before sweeping his hand in a wide arc towards the group of soldiers, who didn't have the common sense not to huddle together like a herd of cattle.

An electro force buzzed past Xavier's face, barely missing him, just as the soldiers flew into the kingdom's security wall. The group fell to the ground in a tangled heap of moaning injured and silent dead. Xavier slowly approached the large man, who whimpered in pain. The blast of the force had hit him with such intensity that it had torn his left arm completely off. He would bleed out in minutes.

"I'm the Chosen, asshole, and you're dead!" he hissed before turning his back on the man and approaching the huddling people. "You need to get to safety!"

"How?" a frail-looking woman questioned, motioning to

the commotion around them. The Dark Army had completely infiltrated the kingdom and dark soldiers and guardsmen were fighting viciously around them. There was no way the group would make it through to safety. He looked back at the dozen or so civilians. He would have to teleport them out of here. But doing so would take too much time, time that he didn't have. Sighing, an outrageous idea came to mind. It was dangerous, but he really didn't have much of a choice. He could leave the group to fend for themselves or take them one at a time, essentially taking him out of the battle. With his mind made up, he stepped toward the group in urgency.

"Look, I'll get you to safety, but you have to get close to one another, like a group hug. I can teleport you if everyone is close and touching each other."

"What? You can do that?" an older man asked, amazement evident on his face.

Feeling unsure, but not wanting to portray that to the frightened people, Xavier smiled sweetly. "Of course, sir. I'm the Chosen. I'm a very strong empowered."

The group's frightened looks disappeared and were replaced with hope and awe.

"You? Our future king is... you're the Chosen?" someone from the group blurted.

"Yes, I am. Now, please! I must help my father fight and defeat the Dark Army. We have no time to waste, so gather close!"

The group quickly formed a group hug, and Xavier inspected them to make sure they were closely assembled before placing his hands on the man's shoulders in front of him. He closed his eyes in concentration. If he could teleport an entire car, surely he would be able to do this. Suddenly, he felt the familiar pull, and someone in the group gasped aloud in surprised. Seconds later, they stood at the palace entrance. Rows of guards stood at attention in front of the gated entrance, and at their sudden appearance, the first row lunged toward them.

"No! Stop!" Xavier ordered firmly, stepping toward the men with his hands up in surrender.

"Prince Wells?" a guard questioned in surprise. "Wh… What…"

Shaking off the guard's confused stuttering, Xavier pointed to the huddled group of civilians behind him. "Get them to safety within the palace walls. The Dark Army has invaded! Be at the ready!"

Immediately, several guards jumped into action, ushering the group within the palace walls. The old man who had spoken to Xavier earlier stopped in front of him.

"Thank you, young sire. Be safe, be quick, be victorious!"

"Thank you, sir. I will." Then Xavier teleported back to the battlefield.

The war was at full force when Xavier returned. The Dark Army and the royal guard were at close quarters, many engaged in hand-to-hand combat. His father's white hair stood out, and he found him among Loren and Ephraim engaged in a vicious fight. Xavier hoped that the blood smeared on their bodies was not their own. If he had just gotten here earlier, before the clash of the armies, he might have been able to stop the war before it ever begun. There was no sense in wishing he could turn back time, as he didn't have that ability. He must deal with the present and help in any way he could.

He raced toward the battle and was immediately engaged in a fight for his life. A smaller man with a quick hand hit him with an electro force that knocked him off his feet. Xavier hit the ground, and his breath was forced from his lungs. Gasping for air, he looked up at the dark soldier's sneering face.

"Well, looky here! Isn't it the great Prince Wells, the *Chosen One,*" he jeered. "Too bad you're the best that Warwood has to offer because you'll be dead in seconds."

"I wouldn't be so sure!" Xavier managed to wheeze out, but the soldier didn't have the common sense to look concerned.

Before the man could complete his next force, Xavier jutted his hand out toward the man and gave a slight twist. The man's shocked face was quickly replaced with one void of life as he dropped to the ground where he stood.

Dusting himself off, Xavier stood and surveyed the fighting around him. Henrick stood feet from him in battle, holding his own, but the young private behind him was not. The dark soldier swept out his leg, knocking the young man to the ground before raising his sword to deliver a mortal blow. Xavier lunged at the soldier and tackled him to the ground. Although he had the element of surprise on his side, he knew he needed to untangle himself from the soldier and get clear to draw his sword if he were to have any chance of surviving. Xavier quickly rolled to the left and sprang to his feet, drawing his sword. The young guard on the ground behind him was injured and panting heavily. He needed a healer and fast! However, the dark soldier wasn't about to let him call timeout to get the man help.

The soldier swung a wide, powerful arc with his sword, and Xavier braced himself for the vibrating clang that would come. Using the impact to create a quick spin, Xavier swung around and struck the dark man in the abdomen, slicing deeply into his gut. As the man cowered in pain, Xavier took advantage of the opportunity to break the man's neck, and he dropped to the ground with a thud. Then he scrambled to the injured guard, who wheezed and gasped for breath but was having a hard time succeeding.

"It's okay. Just relax! I can help you," he told the young

man, kneeling next to him and surveying the injury.

It was a gut wound, painful and surely a death sentence if not dealt with soon. Xavier placed his hands over the wound, applying slight pressure as he closed his eyes to concentrate on the task at hand. Within seconds, he and the guard were ignited in a bright, white light as the rejuvenation power ran its course. Soon the labored breathing lessened and the light evaporated. Xavier opened his eyes and found the young guard struggling to sit up.

"How... how..." he stammered. "You can... can heal? How many powers do you have, sire?"

"I dunno," Xavier shrugged. "I've never counted." He stood and helped the young man to his feet.

"Are you serious?"

Xavier simply shrugged at the man and picked up his sword before asking, "Have you seen my father?"

"He was fighting at the gatehouse earlier. I don't see him now. I'm not sure."

"Okay, thanks," Xavier answered and ran into the chaos of battle near the gatehouse.

As he approached the gatehouse, he saw no sign of his father. Outside the gatehouse, hundreds of dark soldiers gathered around the destroyed entrance, pushing forward in attempts to enter the kingdom. If every last one of the soldiers made their way into the kingdom, the battle would only intensify and become more treacherous than it already was. The group was clustered closely together, unaware that such a formation was a grave mistake on their part. Theoretically, Xavier could take out the entire army outside the gatehouse. He only needed a good vantage point so that no Warwoodian would be on the receiving end of his empowerments.

Xavier looked around at the fighting men. He could get to the front of the fighting lines and expel his lethal empowerment, but that would take time they didn't have. Then he looked up. The kingdom wall was mostly intact on either side of the gatehouse. He could teleport there, but it was risky since he had no idea how wide the ledge was along the top of the wall. He could easily misjudge and tumble over the edge, falling to his death. Sighing, he wracked his brain on what empowerment would get him to the top of the wall. Then he remembered he could fly! He'd never really attempted to engage in his levitation power before, but if any moment required it, it was now. After a moment of focusing on Robbie and how his feelings for her had initiated his first experience with levitation, he elevated into the air above the battle. Concentrating on the wall and where he wished to go, he found himself floating toward the wall. Easier than he thought possible, he soon found himself standing on the wall. He looked back at the battle behind him only to find many, ally and enemy alike, staring up at him in awe. He turned towards the swarm of dark soldiers trying to force their way into the kingdom.

"Turn away and I will show mercy!" he shouted down at the men.

The majority of the dark soldiers looked up at him with a sneer. "Mercy? There will be no mercy when we get our hands on you!" one soldier shouted, his voice full of hatred.

"Please, listen! This is your last chance to walk away from this! End this attack on my kingdom, or I will be forced to kill you all!"

The men below him burst into vicious, scornful laughter. "Kill us? You are only a boy! It would take more than the likes of you to kill us!" the same man shouted, and the group laughed as they doubled their efforts to push forward into the kingdom.

"Stop! I'm warning you!" Xavier shouted, his voice breaking as he raised his hand shakily as he tried to focus on the outspoken dark soldier. Suddenly, a blinding, golden light erupted from his hands, and every soldier in its path was incinerated to ash.

He stared down at his hands before scanning the now empty, ash-filled field. What had happened? He hadn't meant to kill them all! He only wanted to show them what he was capable of so that they would run away. The stillness and eerie silence behind him had him turning his attention to inside the kingdom walls.

Enemy and ally alike stood stone still, staring at the ash remains of hundreds of the dark soldiers. Then panic erupted from the remaining dark soldiers, and they fought to retreat. After the last of the enemy was chased from the kingdom, guards and citizens alike erupted into cheers.

"Long live Prince Wells!" shouted a man from the crowd, and that was all it took for the crowd to begin to chant.

Blushing from the attention, Xavier waved down at the Warwoodians below him as he stepped off the edge of the wall and floated gracefully to the ground. The crowd stared in amazement. Once he touched ground, the crowd converged around him, slapping him on the back and thanking him. When Xavier recognized a sergeant from his training exercises, he grabbed the guard.

"Where's my father? He was here, but we got separated."

"A mayday call came from the palace. A group of dark soldiers made it to the palace gates. He, General Hardcastle, and General Jefferson all went back to the castle."

Xavier felt fear race down his spine. He had to find his father. He had to protect him... but how? The Prophet had never told him the plan to save the king's life. Xavier raced out of the crowd, feeling several thumps on his back as he went. Plan or not, he had to try something. Fear clawed at his gut as he cleared the crowd and teleported to the palace.

Chapter 24

The extraordinary ability that had erupted from him at the gatehouse had scared Xavier. He had little to no control over the ability, and he couldn't afford to conjure the rogue power again. Without the precision needed to wield it, using it again would be like playing Russian roulette.

Once at the palace, he didn't have time to contemplate the unwieldly power. The battle at the palace was fierce and bloody. Dark soldier and royal guard alike lay maimed, dead or dying on the horseshoe drive. Ephraim and Loren fought side by side near the palace's entrance. Xavier made his way toward the men, not even flinching as a dark soldier charged him. He simply extended his hand and made a twisting motion. The man stopped dead in his tracks as his neck snapped, and he dropped to the ground in a heap.

Withdrawing his sword, Xavier approached the dark soldier giving Ephraim a run for his money. The man was quite a talented swordsman, but Ephraim was better. If Xavier had time to watch the fight, he would have enjoyed watching Ephraim cut the man down, but as it was, he had to find his father—the king's life depended on it. As the dark soldier drew back to attack, Xavier lunged his sword forward, impaling the man, who dropped to his knees before dying with a look of astonishment on his face.

"Xavier, good to see you in one piece, boy," Ephraim

stated, wiping the sweat from his brow.

"Where's Dad?"

"Inside. A group of dark soldiers made their way into the palace before we got here. He and a small squad went in to clear the palace of the enemy."

Without a word, Xavier rushed past the generals and into the palace, racing down the hall, up the stairs and through the wide-open residency door. The receiving room was all but destroyed. Signs of battle were all around the room. The dead body of a dark soldier next to the couch was a dead giveaway. A shout from his father's bedroom drew Xavier's attention to the second floor. Gripping the hilt of his sword tighter, he climbed the stairs two at a time until he crept quietly but swiftly towards the king's bedroom. The door stood slightly ajar. Slowly he pushed it open. The room was disheveled, but there was no sign of his father. He could hear the unmistakable sounds of fighting from the patio. He hurried toward the patio door when he saw Lana on the floor, next to the bed. Xavier raced to her side. She was bleeding profusely from a gash on her head.

"Lana? Lana? Are you okay?" he whispered desperately, shaking her. She didn't respond. She needed medical attention! Closing his eyes and breathing evenly, Xavier began a medical scan of her body for internal bleeding or serious injury. Slowly he ran his elevated hand over her body, making mental notes of her injuries. She had a mild concussion. Her arm was broken, but her ribs were intact, which also meant her internal organs were uninjured. She was pregnant, and her legs were uninjured. Wait a second! Pregnant? Xavier moved his hand quickly back to his stepmother's abdomen. A fast, fluttering sound filled his head. Scanning deeper into Lana's abdomen, a baby's image appeared in his mind, and he smiled. He was going to be a big brother! Ceasing the scan, Xavier opened his eyes and looked down at Lana. He put his hand over her bleeding head and quickly healed it shut. A couple of seconds later, her eyes flickered open, and she looked at him with puzzled eyes.

"Xavier? What... where's your father? There are dark soldiers in the castle!" she whispered urgently.

"I know. I'll find Dad, but you gotta get out of the residence. Find Loren and Ephraim at the entrance. They'll make sure you stay safe."

"Come with me, honey."

"I can't. I have to find Dad. This is my responsibility. I have to fight. I have to end this once and for all. Please, Lana, go."

Lana slowly got to her feet and hugged and kissed him. "Be careful, sweetie!"

"I will. I promise!"

After a final squeeze, Lana left the room. Xavier turned and surveyed the room. Henrick lay motionless on the floor next to the mantle. He quickly went to the fallen guard and checked for a pulse. There was none. Pain and remorse stabbed into his chest just as his father's voice shouted from the patio, "Surrender or die!"

Xavier quickly crept to the double glass door and peered out onto the large patio that resembled a garden more than a patio. Twenty feet away, his father stood with his back to him, holding his sword blade to the throat of a fallen dark soldier.

"Never!" the man hissed in response.

"So be it," the king remarked, drawing his sword back slightly and striking the man swiftly. Without a sound, the man fell into a heap at the king's feet. Jeremiah turned, and as his eyes met Xavier's, Xavier felt a chill from the coldness he saw there. Then the king's eyes widened and the coldness was replaced with terror.

"Xavier!" he shouted, his hand raising as if to reach him.

Xavier felt the attack and instinctively dropped to the floor, rolled to his back, and lifted his sword just as a stunning jolt of metal meeting metal rocked up his arms. Danson's evil sneer mocked him.

"So glad you could finally join us, *Prince Wells*. We didn't want to start this party without you!"

"If you hurt a single hair on his body, you will pay," Jeremiah promised, marching toward the man.

Danson only smirked. "Hurt him? Of course not, sire. I wouldn't dream of it." Danson leaned toward Xavier, who struggled to hold the locked swords away from his body. "I plan to kill him."

"Good luck with that. Maybe I should close my eyes so you'll have at least half a chance at it. It wouldn't seem fair otherwise," Xavier chided.

Danson stared at him, and with an ornery grin and a slight nod, Xavier propelled the man out the patio door, barely missing his father, before crashing into a birdbath. The king turned to deal with the dark man, who struggled to his feet, while Xavier turned to face the tremendous energy he felt coming into his father's bedroom. Sure enough, the Sword of the Chosen led the way into the room like a glowing beacon. The Sword of the Chosen had the power to recognize the Chosen and glow in his presence, but it seemed Xavier had the ability to feel when the sword was near. Gripping his benign sword tightly at the sight of it, Xavier readied himself for his destiny. The time was now. It was finally here.

Relief and fear pulsed through his body as Fox LeMasters stepped into the room followed by two very large, burly bodyguards. The older boy stopped at the sight of him while Xavier sized up his enemy. He was a good four inches taller and probably outweighed him by fifty pounds. Fox was no longer a boy. He had grown much bigger since Xavier had last seen him nearly a year and a half ago.

"Well, if it isn't my father's killer. I can't tell you how much I have dreamed of this day."

Then Fox launched himself at Xavier. So much for small talk. If anything, Fox's eagerness to kill him could be used against him.

Xavier stood his ground and waited until the older teen propelled himself toward him in a very sloppy attack. He left his underside too exposed. Xavier stepped forward, knelt, and spun as Fox went flying past him—the Sword of the Chosen swiping the empty air above him. Then, before Fox's feet found solid purchase, Xavier expelled a force at the teen, sending him crashing face first into the king's mahogany bureau. There was a soft crack on impact before Fox fell into a heap on the floor.

Xavier stood, but Fox's bodyguards suddenly grabbed him, jerking him off his feet, and slamming him to the floor, flat on his back. The air was forced from his lungs at such force it left him gasping to regain his breath. One of the goons kicked him in the side, which really didn't help the trying to breathe thing. He didn't even have enough breath to whimper at the pain as a rib cracked in his side. The second goon kicked him in the head. Damn! Was the guy wearing steel-toed boots? Xavier's vision dimmed. The good news was it appeared he was finally regaining his breath as he inhaled a deep, wheezy breath before coughing violently.

"Don't! He's mine!" Fox's overly nasal, distorted voice announced.

Seconds later, Fox's smashed and bleeding face appeared over Xavier. "You will pay for that, boy. You will learn the meaning of dying slowly and painfully."

Fox grabbed him by the shirt, hauled him off the floor, and slammed him against the wall. Xavier whimpered as a slicing pain radiated out from his cracked rib. Fox punched him, and Xavier couldn't stop the scream that erupted from him. Fox sneered triumphantly.

"Why would they believe that *you* would ever stand a chance against me? You're just a little boy," he hissed in Xavier's face, spraying him with spittle as he spoke.

"You know?" Xavier wheezed out, "I might consider surrendering if you'd just stop giving me a shower with your spit." Okay, maybe teasing Fox wasn't a bright idea, but Xavier couldn't help it. The guy was so full of himself and condescending that he rivaled his father's arrogance.

The blow came swiftly and suddenly. Xavier fell to the floor, coughing as Fox stepped back and raised his sword. The hair on the back of Xavier's neck stood at attention as Fox swung the sword downward, but the blow never came. Xavier looked up at the older boy who stared wide-eyed at the sword hovering inches from his skull. Fox's arm shook violently as he strained to control the sword that had suddenly halted the attack of its own accord.

"Wh... What's going on?" he spat, his eyes darting from the sword to Xavier and back again.

"What do you think, numb nuts? It's *my* sword. It won't harm me!" he goaded. It was true. He didn't know how he knew it was true, but he did all the same. Climbing to his feet, Xavier grabbed the hilt of the Sword of the Chosen and waved a hand over Fox's firm grip. With that, he released the sword and staggered backwards.

Twirling the sword with finesse, Xavier had the sword in his hand, and it hummed its welcome. With a large grin, Xavier beckoned Fox with one hand while holding the sword at the ready in the other. Fox relieved one of his men of his sword and attacked. So predictable.

Xavier effortlessly parried the attack, stepped to the side, spun, and sent the older boy across the room with a kick in the butt. Furious, Fox turned and attacked again. This time the older boy controlled his momentum and the swords clashed against each other. Fox was stronger, but he didn't seem to possess much skill with the sword. Grinning, Xavier blocked every advance Fox made.

"What are you smiling at?" he spat, locking swords with Xavier and shoving him against the wall.

"I'm just wondering who the hell taught you to swordfight. You should really consider firing them. You suck, dude."

Using the wall as a point of propulsion, Xavier drove himself into Fox, and the pair flew across the room, taking out one of Fox's bodyguards. The man slammed his head on the corner of the mantle and fell to the floor, motionless.

Xavier positioned himself on top of Fox and smashed his fist into the boy's already shattered nose. The older boy squealed loudly and thrust an electro force into Xavier. The force was powerful and sent him flying across the room. As he crashed to the floor, his sword clattered out of his hand and skidded toward the patio doorway. Fox stood and stomped toward him. When he knelt and grabbed Xavier by a handful of hair, Xavier punched him again. Fox released him and Xavier got to his feet, standing at the ready. His training in hand-to-hand combat didn't seem so barbaric right now. Xavier beckoned Fox to him with a simple wave of his hand.

While hatred flared in his black eyes, Fox swung the first punch, but Xavier easily deflected the strike and delivered an upper cut to his exposed soft underbelly. The air was forced from Fox's lungs, and he staggered away from Xavier to safety. After a couple of deep breaths, Fox spun to face Xavier. The older teen studied him as he stood at the ready. Xavier stood taller at the uncertainty in Fox's eyes. A sudden cry distracted both boys to the fighting on the patio. His father had disarmed Danson and was quickly advancing on him.

"Help him!" Fox ordered the remaining bodyguard, and then, taking advantage of Xavier's distraction, he lunged at him. Fox's shoulder slammed into his ribs, and pain exploded throughout his body. If the initial contact weren't enough, Xavier was tackled hard to the floor, and Fox delivered several hard jabs to his ribcage before delivering a hard punch to the face.

Sounds of intense fighting from the patio reached Xavier's ears. His father was outnumbered! He had to get to him. He had to help him! Finding it hard to concentrate on gathering his powers while being beaten to a pulp, he struggled to escape the older boy's clutches. He kicked out at the boy, but it did little to dislodge him. He was just too big and heavy. His powers were all he had left to protect himself. He had to engage them somehow!

His father's sudden yelp was all the encouragement Xavier needed. Fear coursed through his blood, chilling him to the bone. Suddenly the assault stopped, and he peeked through his battered, swollen eyes. Fox sat above him in mid-strike, frozen like a statue. The only thing that moved on the older boy were his eyes. He glanced frantically down at himself before his eyes settled fearfully on Xavier. Fox was helpless. Xavier could kill him easily, but he had a more important mission. Save his father. Wiggling his way out from under the older boy, he stood and staggered, lightheaded, toward the patio door.

The dark guard and Danson had his father cornered at the rear of the patio. The blood oozing from the king's left side sent adrenaline into Xavier's body, and he raced toward the fight. His father blocked Danson's strike, but in doing so, it left him exposed for the guard's devastating blow.

"NO!" Xavier screeched, lifting his hand as he ran toward

the men. The guard swung his sword as Xavier reacted to the assault. The guard exploded into millions of bloody pieces, spraying his father with the carnage. Unfortunately for Danson, he was standing too close to the empowerment and his left arm disintegrated. With a scream, he fell to the ground and clutched his bloody stump. Within seconds, he bled out.

"Dad!" Xavier gasped, running to his father and hugging him.

"I'm okay," his father wheezed. "Lana..."

"She's okay. I sent her to Loren and Ephraim so they could keep her safe."

Suddenly the king dropped to his knees with a groan, clutching his side.

"Dad! You're not okay. Let me see your wound," Xavier demanded, shoving aside the king's shirt and exposing the large gash there. It looked deep and was bleeding a lot, but it didn't look life threatening. Closing his eyes, Xavier started the healing process.

"Xavier! NO!"

Suddenly Xavier was shoved roughly to the ground. Xavier looked up at his father as Fox LeMasters impaled him with the Sword of the Chosen.

"NOOO!" Xavier screamed as Fox pulled the sword from the king and kicked him to the ground. He crawled to his father, who coughed up blood and struggled to breathe. "Dad?" he moaned.

"Now, we're even. You took my father, and now, I've taken yours," Fox announced smugly. "It's a shame you won't live long enough to truly appreciate the pain of losing a father."

Xavier glared up at the boy and slowly got to his feet. He felt the air pressure around him drop and converge toward him. Fox's smug expression dropped, and he staggered backwards.

"Wh... wh... what... what *are* you? Your eyes... they're... *fire!*"

Xavier drew in energy from every living thing around him until he could feel the energy warring inside him to be released, but he hoarded it inside him a few seconds more, allowing it to grow stronger. Then he released the energy with a yell. The concussion from the release destroyed everything in its path, including Fox, who disintegrated into nothing. The Sword of the Chosen clattered to the ground.

Chapter 25

"**D**ad?" Xavier gasped, rolling the king onto his back. Blood soaked his cloak and torso and a large puddle continued to grow on the floor. "Oh, God! Dad!" Xavier cried pressing his hands over the profusely bleeding wound. It was time. He had failed to prevent his father's death.

"Xavier, don't cry, son. I wouldn't... h... have changed a thing," Jeremiah rasped out weakly. "B... be brave. Everything will... be fine."

"No! It will never be fine!" Xavier cried. "I... I need you, Dad. I can't lose you. I *won't* lose you!" Xavier swiped the tears from his cheeks and raised his hands above the king's abdomen.

"It won't work," a hoarse voice said weakly behind him.

Xavier turned abruptly, an electro force spinning menacingly in his hands. The Prophet, Abraham Vincent, stood tensely at the other end of the patio, his eyes watery and aware. The force evaporated from his hands.

"I can heal him! I can. You don't know what I'm capable of... the powers I have now. My powers are incredibly strong," Xavier argued.

"It won't work," the older man stated again, his voice quavering faintly.

"How do you know? I have to try!" Xavier yelled as fresh tears soaked his cheeks.

Abraham walked toward the boy, his face twisted with sympathy, and something more. "Xavier," he started softly, "your father will die before your healing force can complete its course. It's too late."

"How do you know that? You don't know that!"

"I do know! I know because... I've already tried it."

"You already t... tried? What in the hell does that mean?" Xavier blared, his fear turning to anger. "You said we could save him! You said you had a plan!"

Abraham knelt next to Xavier his eyes never leaving the boy's face. "Prince Xavier, you're a bright boy. Haven't you determined who I am yet?"

Xavier stared at the man kneeling next to him, and suddenly he began to wonder about him, about how the prophet knew so much about him and his life. He wasn't a prophet. He was a time-traveler, but being a time-traveler didn't make him all-knowing about his life, his thoughts, and his feelings. Their first meeting flashed into Xavier's memory. He had mysteriously turned up at the palace with urgent news for his father. Xavier had been intrigued and snuck out of his room and eavesdropped at the library door, where the men had argued cryptically about him. But the prophet had known he was there.

The prophet sighed and continued more calmly, "Now, will you please invite young Xavier, who's eavesdropping at the door, into the room so that I can meet him?"

Xavier hissed a string of curses and opened the door, glancing up at his father with a small grin. "Sorry," he muttered.

"Come here, boy," the old man commanded.

Xavier looked directly at the prophet for the first time and was taken aback. The man's face was grotesquely deformed as if someone had doused his head in acid, causing his skin to melt down his face a couple of centimeters. His mouth drooped at a perversely obtuse angle on one side, and a string of spittle dangled from the corner of his mouth. His snowy hair was tied into a knot at the base of his neck. From Xavier's perspective, the man seemed quite elderly, but he stood tall and proud. He was nearly as tall as Jeremiah, and Xavier could feel the man's strength pulsating in the close air around him. But, as scary and ugly as the man's appearance was, Xavier saw something gentle and oddly familiar in his gray eyes. He slowly approached the man.

The prophet studied him with silent intensity that left Xavier feeling like a rare artifact. Finally, he spoke. "Hello, Xavier. I'm Abraham Vincent. Now I know you heard every word your father and I said, so let's just cut through the formalities, shall we? You mustn't tell anyone, even Robbie, that the Divination is planned for tonight. Do you understand?"

Xavier nodded his head vigorously, intimidated by the man's appearance and the obvious power he possessed. Abe gave him a horrific lopsided smile. At least, Xavier thought it was a smile though it looked more like a snarl.

"Sire?" Abe turned to Jeremiah. "May I speak to the boy alone?"

Jeremiah hesitated briefly and then said, "Ah, sure." He looked at Xavier. "I'll be just outside the door in the receiving room."

Then he left the room, leaving Xavier alone with the hideous man. Abraham studied the timid boy a moment before speaking. "Your father is a good man and a superb king, boy. Watch him, learn from him, so that when your day comes, you will be just as honorable. But," Abraham moved within inches of him, and Xavier could smell his sour breath, "if your Divination goes as I know it will, you will be a far greater, more powerful king than your father ever dreamed of becoming."

Xavier looked up at him in disbelief. More powerful than his dad? It was hard to imagine!

"Xavier, there's another reason why I am here now, and why I did not wait for your thirteenth birthday to perform the Divination. You may not believe me. In fact, I am certain you will not, and that you will not take the Divination seriously at all. But you must be warned." The Prophet paused before continuing in a low, strained tone, "There is great evil oozing its way into the kingdom. The dark seeks to return, and you, your father, and all you value are in grave danger, boy. The Dark Lord will come, and you and your father must take heed!"

Xavier coughed out a nervous laugh. "What? I don't know what you're talking about. Do you always talk in riddles?" he blurted, trying to sound more secure than he felt.

Abraham grabbed him roughly by the collar and hissed irritably, "Don't presume to mock me, boy! Your jokes don't make it any less true. It will happen, and you've begun to sense what lies ahead."

"But I haven't..."

"Yes, you have!" the prophet barked, shaking him. "You've already envisioned the fall of the king, and yet, you and your father have chosen to ignore it!"

"What are you talking about?" Xavier whispered, his anxiety toward the man escalating into fear.

"The dream, boy! The dream! You dreamt of your father's fall two nights ago. You dreamt of Father O'Brien ordering your father's most trusted assistants to beat him while his enemies looked on, buying time to attack."

"How do you know about that?" Xavier questioned, his entire body shuddering.

Not only had Abraham known he was outside the door, but he had known about the dream. He hadn't shared that dream with anyone but his father! He had known the details of the dream as though he had had the dream himself.

Then there were their meetings and conversations at the mountain. The prophet seemed to always know where to find Xavier. He just appeared at the river where Xavier had sat sulking over his father's actions after he broke up with Lana. It never occurred to Xavier then to question how the prophet knew that he would be sitting next to that river. He had been so focused on his own misery and worries.

Finally, after discovering that he was the Chosen, his father, his generals—Loren and Ephraim—and the prophet had cornered him in the fencing room. It was at that moment that Xavier had naïvely decided to return to Warwood to face LeMasters by himself so no one else would die in his name. It was a decision that nearly cost him his life. It was in that decisive moment that the prophet had fallen to his knees in agony.

"Abe! Abe, are you all right? What is it? What's wrong?" Loren yelped, hurrying to the old man's side.

The prophet dropped to his knees in obvious agony. A sudden spasm of pain sent the man to all fours, and he cried out. For several long seconds, he knelt on the cold stone floor, panting and heaving violently. Then another invisible torment slammed him onto his back, and he screamed, clutching his right hip while blood crept to the surface of his trousers.

Loren grabbed Abe and tried to steady his seizing body. "Abe! What's going on?"

Jeremiah rushed over and dropped onto his knees next to the prophet.

"Hold him still, Loren. I'll apply pressure to the wound and try to stop the bleeding."

Xavier wandered toward the men, watching his father press his hands against the bloody wound.

The prophet yelped and swore, perspiration beading on his flushed face.

"Abe, what hap…" Loren began but was unable to finish the question as the prophet's body pitched and arched against another invisible force. Tremors violently threw his body against the hard, rocky floor.

"Hold him, Loren!" Jeremiah yelled as he struggled to keep pressure on the now profusely bleeding wound.

Abe let out a long, loud scream as some invisible force severed the finger on his left hand, leaving a small bloody stump.

"Oh, God! Oh, God!" Abe hissed as a long ugly scar ripped its way across his jaw. There was one last painful shudder as blood oozed over the front of his cloak, and his face grew white and colorless.

Rasping for breath, the prophet's eyes bore into Xavier's as he moaned, "Xavier… d… don't… please…" Before any of them could ask him what he meant, there was a great blinding silver light, and the prophet disappeared.

"What the hell?" Jeremiah hissed, looking to his general. "Loren, what happened?"

The invisible attack on Abraham that day had mirrored the torture Xavier had endured at the hands of William LeMasters. Unconsciously, he rubbed his right hip where LeMasters had impaled him while fighting him at the Academy. He looked down at his left thumb and the white scar that ringed it. His eyes darted to the prophet's hand, and he saw the same scar on the same hand.

Xavier looked up at Abe, who smiled wearily.

"Yes. I know everything about you. I know your thoughts, your dreams, and your hopes. I know everything because I am you," he whispered.

Xavier studied the man, dumbfounded. God he was... old. He was kind of handsome for an old guy, and tall!

Abe snickered. "Thanks, youngling. You're quite handsome yourself for a little boy."

Abe winked down at him, and Xavier started to smile, but a rasping breath snapped his attention down as his father stared at Abe incredulously. He opened his mouth to say something but a sudden spasm violently shook his body and he stopped breathing.

"DAD!" Xavier shook the lifeless king. "NO! DAD! DAD!" He looked pleadingly up at his older self. "Please! Help him! You know I need him!"

"Xavier, I can't! You know the rules that govern my ability. I can't do a thing even if I wanted to. Only you have the ability to save your father now."

Xavier stared helplessly down at his father. Abe was right. Only he had the power to prevent this from happening. Suddenly hopeful, he jumped to his feet.

"How? How do I jump back in time?"

"If you do this, you will seal the time-line, and you'll not be able to jump into times prior to this point. Do you understand that?"

Xavier nodded eagerly. "Yes, yes!"

"And all memory of me will be erased. No one but you will recall me. I will have never existed as the prophet. All my work, my interventions, will be viewed as miracles, unexplainable coincidences. When you return, I will be gone. You will never see *me* again," Abe explained.

Xavier paused slightly at this news before whispering solemnly, "It doesn't matter. Dad has to live!"

Abe smiled, his face mirroring the relief he felt. "Okay

then. In order to leap, you simply focus on a time prior to the attack on your father. However, and heed this warning, you cannot be seen by yourself. If you see yourself it would have unpredictable consequences!"

"But I see you!"

"Ah, but you didn't know who I was until now. Think, boy. What would you do if in the heat of battle you see yourself?"

Understanding, Xavier nodded. "Okay. I'll make sure I'm unseen." He looked at Abraham hesitantly. "Thank you. Thank you for all you've done for... me."

Abe smiled mischievously and winked. "No thanks needed. I did it for the good of the kingdom. I did it for my family. I did it for me. Be careful, boy. I would like a future to go back to."

Chapter 26

Xavier nodded, closed his eyes and began the task of leaping backward in time. Maybe it was because he knew he could do it, but time bending was easier than he thought it would be. He felt a sensation similar to that of teleportation, only stronger and more nauseating. When the sensation subsided, he sat, eyes closed, trying to settle the rollercoaster sensation in his stomach. It didn't work. He threw up on the floor in his bedroom. It was the only place he could think to bend to without being seen, and sure enough, when he opened his eyes, the room was silent and dark. Not sure how far back he had jumped, he looked at his bedside clock. It was just before noon. He would still be at school arguing with Spencer to let him leave to find his father.

Slipping out of his room, Xavier scurried down the hall and into his father's bedroom, but where to hide? The closet! He started toward the closet but cheers from outside drew him to the patio doors. Curious, he stepped out onto the patio as his father's resonating voice echoed from the front of the palace.

"The time is now, men. We've been preparing for this attack for months. We are ready. There will be no retreat this time. We are the last line between freedom and oppression for all of mankind. We cannot fail! We cannot give in! We cannot surrender! This is the moment to show what we're made of: are we lesser men or greater men? This is war for the light and goodness in the world! We will not be defeated, for we are on the side of righteousness. So we must fight through this night of hell, so that the morning will be a glorious day in the light! We will not go gently into the dark, my friends! Rage against the dark so that light may prevail! The time is now, my friends! Who will fight with abandonment for our kingdom?"

Hearing his father's vibrant voice brought tears to Xavier's eyes. He was alive, for now. He *had* to save him! He just had to! Unable to stay focused hearing his father's voice, Xavier closed the patio door. It wouldn't be much longer now. He had jumped too far back in his time stream, but it was better he was too early than too late. He crossed the room to the bedroom closet and opened its mirrored sliding door. It was a large closet and now Lana's things hung on one side next to his father's. Another loud cheer came from outside. Most likely, it was his father introducing him as the Chosen. He smiled at the thought. No sense hiding in the closet just yet. It would be a half-hour or so before his father would return to deal with the invasion on the palace. Xavier sat on the edge of the bed. If he could just succeed, it would all be over, and he and his father could live in peace for the rest of their lives. No more prophecies hanging over their heads. No more attacks on the kingdom. Life could finally go back to normal, whatever that meant.

Lost in thought, Xavier jumped at the sound of the residence door slamming shut. He scrambled off the bed and raced to the closet. He hid in its depths, leaving the door open a crack so he could see what was going on.

"Jeremy?" Lana's desperate call nearly had Xavier stepping out of hiding, but he couldn't. Lana had most likely come from the academy. How would he explain how he had gotten here so quickly?

The bedroom door opened. "Jeremy? Are you here?"

Not receiving an answer, Xavier listened as Lana shut the door and walked away. Releasing the breath he hadn't realized he was holding, he tried to relax and get comfortable for the wait. Then he remembered. He was going to be a big brother! Lana was going to have a baby—a girl! He wasn't sure how he knew the baby was a girl, but he remembered hearing the fast pitter-patting of the baby's heart. He grinned at the thought. He wondered if Dad knew about the baby.

Suddenly a loud bang from the residence entrance stiffened Xavier's spine, and when he heard Lana's scream, a chill shivered down it. He jumped to his feet and sprinted to the door, but when he opened it, he saw a dozen or so dark soldiers trudging up the steps toward him. One carried Lana over his shoulder. She hung like a ragdoll, unconscious. She would be fine. She wasn't killed, but if the Dark Army found him, his father would die! Xavier sprinted away from the door and dove under the bed, having no time to make it back to the closet. No sooner had he crawled to the center of the bed than the bedroom door banged open.

"Put the queen on the bed," an oily voice ordered. He recognized that voice. Danson! "Secure the area. The king will come for her, and when he does, he's ours."

"Sir. What about the boy?"

At first, Xavier thought they were referring to him.

"He's gone straight to the academy to find that murdering prince. Remember, we have our orders. We are not to kill the king until Master Fox returns with the prince. He wants the boy to experience the pain of losing a father as he did."

"Yes, sir," the soldier responded.

The group wasn't in the residence for more than five

minutes when a loud rumble and bang came from the floor below.

"It appears the king is home," Danson snickered and walked across the room to the door, peering out before returning to the soldiers under his command. "It won't take the king long to get past the men posted downstairs. Be at the ready, men. Get to your positions."

The men around him scrambled, some going out onto the patio, one going into the bathroom, one standing guard next to the bed where Lana lay, and finally another going to the closet. Good thing he hadn't had enough time to get to the closet, or he would be so busted now. The clanging of swords and crashing sounds echoed from the floor below. Lana stirred on the bed above him, and the king's heavy footsteps could be heard on the staircase.

"Jeremy! No, it's a trap!" Lana screeched out before Danson scrambled toward the bed and punched her. Lana rolled onto the floor with a thud just as the bedroom door burst open.

"Henrick, you take the ugly cuss on the right. This piece of crap is mine!"

"Yes, sire," Henrick responded and the two men raced into the room. Chaos erupted. Xavier watched the men's feet as they did battle. His father's footwork was light and quick. Danson's heavy and slow. He was most definitely outmatched by the king. Xavier smiled. There was a bright flash of energy. Suddenly, Danson's feet left the floor, and a crash at the far side of the room sounded where he landed. Another flash of light illuminated the room, and there was cry from where Henrick fought against the second man. There were at least two other men hidden in the room, and a dozen or more lying in wait on the patio. Xavier crawled to the end of the bed and peered up at the fighting men.

Henrick was holding his own and had severely injured

the dark soldier, who was bleeding profusely from the abdomen. Danson was scrambling to his feet as the king stomped toward him. Danson managed to conjure a blocking energy as the king sent an electro force at him. The force ricocheted off the block, and Jeremiah ducked just in time to avoid being hit by his own power.

Danson's eyes were wide with fear as the king continued toward him. As the king's hands grabbed him roughly by the collar, Danson cried out, "Attack!"

Suddenly, the hidden men in the room and three additional men from the patio sprang into action. The soldier hiding in the bathroom immediately hit Henrick with a force that sent him to the ground twitching in agony. Xavier recognized the empowerment. Dr. Angelo had used it against him while he was held captive at the Institute. It was a torturous, painful power that contracted muscles until they tore or snapped bones.

As Henrick lay helpless and twitching, the soldier, cocky and confident he had the upper hand, withdrew his sword and approached the lieutenant. This is where Henrick would die, Xavier realized. Taking a deep breath, Xavier reached out toward the dark soldier, who now stood over Henrick with his sword raised, ready to impale him. Closing his eyes, Xavier twisted his hand. Even from across the room, he could hear the man's neck crack and a thud as the man dropped dead to the floor. Xavier opened his eyes and met Henrick's staring back at him. Gesturing for Henrick to remain silent of his presence, the guard nodded weakly before passing out.

Xavier looked toward the patio doorway. His father had taken the battle outside. Fearful that his father was outnumbered, Xavier squirmed out from under the bed and crept to the doorway. His father wielded his sword expertly with jaw-dropping finesse. Six dark soldiers and Danson had the king surrounded, but his father didn't look at all worried. Holding his sword in one hand, he extended the other toward an attacking solider, making a twisting motion. The man dropped to the ground like a stone just as the king parried a complex move from another soldier while Danson stood back and observed. In no time at all, the king countered the attack with a feint to the abdomen before slashing the man's head clean off. Xavier took a step back at the brutality of the action, but quickly dismissed it. After all, this army under William LeMasters' command did the same to Dublin Minnows. Satisfaction filled him as he continued to watch his father take out one soldier after another until only Danson and one soldier remained.

Danson suddenly looked in his direction, and Xavier quickly ducked behind his father's lounge chair next to the patio door. Downstairs, Xavier heard the door shut. It could only be one person. He was about to see himself racing into the room. Suddenly, Danson raced into the room and quickly clambered into the closet. Damn! He was sure glad he didn't hide there. Moments later, *past* Xavier entered the room.

"Lana? Lana? Are you okay?" he heard himself whisper as he knelt next to Lana.

A few moments past before Lana answered, "Xavier? What... where's your father? There're dark soldiers in the castle!"

As his past self talked Lana into going to safety without him, Xavier peered out onto the patio where his father had disarmed the dark soldier.

"Come with me, honey," Lana was pleading.

Xavier tuned out the remainder of the conversation as his mind reeled to come up with a plan to save the king.

"Surrender or die!" his father ordered.

Past Xavier crept to the double glass door and peered out

onto the large patio.

"Never!" dark soldier responded.

"So be it," his father responded, killing the man.

The events that followed happened quickly. Danson, hiding in the closet, opened the door and crept up behind past Xavier.

"Xavier!" his father shouted.

He watched himself drop to the floor, roll to his back, and lift a sword just in time to block Danson's strike.

"So glad you could finally join us, *Prince Wells*. We didn't want to start this party without you!"

"If you hurt a single hair on his body, you will pay," his father warned as he approached them.

"Hurt him? Of course not, sire. I wouldn't dream of it. I plan to kill him."

"Good luck with that. Maybe I should close my eyes so you'll have at least half a chance at it. It wouldn't seem fair otherwise," past Xavier responded confidently.

Suddenly, Danson flew out the door and crashed into a birdbath. His father turned to deal with Danson while past Xavier faced Fox LeMasters. Xavier remained hidden behind the chair, his mind analyzing when he could get to his father to save him. Then he realized he didn't need to save the king, he needed to kill Fox. But that still didn't prevent the wound Danson inflicted with the aid of Fox's bodyguard. Past Xavier's fight with Fox was pushed to the background as Xavier contemplated his options. He didn't have much time to work something out.

Suddenly, Fox and his past self slammed into the bureau near him and he hunkered down out of sight. How was he going to get out onto the patio with his former self and Fox fighting in plain sight? The solution suddenly came to him, and he was tempted to slap himself in the head. His abilities! Why did he forget about how powerful he was? He had the ability of invisibility! Xavier was no longer surprised by how easily his abilities came to him, and with the mere thought of being invisible, Xavier looked down at his missing body. The only drawback with this ability was that he would have to remove all his clothing in order to sneak out. He would be naked. Not liking the idea but with no other option, he quickly stripped and slowly stood from his hiding spot.

Fox had his past self pinned against the wall.

"Why would they believe that you would ever stand a chance against me? You're just a little boy," Fox hissed.

"You know?" past Xavier wheezed, "I might consider surrendering if you'd just stop giving me a shower with your spit."

The comment earned a punch to his already bruised ribs and he fell to the floor. Fox swept the sword in a wide arc, his intentions obvious to Xavier as he watched, invisible from his vantage point. It occurred to him then that the sword hadn't stopped on its own accord. Thrusting his hand toward the Sword of the Chosen, he locked it in his telekinesis power just inches from his past self's head. Fox fought against the force, trying in vain to use brute force to continue the kill strike.

"Wh... what's going on?" he exclaimed.

"What do you think, numb nuts? It's my sword. It won't harm me!"

Then Fox and his past self began to fight until Danson's cry sent all eyes to the fighting on the patio.

"Help him!" Fox ordered his bodyguard.

Leaving his past self to continue the fight with Fox, Xavier quickly slipped out onto the patio ahead of the burly bodyguard. He slipped behind some shrubbery as the bodyguard approached the king, who had a hand wrapped around Danson's neck. It appeared that the king had settled for killing Danson the old-fashioned way. The guard withdrew his sword and had every intention of stabbing the king in the back. With a quick flick of his finger, Xavier tripped the large man. However, he unexpectedly stumbled directly into the king, and the men fell in a heap onto the ground.

The king let out a grunt as the large guard fell on top of him. The men fought and wrestled around the ground for several minutes until finally his father punched the guard, pinned him to the ground, rolled free, and sprang to his feet. Danson and the guard scrambled to their feet and faced down the king, who smiled cockily at the pair.

"So? Who's going to make the first move? The second best brother or the substandard guard who could only successfully attack me with my back turned?"

Both men attacked at once. The guard lunged at the king while Danson swung his sword. The result was catastrophic for the guard. Danson's sword caught the larger man across the chest, and the man jerked backwards with a yelp. The king looked somewhat shocked by the turn of events before a booming laugh exploded from him. Xavier couldn't stop the snicker at the sight. The pair of dark men looked like bumbling idiots. With a quick twist of the king's hand, Danson dropped to the ground. The bodyguard lunged at the king but never made contact as Xavier instinctively sent a force at the man and sent him flying over the patio wall, plummeting to his death.

The king's gaze jerked in Xavier's direction, and he ducked, forgetting he was invisible.

"Dad!" past Xavier gasped, running to his father and hugging him.

"I'm okay," his father responded. "Lana..."

"She's okay. I sent her to Loren and Ephraim so they could keep her safe."

"Good. Good."

Fox suddenly appeared behind past Xavier, his sword raised at the ready.

"Xavier! NO!" his father yelled, shoving him aside.

Hidden and invisible Xavier watched the entire episode unfold, again! He couldn't let his dad die! He couldn't!

"NOOO!" he screamed, thrusting his hand toward the Dark King. Just before Fox plunged the sword into the king, a gravitational force slammed the older boy to the ground with such force that Fox was crushed on impact.

Jeremiah looked down at the puddled mess that was once Fox LeMasters before jerking his eyes in invisible Xavier's direction again. With a sigh of relief that the job was done, Xavier released his hold on the past and found himself in the exact spot he had been in when he bent time. Still naked, but no longer invisible Xavier scrambled to find his clothes. They were exactly where he had left them, behind the chair. Grabbing his pants, he pulled them on and looked around the room. His father sat on the bed, looking at him.

"Dad," he whispered, relief pouring into his voice as he raced to him and launched himself into his arms.

"It's okay, Xavier. I'm okay." He pulled him to arm's length and studied Xavier's face. Then he stroked the boy's face and smiled. "You are extraordinary. The prophet... he's you, isn't he?"

Xavier was taken aback. No one was supposed to remember Abraham Vincent. How did his father remember? He started to answer but found himself speechless.

"I remember because I have omniscience. I see all truths. I always have. Whenever Abraham intervened in our time stream, I could see the results of what would have happened if he hadn't. I remember him because there's a trace of time-bending in me, but I'm surprised at myself for not figuring out who he was sooner." The king shook his head with a dry smile.

"Did you like him... me?" he wanted to know. For the few interactions between his father and the prophet, Xavier had the impression the pair didn't get along. "I mean, you both seemed to fight a lot."

Jeremiah paused in thought before answering. "Xavier, I liked the prophet, but you must understand, there were ways he handled things I felt were a bit... ruthless."

Xavier felt disappointed. He didn't quite understand why, but it felt as if his father was criticizing him. Well, he was, kind of. "What do you mean?"

"I disliked how he handled you. He was too abrupt, too harsh."

Xavier thought back to his first encounter with the prophet. He could see what his father meant. Even he hadn't liked the prophet much then, but there were other times he had been more comforting and helpful. However, the king wasn't aware of those moments. They had been just between the two of them.

"Now that I know his identity, I understand him and his actions better. I still don't agree, but he didn't have my guidance as he grew into a man. It is, however, comforting to know that you grew into a strong, just ruler without me."

"I won't have to now," Xavier whispered. "Abraham didn't want me to. Even though your death wasn't a catastrophic event, he knew I needed you. I'll be a better king because of it. You'll see. I'll be even better."

The king squeezed him tightly in a bear hug just as the door sprang open and Loren and Ephraim raced into the room.

"All right?" Ephraim asked the pair.

"Yes. We're unharmed, and the Dark King is dead. It's

over."

The generals visibly relaxed and sighed out the tension they had penned up in their taunt bodies. Loren stepped forward and ruffled Xavier's hair.

"Well done, little king."

Xavier smiled up at Loren.

"Is the Key still safe, Loren?" the king asked.

"Yes, not sure why, but those idiots thought we'd place the Key back into the vault. Of course, they found nothing when they broke in."

"Where is the Key," Xavier asked, curious.

Loren grinned. "On my mantle, in plain sight, but now that the war is over, I suspect the Key should be returned to its owner."

"Who's that?" Xavier asked.

Loren looked at the king with a knowing grin before looking back at the boy. "You, young sire. The Key is yours."

"Mine? Wait. Do you mean because it's the King's Key, it goes to me because I will be king someday?"

"No, young sire," Loren answered. "It's your Key. You created it... or at least you will create it."

Xavier looked between the men. Both the king and Ephraim seemed to be just as confused as Xavier, which was some relief. He looked back at the tall general. "Loren, you're not making sense. What do you mean?"

With a sigh, he asked, "Do you know who the prophet truly was?"

"The prophet?" Ephraim asked. "What in the hell are you talking about, mate? What prophet?"

Xavier was shocked to see that Loren knew of the prophet. Ignoring Ephraim, he looked at Loren. "Yes. I do. Do you?"

Loren nodded, and the king spoke then. "Loren, why didn't you tell me?"

"I couldn't, sire. It would change the way you interacted with him, and King Xavier didn't want that. He said it could cause more harm than good."

"Okay, okay!" Xavier announced, frustration filling his tone. "Loren, explain what you mean that the Key is mine."

"You, future you, will create the Key to send you back in time. It was intended that your father would need extra abilities during your influx year. If your father had died during the first invasion, your influx year would have caused great harm to you. That is why when you first met the prophet, he was so horrifically scarred from the burns. Robbie died in the fire in the Woods during the peak of your influx, Xavier. Your father wasn't there to carry her out, and as a result of your attempts to save her, you suffered severe burns over seventy-five percent of your body. It was a miracle you lived. However, after that future was averted, Robbie survived because of your father, and you didn't suffer the burns."

Jeremiah moaned, "Dear God."

"You created the Key. You took metal from King's Mountain and forged the key from that metal. Then you transferred a copy of your powers into the key. You knew your father needed access to the powers you had in order to protect himself, you, and the future of this great kingdom."

Xavier was speechless. He had created the all-encompassing object of power!

"Could someone tell me what the hell is going on?" Ephraim blared.

As Loren tried to explain who and what the prophet was to Ephraim, the king and his son stared at one another, dumfounded.

Chapter 27

When the king, prince, and the generals exited the palace, royal guards were busily cleaning up the aftermath of war. A lot of Warwoodian lives had been lost, mostly royal guards, but the carnage of the Dark Army outnumbered that of the kingdom. Telekinetics busily piled up Dark Army bodies ready to be burned. The dead royal guards were treated with more care and respect. Their bodies lined the horseshoe-shaped drive with their royalty cloaks draped over their bodies, awaiting their families to collect them. The wounded dark soldiers and royal guards alike were taken to the infirmary for treatment.

"I'll help dispose of the Dark Army bodies. There's no need for our people to smell burning bodies into the night," Xavier stated and walked away from the men toward the guards preparing to set fire to the bodies.

Ephraim questioned watching the boy approach the men, "How's he going to prevent that?"

A young guard overheard the general and stopped in his tracks. "Sir? In a blink of an eye, the prince incinerated over a hundred dark soldiers into ash at the gatehouse. We would have been overrun by the enemy if he hadn't. It was... amazing."

The men looked at one another in shock.

Loren was the first to speak. "I've got to see this!" He

hurried to where the prince stood talking to the royal guard in charge of the disposal of bodies. Loren clapped Xavier on the back and spoke. Xavier grinned and nodded.

"Jeremy!" Lana's relieved voice cried from behind the king. He turned and swept his wife into his arms as she launched herself at him. "Oh, thank God!" Then she began to cry into his chest.

Jeremiah soothed his wife, stroking her head and kissing her forehead repeatedly. "It's okay, sweetheart. Everything is going to be okay."

"Xavier?" she gulped.

"He's just fine," the king answered, turning her so she could see the boy talking to Loren and the guard in the center of the drive.

"I was so worried. He wouldn't leave with me! I was so afraid you'd both die!"

Jeremiah hugged her close and kissed her forehead again. "Naw. It'll take a hell of a lot more than one measly army to kill us," he joked.

"You can really do that?" the guard asked the boy, astounded.

"Yes, sir. I can. I don't know about you, but I don't want to be smelling these carcasses all night."

"Agreed," the guard nodded.

"Let me clear it with my men. I'm sure they'll be ecstatic to be relieved of this duty."

As the guard walked away to organize his men, Loren sidled up next to Xavier. "I've got to see this."

Xavier looked up at the general. "I'm a little afraid to use it." He glanced back at his father hugging Lana. "Loren," he continued in a whisper, "I didn't even know it would happen. The... the dark soldiers wouldn't listen! I tried! I really tried to get them to listen and leave Warwood, but they wouldn't. Then one of them... well, he taunted me. I got mad. I figured if I could do something big... something really scary, they'd just leave."

"Well, I'd say your mission was accomplished!" Loren responded with a grin, but when he saw the tears on the boy's face, his mirth dropped. "Hey, now. Xavier, it's okay." He hugged the boy. He was only a boy. How old had he been when he had to kill his first man? Twenty? Twenty-one? Lord, how he struggled with it! How much more difficult would that be for a fourteen-year-old?

"I didn't mean to kill all of them!" the boy muttered against the general's chest. "I only meant to kill the one that was teasing me so that the others would be afraid and run. The power was so strong... I couldn't... I didn't know how to... channel it, stop it. Please! Please, don't tell Dad. Please!" he pleaded.

Loren pushed the prince to arm's length and met his eyes before stating, "Young sire, war is messy. Nothing goes as planned or as we'd like. In the first invasion, I..." Loren paused to clear his throat, "I killed a kid. He was a dark soldier, but he was still just a boy. However, if I hadn't stopped him, he would have killed an unarmed woman with a small child. Bad things happen in war, but it doesn't make us bad people. As for not telling your father, I think you're worried over nothing where he's concerned. If anyone understands what you're going through, it's him."

Xavier nodded and quickly wiped away his tears as the guard returned. "Prince Wells? If you give my men another half hour or so, we should have all the dark soldiers ready to go."

Xavier gave the man a quick nod. Then, remembering Fox's bodyguard who had plummeted off the side of the palace's patio, he added, "Sergeant? There should be

another body on the east side of the palace. A dark soldier...
ah... fell off the patio."

A smirk filled Loren's face. "Fell, huh? Bet he had help
with that fall."

Xavier smirked back at the general. "Of course he did."
That was one death he didn't feel one iota of guilt over.

Nearly a half-hour later, Warwoodian citizens started to
return from hiding, including the teachers and children
from the academy.

"XAVIER!" Robbie screeched.

Xavier turned to see Robbie sprinting toward him, her
face red and tears streaming down her cheeks like rivers.
Something in his gut twisted at the sight of her distraught
face. He felt guilty for making her worry and causing her any
kind of pain. As she reached him, Xavier scooped her up,
hugged her close, and spun her in circles.

"I'm okay! I'm okay," he whispered as she muffled her
racking sobs in his shoulder.

He set her to her feet and cupped her face in his hands.
He could feel his own tears now. "I'm okay. It's over, Robbie.
It's all over." He kissed her tenderly, but her emotions were
too raw to keep the kiss tender. He could feel her love, her
desperation, and her relief in her kiss, and it made his knees
weak.

When they finally withdrew, Robbie giggled. "You're
glowing."

For once, Xavier didn't care. He didn't care who saw him
glowing. He wanted the entire kingdom to know that he
loved this girl. With a smile, he kissed her back and felt her
surprise and something else as he put his whole heart into
that kiss. She whimpered as he withdrew, and he smiled at
her again.

"I've got some work to do. I... I'm not sure you should
watch though. It's... it's not a very... pleasant task."

"No, Xavier. I'm not leaving your side again," she whispered, and together they watched the guard finish piling up the enemy bodies.

Nearly thirty minutes later, the sergeant approached Xavier.

"Are we ready?" Xavier asked him.

The guard gave him a nod and saluted him. Xavier felt his father's presence behind him long before the king's hand grasped his shoulder reassuringly. Closing his eyes briefly, Xavier imagined the pile of bodies turning to ash. Almost instantly, the group around him expelled sounds of awe and surprise, and when Xavier opened his eyes, the bodies were gone and in their place was a pile of ash.

Later that night, Xavier sat on the sofa in the receiving room lost in thought, and oddly, feeling extremely lonely. Although the dark soldiers had left him with no other choice, killing them the way he did left him feeling guilty and alone. No one could understand how he felt. He was still a freak among freaks. He was the king of freaks and many people acted awkward or even fearful around him. Would he ever fit in?

"Son?" his father called from behind him.

Xavier turned and found his father and Lana with an arm around each other giving him looks of sympathy.

"Don't look at me like that," Xavier murmured, turning away from his parents.

The pair entered the receiving room and sat next to him on the couch. His father pulled him into his arms like he was a toddler. He felt awkward at first. He was nearly fifteen for crying out loud, but the comfort he so sorely needed was there, in his father's arms. So he allowed it.

His father stroked his head as he spoke, "Son, I cannot imagine having to do what you had to do at fourteen.

Everything you faced today was more than most men could tolerate. I'm proud of you. But I want you to know something."

Xavier sighed and muttered, "What?"

"You are not alone. Everything you're feeling right now is perfectly normal. Son, I'm feeling those same feelings. It's never easy to kill a man, even when you have no choice. It's okay to feel bad about it. It's okay to feel guilty. You care and respect human life, so these feelings are only natural. Unlike you, however, I've had practice in dealing with these feelings."

Xavier looked up at his father, curious. "What did you do to make it go away?"

"It never really goes away, but it will fade in time. Being around the people you love will definitely help. You shouldn't be alone."

Xavier nodded.

His father kissed his forehead before telling him, "You better get the door, son. It's for you."

Suddenly there was a loud knock at the door. Xavier looked at his father's grinning face suspiciously before standing and going to the door. When he opened it, he was suddenly tackled by a half dozen bodies. They tumbled to the floor with a thud. Then someone stuck a wet finger in his ear.

"Hey there, Mr. Bigshot!" Garrett's voice announced before the group giggled and wrestled around with each other.

Slowly the kids began to climb off Xavier, who was grinning from ear to ear. "Hey! What are you guys doing here?"

"Your dad invited us to spend the night in the palace. How could we say no to that?"

Xavier looked at each face and stopped at Robbie's. He

turned to his dad.

"Really? They're *all* staying?"

The king nodded. "Yep, but each person *will* be in their own sleeping bag, and Loren, Lucy, Ephraim, Rebecca, Lana, and I will be supervising. So there will be no hanky-panky!"

"Good thing!" Xavier blurted, eyeing his father with mirth. "You and Lana would embarrass the crap out of me if you started that nonsense in front of my friends."

The king's bellowing laugh had the entire group giggling.

"Touché, son."

In the next couple of weeks, life in Warwood returned to normal. Xavier continued his lessons at the academy in the morning and his lessons on kingship with his father in the afternoons. The feelings of guilt and loneliness began to subside just as his father said they would.

"Well, that's it for the day," his father announced from behind his desk. "What have you learned?"

"I've learned that you must read a proposal aloud three times before it can be voted on by the legislative body. I've learned that Warwood is not completely self-sufficient in our food sources, and that we depend on local common farmers and fishermen to help provide for our food needs."

"Good, and what have you learned about our laws in today's discussions?"

"Ah, that it's illegal for the king to intimidate or bully any citizen into breaking the codes or passing laws that the king sees fit. If the king wants to present a new law, he must do so himself without intimidation."

"Good! Now, what would you like to work on in combat training today?"

Xavier had been thinking about this for weeks, since he saw his father in action during the War of Kings. He would never know if his father was as good as he seemed to be if he didn't have a bout with him. The few times he fought his father at the mountain, he had always held back. Although Xavier hadn't realized it at the time, he knew it for certain now. His father was a very powerful man in his own right.

Xavier grinned. "You, Father. I want to bout with you."

The king laughed loudly. "Are you sure about that, kiddo? I won't hold back. I will hurt you."

Xavier grinned cheekily. "Well, I'll hurt you, so we'll be even."

Again the king laughed. "Well if you're sure..."

"I am."

"You know what they say, 'Be careful of what you wish for.'"

Nearly an hour later, the king and prince stood in the center of the rugby pitch suiting up their armor and preparing for the training exercise. When Xavier's friends realized who he was fighting, Frankie ran out of the arena and returned with a never-ending line of people. Soon the arena was nearly half full of spectators and observers, all of whom were freakishly silent.

"Ready, son?" the king called from across the field.

"Nearly," Xavier answered as he tried to get his head into the exercise and off the crowd gathered to watch them.

Jeremiah approached the boy confidently, placed his hands on his shoulders, and looked him in the eye. "Xavier, forget about the people. Pretend it's just you and me at King's Mountain messing around and having a quick bout."

Xavier nodded and did his best to do as his father suggested. He lost all concentration, however, when Robbie screamed from the sideline, "Go, Xavier! You can do it! I believe in you."

He looked over at his girlfriend grinning like a fool. *Just one kiss for luck*, he thought and jogged over to where Robbie stood.

"Hey," he breathed out as he stopped in front of her.

"Hi," she answered with a large smile.

"Kiss for luck?" he asked, smiling bashfully.

"Oh, I'll kiss you for anything, anytime, anywhere!" she whispered before planting a breath-stealer on his lips. "Good luck," she whispered, separating from him.

With an enormous grin, Xavier jogged back to the center of the pitch across from his father, who was shaking his head.

"What? It was for good luck," Xavier responded indignantly.

His father laughed loudly. "You're going to need it, son," he teased, giving his son a cocky smile.

"We'll see, old man. Bring it!" he challenged back, beckoning his father with a simple wave of his hand.

The king's grin broadened, and he approached languidly. Xavier immediately scanned his father's approach, looking for an opening. He saw it and immediately went into attack mode by faking a low blow then going high. His father blocked the attack with a grin.

"Nice try," he goaded.

Great! His father was going to rub in any mistakes. Well, two can play that game!

The king stepped backward and returned the confident beckoning gesture Xavier had given him just a moment before. Trying not to laugh, Xavier swung low in a direct attack, trying to swipe the king's legs out from under him. The king jumped backwards, and before Xavier's swing even finished, the king went on the attack with a wide arc of his sword. Xavier barely had a chance to move out of the path of the strike let alone block it. His father's sword nicked his shoulder. Clenching his teeth against the sting, he attacked the king recklessly. The king anticipated the attack and sent him stumbling past with a kick to the butt.

Rubbing his butt, Xavier glowered at his father as snickers from the stands filtered down to him. Reminded that hundreds of people were in the stands watching sent heat spreading across his cheeks. Regaining his composure, Xavier and the king studied one another, waiting for an opening. The king suddenly lunged at his son. Xavier, startled by the attack, stumbled backwards, lost his footing, and fell to the ground. He managed to lift his sword in defense as the king's sword swept down at him. The clang of metal against metal echoed around the arena, and several appreciative groans came from the stands. Xavier rolled quickly to the right, sweeping the legs out from under the king. His father fell to the ground with a grunt, buying Xavier time to spring to his feet. He spun and swung his sword at his father, but it never made contact. The king had used telekinesis to cast the sword out of his hands. It flew twenty feet away and landed blade down, wedging itself deep into the turf.

In the time it took Xavier to realize his sword was missing and its location, his father was on the attack again. As the king barreled down on him, Xavier teleported directly behind the king, but the king seemed to know his every move and instantly spun, backhanding him to the ground. Xavier could taste the blood from his busted lip. Feelings of betrayal and hurt flooded his body, and the king lowered his sword a fraction.

"Son, you wanted this. What kind of king would I be, what kind of father would I be if I just let you win?"

Understanding, Xavier nodded and pushed his feelings aside. Then it occurred to him. His father was not anticipating his every move, he was monitoring his thoughts and feelings!

"You cheat!" Xavier spat, jumping to his feet and stepping angrily up to his father.

"No, it's not cheating, son. You could prevent me from knowing your every move if you'd bother to practice your impediment."

He was right.

"Damn right, I'm right!" his father answered his thought. "Now, quit whining and fight me. You wanted this!"

Xavier reacted without thought, and as a result, the king was caught off guard as Xavier propelled him twenty-five feet across the field. His father landed awkwardly, injuring his shoulder. Xavier turned, spotted his sword, summoned it to his outstretched hand, and turned just in time to parry his father's attack. He countered with a complex move Ephraim had taught him a year ago. It sent the king reeling in defense, leaving his abdomen opened for a sharp uppercut that forced the breath from his lungs. The king reacted by stooping forward, which allowed Xavier to punch him squarely in the face. The king dropped to the ground as blood gushed out of his nose. Xavier raised his sword to finish with a kill strike, but the king sent him to the ground with his gravitational powers. Xavier squirmed but found he couldn't move, and the pressure hurt!

Groaning, he closed his eyes, conjured his immolation ability and sent a wall of flames around him. The heat of the power broke the king's concentration, and Xavier was released from the gravitational pull. Xavier stood and grabbed his sword, which had fallen a few feet from him when the gravitation had hit. Unfortunately, the sword had been in the line of fire, and the heat from his power had melted the sword so that it was no longer usable.

"Great!" Xavier muttered. So much for sword fighting.

The king approached, saw the state of his son's sword and smiled. "So, we're going without swords now? Ready for a little hand-to-hand combat?"

No! He wouldn't stand a chance in hand-to-hand combat against his father.

The king threw his sword to the side and took off his armored vest and mask. Xavier mirrored his father's actions. Without swords, there was no need for the armor. It would only get in the way and make his movements more cumbersome in hand-to-hand. His father was the first to attack. His first punch made contact with Xavier's abdomen. With his breath knocked out of him, Xavier staggered in retreat, but his father kept advancing. Another punch came quickly and grazed his right temple. It would have knocked him out cold if he hadn't dodged at the last second.

His father threw a left hook, and he threw up his forearm to block the punch. It only slowed the punch and nearly broke his arm in the process. Hand-to-hand was a losing battle. Xavier had to get some distance between them and resort to empowerments. At least with empowerments, he had the advantage.

Xavier thrust his hand into his father's chest, but the king knew what was coming and turned his body at the last second. Xavier's empowerment only grazed the king and sent him stumbling back a step or two. The king grabbed him, trapping his arms to his side in a strong bear hug. Barely able to breathe, Xavier squirmed to get free, but his father simply lifted him into the air so he had no purchase to throw him off balance. He began to kick the king anywhere he could. After making several solid, painful contacts to his father's shins, the king took him to the ground, nearly squashing him under his weight. Chuckling, his father whispered in his ear, "Do you yield, son?"

"Never!"

The king chuckled louder. "All right, son. You've brought

this on yourself."

Suddenly his father pressed his fist against Xavier's lower back, and Xavier cried out in pain.

"The kidney is an easy pain receptor. It can be used to subdue any opponent," his father told him, easing up on the pressure he applied to Xavier's back.

"Really. That's good to know," Xavier managed past a grimace.

"Do you yield?" the king asked again.

"Never," Xavier hissed and tried in vain to buck his father off him, but it was like trying to move a brick wall. He tried to use his telekinesis to remove the king from on top of him. The king simply pressed his palm to Xavier's forehead, and suddenly a cold sensation snaked through his body. Great! He had just taken his powers! Now what?

"Do you yield, now?"

"No!" Xavier's thoughts reeled for a plan, but nothing came to mind. Suddenly he blurted with a grin, "What are you going to name the baby?"

The king froze and stared down at his son.

"What are you talking about?"

"My sister. What are you going to name her?"

"You don't have a sister."

Xavier's grin widened. "No, not yet, but in a few months, I'll have a baby sister. Lana's pregnant."

The king sat up suddenly and looked as though a feather would blow him over. Xavier took advantage of the king's shock by knocking him to the ground, reaching into the king's cloak and withdrawing a knife, holding it to the king's throat.

"Do you yield?" Xavier asked with a smirk.

Surprised by how quickly the boy had gotten the upper hand, he gave him a nod. Xavier stood and helped his father to his feet. Jeremiah continued to stare at his son. He knew the answer to the question before he asked, but he asked anyway, "Were you telling me the truth about Lana? Is she... is... is she really pregnant?"

Xavier grinned broadly. "Yeah. I wasn't making that up. I found out when I found her unconscious on the bedroom floor and I scanned her."

The king suddenly raced from the pitch.

"Dad! Where are you going? Lana's in the stands!"

The king froze and scanned the stands. He couldn't see her, so he called to her above the growing whispers of the onlookers. "Lana Wells? Lana?"

Lana stood and began to make her way out of the stands to the king, but it appeared the king couldn't wait that long. He jumped the six-foot wall, grabbed the ledge and hauled himself into the stands. He took the steps two at a time until he had her in his arms.

"Is it true?"

Lana gave him a puzzled look. "Is what true?"

"Are you pregnant?"

Lana glanced around, suddenly aware that everyone listened intently to their conversation. "I... I was going to tell you this evening. I found out this morning at my appointment, but yes, Jeremy, I'm pregnant."

Jeremiah let out a loud whoop, scooped the woman he loved into his arms and kissed her. The stands erupted in cheers and laughter.

Xavier watched his parents from the field with a large smile on his face.

"Xavier! Xavier! Did you hear them?" Robbie blurted, racing toward him. "Lana's pregnant!"

Xavier caught Robbie as she threw her arms around him. He hugged her close, spinning her in circles.

"I know. How else do you think I won this fight? I was a goner, so I played dirty and told my dad Lana was pregnant."

Robbie giggled. "Well, didn't your dad always tell you all is fair in love and war?"

Xavier smiled down at her before whispering, "Yep."

He kissed her then and felt her melt against him. It was at that moment Xavier realized how right his father had been. Love and friendship were cures for loneliness and a broken soul. He had never felt so complete in his life. He had never felt so loved or at such peace. He was home! He was finally home.

www.ingramcontent.com/pod-product-compliance
Lightning Source LLC
Chambersburg PA
CBHW071254170626
46809CB00001B/222